Also available from J

Gulls!
Buddha's Big Book of Short Stories

By Phil Hodgkiss and Red Mackenzie

Through The Eyes of The Skull

Dedicated to Archie Hodgkiss, the best dad in the
world

First Published in December 2014
Copyright *Phil's Writing*

Chapter 1

The sun was out and a fresh breeze, not quite stiff enough to ruffle the waves, blew across the bay. Jenny slowly climbed the rocky path leading up from the pebble beach to the heather covered cliff top above her. Despite the coolness of the air, a slight film of perspiration had formed on her brow; the weight of the rucksack on her back adding to her exertions.

From the moment the alarm had woken her that morning she had felt the need to get out of her cottage and away from a home that was now harbouring two obnoxious male students who, since their arrival the night before, had invaded her sanctuary and trespassed on the tranquility that she had grown accustomed to. Overnight she had once again become a stranger in her own home and now she wanted nothing more than to escape the oppressive air the selfishness those immature alpha males had infected her peaceful existence with.

As had been his habit over the last few months her son, Stuart, had arrived unannounced, friend in tow, with the unashamed intention of using her seaside home as a hotel. Ever since she had become the sole occupant of the cottage following the sudden death of her second husband, Alan, less than twelve months ago, her son had been turning up like the proverbial bad penny on a regular basis.

Jenny could probably have tolerated this – she was his mother after all - but she found Stuart's visits all the more galling considering he had been an infrequent visitor while Alan was still alive. When she had finally plucked up the courage to walk out on her cruel first marriage he had stayed with his father and kept any contact with her to a bare minimum.

In their relatively short time together Jenny and Alan had only one argument of note; it being over Stuart and involving her giving him money. It wasn't that Alan begrudged Jenny helping out her son in this way but he deplored the cheap way Stuart played on his mother's emotions to get it. Her son had perfected the ability of making Jenny feel guilty about 'deserting' the family home; a guilt Alan argued without success that she had no reason to feel. He tried to make Jenny see that this was all her good for nothing son wanted from a relationship with her and that without the money, he would have no interest in her whatsoever. After all, Jenny owed him nothing after the way Stuart had treated her not only since the separation from his father but for all the years prior to that. However, Jenny was resolute about it all so Alan resigned himself to conceding that he could do nothing but stand by and support Jenny, however much it irked him.

As she made her way to the cliff top Jenny, unsurprisingly, found herself thinking back to Alan and the short time they had together. There was something important she had to do and she had decided that today was the day to do it.

Chapter 2

Jenny and Alan had moved to the coast to start a new life. Their decision to quit the village that they were both living in was made all the more easier by their desire to escape the memories of their unhappy pasts with their first spouses.

Jenny had met and fallen in love with Alan while they were both still married. At that point in their lives their lifestyles couldn't have been following such different paths. He lived with his rich wife in a large five bedroom house in the countryside just outside the village; she with her bullying husband and son in a two bedroom council owned town house in its centre. Despite these conflicting existences though, there was a common thread that eventually drew them together. They were both in relationships that made them extremely unhappy and left them wishing for more from life.

Jenny's first husband, Tom Barnes, had been a tyrant. He was an insanely jealous man and kept his wife as close to him as possible, convinced that if she was left alone she would be unfaithful to him. From early on in their relationship Barnes would become aggressive with her whenever he felt that she had stepped out of line. Barnes would constantly shout at Jenny and put her down at every possible opportunity. He ruled her with a tirade of verbal threats and did his level best to keep her on a tight leash.

In the early days of their relationship his abuse was sporadic brought on mainly due to his excessive drinking. But when he was laid off from his job as a car salesman at a dealership in the local town it became increasingly torturous. Because of this, Jenny had withdrawn into herself. Any of the villagers who saw her if she was out and about around the village saw a timid, shy woman who held her head down low. As a result there were not many who took the time to speak to her.

For Jenny's part, she scurried through the village, always seeming to be in a hurry and making sure she wasn't out of the house for too long. If she was away for more than an hour without good reason Barnes would whip himself into a fury fantasising about what she might have been up to while she had been away from him.

From an early age Stuart sensed her timidity and played it to his advantage. At the age of seven he realised that to gain favour with his father all he had to do was inform on his mother. He would report back when Jenny hadn't done something he had heard his father ask her to do or that she had been doing something that Barnes had told her not to. By doing so Stuart managed to avoid the mental anguish he had seen so cruelly dished out to his mother. He soon realised that he could get whatever he wanted from his mother by threatening her with his father if she didn't give him what he desired.

Barnes, likewise, cultivated an attitude of betrayal in his son which he rewarded each time Stuart informed on his mother's *indiscretions*. Stuart became very good at playing this betrayal game, even going as far as to make things up about his mother to please his father. Barnes, always ready to believe the worst of his wife, was happy to take everything his son said to him as the truth.

All in all, Jenny lived in a brutal loveless marriage, with a heartless, unloving son and with nothing in life to look forward to. Her only escape in life was her love of reading, liking nothing more than to lose herself in the books she invariably borrowed from the mobile library van that visited the village once a month. However Barnes, if he caught her in the act of reading, would scold her and call her a *lazy good for nothing* so she reserved such scant luxuries to the rare moments she was alone.

The turning point in Jenny's life came when their financial situation took a marked turn for the worse. The money from her husband's redundancy finally began to dry up as, in the months since being laid off from work, he drank or gambled his way through most of it. He found it increasingly harder to find new employment and those jobs that he did manage to get he could not hold on to. The longest he lasted was four weeks before his employer had to *regretfully* let him go due to his increasingly bad time keeping; a result of him frequently being too hung over to be bothered to get himself up for work. On the whole though, he would go to work one day and then not bother going back the next, citing that the job was *not for him*. Unsurprisingly, the longer this went on, the more unemployable he became.

As the weeks went by it became more challenging for Jenny to put food on the table and keep up with the monthly bills. Finally, with a great deal of courage, she broached the subject of her getting a part time job to help make ends meet. She had seen a cleaner's job advertised at the local primary school and thought this was something she could do without being too exposed to the glare of the people in the village. Besides, she wasn't afraid of a little hard work. She was, after all, used to cleaning up after her son and husband so she was sure she could cope with whatever needed doing.

Her husband didn't appreciate this suggestion at all. He flew into a rage and told her in no uncertain terms that no wife of his was going to go out to work, especially cleaning up after other people, and show him up. A woman's place, he had drummed into her ever since they had been married, was in the home looking after her family making sure that the house was clean and that there was food on the table. He didn't want the shame of the village thinking he was unable to support his good for nothing wife and son. However, after a couple of weeks of being barely able to scrape together enough money to buy alcohol and no likely change in his job prospects, he suddenly had a change of mind.

One Saturday night, after raiding what remained of the money Jenny kept aside for the housekeeping and taking himself off to at the local pub, he staggered in with a self-satisfying grin on his face and informed Jenny that he had found her a job as a barmaid.

Jenny was mortified.

She was horrified at the idea of having to work in a pub particularly as she would be serving the very people in the village that passed her by in the street. The thought of having to stand and serve them made her feel physically sick. However, Barnes angrily waved away her protests and told her that he had arranged that she start work the following night. He had agreed with the landlord that she could work every night except Fridays and Saturdays and that her wages would be paid straight to him on a Saturday night. Jenny was well aware that Friday and Saturday were his nights at the pub so it was obvious that he didn't want her there when he was. She was also under no illusion that the majority of any money she earned would more than likely be ploughed back into the pub having been spent on his drinks. In truth, she was doubtful that she would get to see a single penny of it. However, being too frightened of her husband to argue with him and face the consequences, she reluctantly resigned herself to doing as he commanded.

Chapter 3

Jenny spent the entire next day dreading going to work at the pub. Her experience of men convinced her that the landlord would be yet another male tyrant who would bully her and that she would embarrassingly dry up the minute a customer asked her to serve them. She told herself that she wouldn't be able to operate the till; that she would either short change or over-charge someone so causing an argument that would end up with her being shouted at and reduced to tears. In short, she was convinced that she would make a real fool of herself in front of everyone.

She imagined, irrationally, that the entire village would turn up to poke fun at her as she fumbled her way behind the bar and that she wouldn't be able to walk the streets of the village without being further ridiculed by all and sundry. She worked herself up into such a nervous state that when it was time for her to leave home and walk up to the pub Barnes had to physically push her trembling out of the door, threatening her with what he would do to her if she didn't go to work. Heaping more pressure on her, Barnes told Jenny not to get flirting with any of the customers. He made it clear to her what would happen if he found she'd been *over-friendly* with any men.

Jenny felt as if she was caught between a rock and a hard place. Never had such a phrase been so apt at describing her situation. If she didn't go to work then Barnes had made it quite clear that she would suffer grievous consequences. However, she was convinced that if she did go, her inability to do the job would cause her to lose it and be sent home to what would amount to a similar fate. Facing such a dilemma she felt she had no choice but to go to the pub and risk facing the ridicule.

Slowly, she walked the short distance up the steep road from her home to the pub; her stomach turning over every time she thought about what the night ahead was going to hold for her. She arrived at the door well before she was due to start and was standing outside still deliberating whether to enter or go home and take her chances with the wrath of Barnes when she heard the locks being drawn back. The door swung inward and the big, round, smiling face of a woman peered out onto her.

"Jenny?" The beaming woman asked, her voice full of enthusiasm.

It took a monumental effort from Jenny to resist the urge to turn tail and run back down the hill. Hugging herself in an attempt to stop herself from shaking she nodded a quick confirmation to the larger than life ruby faced woman in front of her.

"Come in, my dear." The woman said in a friendly West Country voice that seemed to have an instant calming effect on Jenny. "Welcome to the Red Lion. I'm Maisie. The landlady."

Jenny felt mesmerised as she followed Maisie into the pub. Each step seemed to take a supreme effort and she thought that her legs were going to give way under her they were shaking so much.

Tentatively she moved across the room taking a moment to look around her. She had never been allowed to visit the Red Lion, or any other pub for that matter, with her husband. He constantly told her he didn't want her miserable face putting a dampener on his night out. Therefore, being inside a pub was a completely new experience for her.

Jenny breathed a sigh of relief that it was empty. At least she had been spared the embarrassment of being stared at when she walked in.

Strangely, she found that her curiosity began to get the better of her fears and she started to take in her new surroundings. Low oak beams and alcove seating areas gave it an intimate yet homely feeling. It had a not unpleasant musty smell which reminded her of a museum she'd visited all those years ago when she'd been at school. However, this had the underlying smell of beer which she found surprisingly pleasant, given the fact she couldn't stand the staleness of the smell on Barnes' breath after one of his heavy drinking sessions.

All-in-all, Jenny found the pub quite quaint and felt herself begin to relax slightly; her nervousness draining a little.

Maisie came to a sudden stop halfway across the room next to an open unlit fire place where she proceeded to call out.

"John! John! She's here!"

Jenny stared across to where Maisie was directing her voice. She appeared to be addressing the pump laden bar that now stood in front of the two women. Jenny heard a loud thud followed by a strangled mutter of pain as a plump red faced man stood up from behind the bar, rubbing the top of his bald head rapidly. Despite her nervousness, she couldn't help but find this funny and put her hand to her mouth to stifle the laugh that was trying to force its way out of her. However, when she realised that the landlady standing next to her was roaring herself, she couldn't help but let out a shy giggle.

"Thanks for the sympathy, Maze!" The man behind the bar said half grimacing, half smiling.

"I'm going to get you a crash helmet, my love!" Maisie exclaimed when she had managed to calm her laughter. "How many times have you done that?"

"Only every time you call out when I'm not expecting it. That's how many." The man that Jenny now took to be Maisie's husband and, therefore, the landlord said.

"Well, when you've stopped messing around and making dents in the bar, this is Jenny. The new barmaid." Maisie said, placing her hand on Jenny's shoulder. "And this buffoon is my husband, John."

"It's very nice to meet you." A friendly-faced John said coming from behind the bar and thrusting out his right hand. "And welcome. Have you worked in a bar before?"

"Erm, no." Jenny whispered, nervously taking his hand and matching his firm grip with a timid handshake of her own.

Despite the apparent geniality of the man in front of her Jenny still felt very cautious of him. However, there was something about his friendly manner that seemed to dispel her fear that he would be the tyrant her husband was.

"That's alright. No problem at all." John told her kindly. "There's nothing to it. Maze here will show you the ropes. She'll be working with you most nights to begin with until you get the hang of it. She's been doing it for years so you just watch her and learn."

"Thanks! You make me sound like a right old mare!" Maisie said giving her husband a friendly thump on the shoulder.

"Aye." John replied oblivious to Maisie's attempt at indignation. "But you're a beautiful old mare and you're mine."

Maisie inclined her head slightly, narrowed her eyes and feigned a hard stare for a few seconds. Then, smiling, she turned to Jenny.

"Right. We open in fifteen minutes so we had better put a shimmy on and go through some of the basics."

With that, Maisie led Jenny around to the rear of the bar, indicated to her where she could hang her coat and then began the task of showing her how to operate the hand pumps, optics and till.

Chapter 4

Jenny was amazed at how much she actually felt comfortable working behind the bar. To her surprise, it didn't take her long to grasp the fundamentals and with Maisie's encouragement she was soon shyly joining in with the friendly banter that took place while she was serving. However, she was still very careful not to say anything that Barnes could construe as flirty. Her fear of the village appearing *en masse* to taunt her never materialised and she was surprised at how friendly everyone who came in was. John and Maisie, for their part, kept telling her how well she was doing and that she was a natural.

She had a few problems with the lager pumps, producing pints of froth. But Maisie was patient with her and gradually she mastered how to pull a full pint of the amber liquid. Her first success was greeted by a friendly round of applause from two young lads who had called into the pub for a quick pint on their way to town. They had gallantly stood by the bar encouraging Jenny as the first two pints of froth ended up in the slops tray. When they finally got their pints with the requisite amount of beer in them, Maisie offered to let them have them for free. Both insisted that they paid stating how much they had enjoyed the light-hearted entertainment. As they left the bar they wished Jenny luck in her new job and told her to persevere with the lager pulling.

Likewise, her experience with the till was not as traumatic as she expected either. She found she had a surprisingly good head for figures; something she put down to having to balance the meagre household budget. Once Maisie had shown her how to operate the till she had no trouble in ensuring that the customers left with the correct amount of change in their pocket.

All in all, Jenny thoroughly enjoyed her first shift at the bar to the extent that when she left the pub that night she was on a high, skipping like a school girl all the way home. As she walked down the pathway to her front door she still couldn't believe that she would have ever got so much pleasure out of working behind a bar. She was already looking forward to her next shift at the pub. Even Barnes' surly reception when she got in and the fact that he had left a pile of dishes for her to wash couldn't dampen her spirits. She threw on an apron and, singing quietly to herself, ran the hot water ready to wash the dirty crockery. She filled the wash bowl and with an exaggerated flourish, squeezed in a generous amount of washing up liquid. She released the water onto the dishes and set to scrubbing them. By the time she had them all stacked and draining she had finished singing and was now softly humming to herself. She removed her apron, switched the kitchen lights off and then headed towards the stairs.

Jenny popped her head into the lounge and told Barnes she was tired and was going to bed. He could only grunt a reply but that did not stop her going upstairs that night feeling as good about herself as she had done in a very long time.

After her shift had finished on the Thursday of her second week John took Jenny aside and presented her with a brown envelope.

"What's this?" Jenny asked smiling though looking a little puzzled.

"Your wages. We do pay our staff you know." John teased grinning.

Jenny's face dropped and, shaking her head, gave the envelope back to him looking more than a little alarmed.

"You have to give this to my husband on Saturday." She said hurriedly reaching for her coat and then turning to go.

"Jenny this is yours. You've earned it."

"But I can't take it."

"Why not?" John asked looking perplexed.

"I just can't. The agreement was to give it to my husband so you must do that."

With that she said goodnight and rushed home.

When Jenny turned up for work the following Sunday John was waiting for her. He couldn't help but notice her quiet mood.

Her husband had returned home drunk from the pub the night before well after Jenny had gone up to bed. He hadn't woken her, as was his usual routine, but had gone straight off to sleep himself. Although this was a welcome change to his behaviour, anything he did out of the ordinary always left her feeling a little uneasy.

When she woke and got out of bed the following morning he was still fast asleep. With no sign of her wages to be seen she was convinced that her greatest fears had been realised and that her husband had drunk himself into oblivion at her expense.

However, as she now walked into the pub, she could see that John had the brown envelope in his hand.

Jenny frowned.

"Your money." Was all he said.

He placed the envelope on the bar and walked away from it.

"Wait!" Jenny cried. "What? How?"

John returned to the bar, picked up the envelope and placed it in Jenny's hand. He gently closed her fingers around it.

"It's yours. As I told you on Thursday you've earned it."

"But my husband ..." she started to say.

John brought his finger to his lips to quieten her.

"It's all sorted. I've done a deal with him. I give you the money. All of it. And while you work here, within reason, he gets to drink for free. However, if I suspect, shall we say, any wrong doing toward you then the deal is off. I also made it clear that if I do suspect any such wrong doings to you then I would ensure they return to him tenfold."

"He agreed to that?" Jenny said stunned, amazed that such a mild mannered man as John could have such a hard streak in him.

John just smiled and nodded.

"And he knows it's no idle threat. I made sure of that. So he'd be a fool to even think of going back on our deal."

Jenny stood there amazed. She couldn't remember the last time anyone had stood up to her husband like that. The sheer fact that Barnes hadn't woken her when he came home and taken issue with John's threat seemed reassuring. No one had looked after her like this ever. Her life had been miserable for as long as she could remember yet here was this man who she had only known for just over a week showing her such kindness.

A sudden thought occurred to her.

"How did you know?" she said looking quizzically at the landlord and then, dropping her gaze to the ground feeling a little ashamed and very embarrassed, added. "About the ..."

"I can spot the signs." He replied shaking his head, a mixture of sadness and anger rippling across his face. "You get to recognise them, especially in this job."

Jenny couldn't help herself and threw her arms around John's neck. She kissed the top of his bald head and swung him around laughing.

"My! My!" Maisie said as she walked into the bar. "What's all this then?"

"It's your husband!" Jenny exclaimed skipping over to Maisie. "He must be the most wonderful man in the world!"

"Of course he is, my dear!" Maisie said smiling "Why do you think I allowed him to marry me?"

John rolled his eyes up into his head while Jenny grabbed hold of the land lady and hugged her too. She held her so tightly Maisie thought she was never going to let her go.

Chapter 5

Alan walked into Jenny's life during one of her Wednesday night shifts at the pub. From the start, everything about him told her that he was a gentleman. In fact, the more she got to know of him the more she saw he was everything that Barnes was not. He was kind, caring and always polite to her when he came to the bar to order. He always took time to speak to her and always spoke to her like a human being and not some kind of pet animal that existed only to be abused.

At that time Alan was married to Stella, the daughter of a local self-made multi-millionaire business man. She was well known throughout the village and had over the years used her father's status to her full advantage. She was calculating and ruthless managing to position herself on all the high profile committees in the village and surrounding area including the Parish Council. Here she wielded her power to the full in order to fulfil her own political desires. Everyone who thought they were anyone in the village went out of their way to move in the same circles as Stella and aligned themselves with her on anything she even remotely deemed important. Likewise, anyone who dared to oppose or disagree with her felt the full force of her retribution. Hardened business men were known to show outward signs of trepidation in her company.

Alan was completely the opposite. He was a humble but proud man. Like Jenny, he too was quite shy underneath and the years spent with his overpowering wife had gradually removed a little of the spark from his once vivacious personality.

From the moment they had married Stella had refused to allow him to work. She wanted him not only as a house husband but also as someone she could trot out as an ornament if need be at one of her social occasions. However, even his role in these *ceremonies* had become less frequent the more assured of her power and influence Stella became.

She had burst into his world not long after Alan had bought himself a small garage on the edge of the village. He had ploughed everything he had into it and, though he owned the business, he didn't turn over enough income to be able to afford to employ any extra staff. As a result he was not only the boss of his own company but also its sole mechanic too. He worked from early morning to late at night determined to make his business a success. On the modest wage that he drew for himself, he couldn't afford to rent or buy accommodation nearby so he lived in a small room above the workshop. However, despite these difficulties, he prided himself on the fact that he was never late paying any of his bills and always quoted fairly on any work he was asked to do. This resulted in him being known throughout the village as a fair and honest man.

On the fateful day his wife-to-be entered his life, Alan was working inside his garage on the particularly stubborn brakes of a saloon car. Whilst he was hammering away at them he heard a loud bang outside followed by the screeching of tyres. He dropped his tools immediately and ran out to see what had taken place. He found a black Porsche convertible, rooftop down, sitting in the road at ninety degrees to the hedgerow. Emerging from the driver's side was the most sharply dressed woman he had ever set eyes on. With her dark sunglasses, wide brimmed hat and short but fashionable white dress, she looked every inch a film star.

Alan was suddenly conscious of the fact that, as he had been working in the heat of his garage, he had peeled his overalls down to his waist to keep cool. His exposed greased stained muscle top was soaked with the same sweat that now glistened on that skin which was exposed. Despite his self-consciousness he was quietly thrilled to see that this obviously sophisticated lady could not take her eyes of his well-toned body. He deliberately flexed a bicep as he wiped the sweat from his brow and felt a slight twinge of arousal when the girl gently bit down on her bottom lip while not taking her eyes of his muscles.

Alan glanced over at the car. It was obvious to him that it had suffered a blowout. He could also tell by the length of the tyre marks and the shredded rubber in the road that the girl must have been racing along the lane at quite a speed. The front passenger side tyre had disintegrated and the wheel itself was buckled. However, it was obvious from the way the car had been brought to a halt with the minimal amount of damage inflicted to the body work that the lady was more than capable of handling a powerful sports car.

To his amazement, the girl didn't look the least bit concerned or ruffled by what must have obviously been a frightening experience. Instead, she was looking at Alan in a predatory way that gave Alan the urge to have her there and then. In time, Alan grew to recognise this as the look his wife would get whenever she came across something she had decided she wanted and was prepared to stop at nothing to get. But on this first encounter all he could see was this drop-dead gorgeous woman who was looking at him with unashamed desire.

The girl introduced herself as Stella. With a demure drop of her eyes she rubbed her hand seductively along the front bumper of the Porsche and asked him if he would be able to fix the car for her. Unable to suppress a laugh he informed her that, to his great chagrin, his garage was fresh out of wheels suitable for a Porsche. However, on a serious note, he did have a friend who owned a recovery truck and told her that if she wanted, he could ask him to come over and take the Porsche to a garage in town which would be much better equipped to deal with the damaged sports car.

Stella agreed to this and Alan was soon arranging for it to be picked up for her. When the rescue lorry finally arrived the girl told him that she would pay his friend whatever it took to get the Porsche to the dealer she used forty miles away. Alan couldn't help but be impressed by this open display by the woman that money was no object in her world.

Alan helped load the stricken car onto the recovery vehicle and, as it drove off down the lane, asked Stella if he could give her a lift back home or on to wherever she was heading. She told him that would be very gallant of him and she would like that very much.

Stella waited for him at the entrance to the workshop while he went inside the small office to clean up. While he rinsed the majority of the grime from off his face and torso he could feel Stella's eyes burning into his back as she watched from the garage doorway. She kept her eyes on him as he opened a cabinet in the corner of the office and grabbed a fresh t-shirt and clean jeans. Conscious that he was under scrutiny he pulled the office door to so that he could change unobserved.

Alan came out of the office making final adjustments to his attire and, feeling a slight chill of excitement, he joined Stella outside. After closing the garage doors behind him and locking them, he disappeared around the back of the building.

A couple of minutes later, and with no little embarrassment, he brought his beat up old pickup truck around to the front of the garage. Jumping out of the driver's seat he ran around the truck to open the door for her, helping her up into the passenger seat. He had draped a clean sheet across it to try and protect her dress from the grime that had accumulated over the months of use.

Once she was in he closed the door and strode back around to the driver's side where he climbed back in behind the steering wheel, fired up the engine and then set off back down the lane as directed. He was amazed when, after they had gone about three miles down the road, Stella asked him to turn off onto a long, winding driveway that he knew led down to the mansion of a newly resident millionaire businessman. When he asked her if she was a friend of the family she laughed and informed him that she was family. She was the businessman's daughter and had just moved in with her father after spending some time abroad. Alan laughed nervously but was reassured when Stella told him how grateful her father would be that he had been her knight in shining armour.

Alan drove into the courtyard of a grand looking house and brought the pickup truck to a stop outside. The porch entrance was elaborately designed with two Romanesque columns standing sentry either side of it. Stella waited patiently with her hands in her lap for Alan to exit the vehicle and make his way around to her door. As he helped her down her short dress rode up considerably to reveal soft, smooth, suntanned thighs. She caught Alan staring at them and with a seductive smile, slowly straightened her dress again. Looping her arm around Alan, she marched him through the grand entrance and into a reception hall that he was sure wasn't far off the size of his garage. He was awestruck.

Stella led him into the lounge to meet her father and over dramatised Alan's part in her rescue. As predicted, her father heaped elaborate praise on him and wouldn't take *no* for an answer when he demanded that Alan stayed for afternoon tea. Alan finally agreed and from that day forward his life moved on at a blistering pace. He spent more and more time with Stella and less and less time at his garage. The business began to suffer and eventually he sold it for half of what it was originally worth. Surprisingly this didn't seem to matter to his new found girlfriend or her father and, barely a year after meeting, they were announcing their engagement.

At first, Alan was excited at the prospect of marrying Stella. She was the most beautiful, self-assured woman he had ever come across. However, he soon began to feel as if he was being sucked into something he wasn't a hundred percent sure he wanted. He raised his concerns about the speed of their impending matrimony with Stella a number of times but each time he did so, she told him that once she had made her mind up about something she didn't like to wait. So Alan woke one summer's morning in June on the French Riviera to find that he was not only a married man but married to probably the richest woman in the County.

They returned to setup their marital home in a separate wing of his father-in-law's house. Life was bliss for the first few months. But when Alan started to get bored and finally began to get the urge to work again, his new wife threw a tantrum and told him in no uncertain terms that she would not permit it. She wanted him at home where she could keep an eye on him. Besides, she told him, there was no need for him to work anymore. If he wanted anything all he had to do was ask and, as long as she thought it was appropriate, she would make the money available to him.

Alan began to feel miserable. Every time he tried to exert any authority on their relationship, his wife would shout and scream at him, threatening him with telling her father how badly he was treating her. Unsure of himself in such a powerful household, Alan always backed down letting her get her own way. It wasn't long before he started to feel trapped in his own life.

When Stella's father unexpectedly died two years into their marriage she got to inherit his fortune. With a vast amount of wealth behind her she became more power hungry and Alan became even more of a sideline to her. She devoted the majority of her time to the local politics of the village and sought as much power as she could possibly get. Life became intolerable at home for Alan and barely three years after their wedding day she moved him out of her bedroom and into one of the spare rooms.

Chapter 6

Despite feeling sorry for himself, Alan managed to carve an escape away from his humdrum life. He began playing golf every Wednesday with two local businessmen who just also happened to be married to two of his wife's political associates. Stella naturally gave her blessing and actively encouraged this new pastime of Alan's. She saw these new found relationships of his as the perfect opportunity for him to feed back to her any information the husbands may let slip about their wives that might prove useful. She was also more than happy for him to go out with them to the local pub afterwards for a few drinks thinking that would be where they might be at their talkative best.

Alan, for his part, was very careful about what said to Stella. He was not comfortable with the idea of spying on probably the nearest he had left in the world to friends. He always fed back a lot of positive comments that put his friends' wives in a good light ensuring that nothing got back to Stella that she could use against them

Jenny had been working in the pub for a few weeks when Alan walked into her life. By then she had become comfortable with her surroundings and was beginning to develop an ever increasing inner confidence. This was in stark contrast to the meek and mild woman that still lived in fear of her husband when she was at home. But, while she was at work, she felt safe. This was a feeling she credited wholly to

Maisie and John who treated her like a surrogate daughter.

Alan had just returned from a holiday in Mexico where, though he had accompanied Stella, she had booked them separate apartments. As a result they spent two weeks having as minimal contact with each other as Stella deemed necessary. She went on sightseeing trips while Alan was left to sit alone by the swimming pool reading.

In truth, Alan was quite happy to sit in solitude and catch up with the latest novels he wanted to read. But there were times when he needed to be with people, even if it was the unrewarding company of Stella. However, whenever he did make the effort to get close to her she would push him away telling him to *go and enjoy the holiday she was paying a fortune for.*

Jenny was refilling one of the spirit optics when Alan came over to the bar. She turned around to serve him and immediately felt a rapid flutter in her chest. It was a feeling she hadn't had since her first schoolgirl crush. It caught her completely by surprise as it was a feeling she had never expected to experience in her life again.

The sun bronzed man in front of her had a handsome but sorrowful face. When he smiled at her she felt a warm feeling build up inside her.

Alan, for his part, gazed straight into Jenny's eyes and fell madly wholeheartedly in love with her. As he looked into them he saw a hint of the pain and suffering they held. But he also saw something else. Deep down, beyond the misery, he recognised a spark of life and passion that was there just waiting to be ignited.

Standing at the bar he was suddenly lost for words and Jenny had to prompt him for his order.

"Do I have to guess or are you going to tell me?" She said teasing him.

"Sorry?" Alan said looking quizzically at her.

"Let me see, you don't look like a lager lout. Nor a cider drinker either. I would hazard a guess at a real ale drinker?"

"Oh, err, yes... Sorry." Alan said stumbling over his words. "That's two Paddy's and a large coke for the driver."

"And are you the driver?" Jenny asked, taking a pint glass from behind the bar, placing it under the hand pull and then starting to pump out the dark liquid.

"No, I'm Paddy's." Alan said, still reeling inside from his first contact with the new barmaid.

"Well, nice to meet you, Paddy." Jenny smiled teasingly, reveling in her new-found confidence. "I'm Bacardi."

Alan stared at Jenny for a moment then realised what the barmaid was saying

"No, my name's Alan." He hurriedly explained. "I drink Paddy's."

"I see." Jenny said slowly nodding her head smiling.

"It's nice to meet you too, Bacardi...." Alan began then pointed his finger at Jenny. "Wait a minute. You're mocking me, aren't you?"

Jenny pointed at herself and pretended to look shocked.

"Who me?" She said her eyes wide and bright causing Alan's heart to melt further.

"Yes, you!" He replied giving her a look that told her he wasn't buying the *little miss innocent* act

Jenny smiled at him and if there had been any lingering doubts about that hidden fire he had experienced when he had looked into her eyes, the smile now lighting up her face erased them all.

"Well. There was a character in one of the novels I've just read called Bacardi." He explained, trying not to look stupid.

"Let me guess?" Jenny interrupted him. "Scarpetta? Patricia Cornwell?"

"Yes!" Alan said looking amazed. "How did you know that?"

"Well, despite being a lowly barmaid I do possess the ability to read." Jenny said trying to look offended but only managing to look more appealing in Alan's eyes. "I borrowed it from the library van and I've just finished reading it myself. That's what gave me the idea. My real name's Jenny by the way."

Alan gave her a wary look.

"No, honest. It is." Jenny said crossing her heart with the index finger of her right hand which Alan thought was the cutest thing he had ever seen.

"Well. That's a much fairer name." Alan said in a way that pleased Jenny.

"Why thank you, kind sir." Jenny said as she curtsied behind the bar giggling causing Alan to laugh.

For the next few minutes they talked about the books they had read before moving on to who their favourite authors were. They found they had similar tastes though disagreed on which novels they thought were the best. Their conversation was finally interrupted by one of Alan's golf buddies coming over in search of his lost pint. Alan thanked Jenny and went off to join his party. The barmaid watched him walk across the room, the flutter in her heart still there.

Chapter 7

From that night onwards Jenny looked forward to working on a Wednesday more than any other night of the week. She began to treasure the brief moments she managed to grab with Alan when he came to order at the bar. Her heart swelled when he walked in and sank as he left. The more she saw of him the more she found herself wondering what life would be like with him.

Alan found his Wednesday night trips to the pub were becoming the highlight of his week too. Jenny was constantly in his thoughts and he, too, began to wonder what it would be like to be out of the sham of a marriage he was in and with her.

One night, Maisie caught Jenny staring longingly from behind the bar at the table Alan was sat at.

"You know, he deserves better." She said to the love struck barmaid. "And so do you."

"I...I...don't know what you mean." Jenny said turning back to the bar and starting to dry a glass rigorously with a towel.

"Jenny, it's obvious." Maisie said kindly. "I see the way you look at him. I see the way he looks at you. There's chemistry there."

"It's just friendship." Jenny hurriedly said placing the now highly polished glass on its designated shelf. "He's married to the richest woman in the county. And I'm married to a homicidal maniac that would probably kill us both if he found out we've even been talking!"

"Things don't have to be like that." Maisie said looking straight into Jenny's eyes. "You're both unhappy with what you have. Why not gamble and reach out for something better?"

Jenny looked horrified for a moment. What Maisie was talking about scared her. She was a married woman and all this talk about having feelings for another man, also married, should not be taking place. She should politely ask the landlady not to raise the subject again and then suppress her feelings for Alan. But something in the landlady's knowing gaze had her dropping her elbows onto the bar and sinking her chin into her hands. Finally, she gave in to those feelings.

"I don't even know if he feels the same." Jenny said. "We chat about books when he comes over to the bar to order but nothing more than that."

"Jenny, your eyes light up when he comes to the bar." Maisie said. "There's a definite sparkle there. I can see that and I am sure he can see it too. He stays much longer chatting to you than any of the other customers and then all he does all night is keep glancing over at you. I've watched him. He's oblivious to anyone or anything else around him"

Jenny's head sank lower into her hands. She thought she had never felt so confused in her life. There was a definite spark between them; that she couldn't deny. But again it came down to the plain fact that they were both married and any such feelings just had to be wrong.

Hadn't they?

Jenny looked up despairingly at the landlady hoping for guidance. Maisie just nodded towards the table Alan and his friends were sitting at.

"Look, he's coming over." She said, her back to Alan so he couldn't see her talking about him. "Why don't you try and arrange to meet him outside of here or something? Be bold."

Jenny opened her mouth to protest but Maisie scuttled away, leaving her facing Alan with her mouth wide open. Alan stopped dead in his tracks and looked puzzlingly at Jenny.

"Am I that scary?"

"What?" Jenny said closing her mouth.

"You looked startled as I came over."

"No, it was something Maisie said to me." Jenny hurriedly explained and then tried to divert the conversation. "Do you want the same again?"

Alan nodded.

"I was wondering ..." he began to ask laying the empty pint glasses on the bar.

He seemed to be battling to get his words out. He took a deep breath and then puffed it out of his lips.

"I was wondering if you are you doing anything tomorrow night." His speech was hurried as if sheer speed of delivery would help him get out what he wanted to say. "Only I have two tickets to a book launch in town and my wife has let me down. Again. It's a local author. She writes historical novels based on the local area. Only I thought that with your interest in reading you might like to come with me."

Alan looked a little flushed when he had finished but his complexion was pale in comparison to the colour Jenny was now turning.

"I'm supposed to be working tomorrow night." Jenny mumbled back at him suddenly feeling as if the room had got warmer.

Alan looked as if he was thinking for a moment.

"Well, I suppose that's not an outright *no* which is promising." He said more to himself than Jenny before looking at her and smiling. "I'm sure Maisie and John won't mind. You must be allowed some time off?"

"But my husband? Your wife?" Jenny spluttered.

"My wife has an Extra Ordinary meeting of the Parish Council tomorrow night." Alan said with a little resentment. "We were supposed to go to the book launch together but as usual she has found an excuse not to spend any time with me. Unfortunately the author does not hold enough political influence for Stella to be bothered with."

"But my husband." Jenny repeated.

"He'll think you're at work."

"I don't know." Jenny said looking anguished. "It all seems a little deceitful. And if he found out…"

"It's only a friendly night out." Alan continued trying not too seem to pushy. "If you don't want to I'll understand. But if you did you would be doing me a great favour as well as brightening up my evening."

Jenny felt confused. Her heart wanted her to say *yes* but her head rang all sorts of warning bells, telling her she would be in a heap of trouble if she did go with him. Jenny had no doubts that if, judging by their earlier conversation, she were to ask Maisie for the night off the landlady would willingly oblige, especially once she knew why Jenny wanted the time off. But she was also aware that if her husband found out she had been off gallivanting with another man then, threat or not from John, she would be in severe trouble.

"Can I have a drink while you're thinking about it?" Alan's voice broke into her thoughts.

"Err… oh… yes… sorry!" Jenny replied hurriedly reaching down for a glass.

Her confused state of mind conspired to make her a little clumsy and she knocked a tower of pint glasses off the shelf below the bar and onto the floor. There was a loud crash as the glasses smashed sending a shower of destruction across the floor behind the bar.

"Oh, no!" She cried out and hurriedly bent down to start clearing up the mess.

In her haste, she failed to notice a jagged piece of glass from the base of a pint pot sticking up from the floor and ran the palm of her right hand down it. She let out an anguished cry and stood up quickly holding her injured hand, a small trickle of blood beginning to flow from between her fingers.

Alan leaned over and swiftly grabbed a clean beer towel from the side of the bar. He quickly wrapped it around Jenny's hand and held it firmly in place. Despite the throbbing pain of her wounded hand, Jenny felt soothed by Alan's gentle touch. For a split second she felt the urge to withdraw her hand from his. But something in the comforting way it felt stopped her.

"Are you alright?" Alan asked her with concern.

"I am now." She replied, liking the way Alan's hand gently cradled around hers.

After a moment's hesitation, she added, "I will come with you tomorrow night."

Alan gazed into Jenny's glistening eyes and his heart soared. Jenny looked back at him with mixed feelings of excitement and panic, not understanding how or why she had suddenly made the crazy decision to take up his offer.

Maisie came over breaking the spell of their first intimate moment.

"Let me have a look at that cut." She said, peeling Alan's hand from around Jenny's.

"I am so sorry." Jenny said tearing her eyes away from Alan to look at the landlady. "I'll clear up and pay for all the damage."

"You'll do no such thing, dear." Maisie said softly and gave her a reassuring smile as she began to remove the beer towel.

Jenny grimaced as a sharp pain shot through her palm and up her arm. The cut was deep but Alan's prompt action had stemmed the majority of the flow of blood for the time being.

Maisie's pronouncement on the wound was that it would most likely need to be stitched and that Jenny would have to go to the hospital in town. Alan stepped forward and offered to take her but Maisie reminded him that not only had he already had three pints and was therefore not fit to drive, he had also left his car at home.

Alan retraced his step backward sheepishly.

Jenny didn't argue when Maisie said she would run her to the hospital and stay with her while she was treated. The landlady called up to John who had been working on the pub's accounts in the living quarters upstairs and explained to him what had happened. Teasing him, she announced that he would have to look after the bar on his own for the rest of the evening and hoped he would be able to cope. The robust landlord, with good humour, came down the stairs and assured his wife that he had been running pubs long enough to feel that he might just be able to survive; if they weren't too long that was. The banter between them brought a smile out of Jenny which lit up her pallid face.

"I'll pick you up from here at seven tomorrow." Alan said to Jenny.

A wave of uncertainty washed over the barmaid but she nodded back at him.

Maisie looked quizzically at Jenny.

"I'll explain in the car." Jenny told her as John appeared with her coat and began helping her into it. Quickly they left the pub leaving John to sweep up the broken glass.

Chapter 8

The moment the two women were in the car Maisie quizzed Jenny about Alan's parting comments. Embarrassingly Jenny explained to the landlady how she had somehow managed to agree to go with him to the book signing the next night.

"Well, *hurrah* for that!" Maisie exclaimed banging the steering wheel in front of her with both hands not even trying to hide her delight. "I'm glad one of you has taken the bull by the horns."

"It's only a book signing." Jenny replied shyly. "It's not as if it's a night of mad passion."

"It's a start." Maisie said, her round face lit up with pleasure.

"Doesn't it bother you that we are both married and being deceitful?" Jenny asked looking warily at the landlady sitting beside her.

"It's only a book signing." Maisie threw back Jenny's words to her laughing. *"It's not as if it's a night of mad passion."*

Jenny couldn't help but smile herself until a sharp pain shot up her injured arm making her grimace.

"Right! Let's get you to the hospital." Maisie said turning the ignition key to fire up the car.

She drove off the pub car park and put her foot down on the accelerator.

"We need to get you patched up for your big date!" The landlady said with an impish grin.

Jenny looked at Maisie and shook her head in despair.

Maisie and Jenny spent two hours in the hospital casualty department waiting to be seen. Luckily, the bleeding had stopped but every so often Jenny was hit with a shooting pain that went from her hand all the way up to her shoulder causing her to gasp. Finally a short, plump nurse called her name and then guided her to a cubicle. Jenny then had a further wait until a female doctor arrived who proceeded to clean the wound by squirting a small syringe of sterile water into it making Jenny wince. After a quick visual scan of the wound she announced that it was clear of glass and asked the nurse to stitch and dress it. Jenny emerged from the cubicle twenty minutes later with five stitches in a hand now protected by a wrist length bandage and tucked inside her coat.

Maisie drove Jenny home dropping her outside her front door.

"I know you probably think it's not my place to say this," The landlady said as Jenny started to get out of the car, "but it seems to me that you have a chance here to do something that will make you both happy. But only you can decide if that chance is worth taking."

Jenny sat back for a moment staring out the windscreen into the dark. Then she turned to Maisie.

"Thanks for your help. You've been so kind to me."

She climbed out the car and stood on the path, giving Maisie a short wave with her uninjured hand as she drove off. Then she turned to the front door, took a deep breath and walked in.

Jenny could hear her husband in the kitchen when she entered the hallway. She took a deep breath and then went to join him. He was closing the fridge door having just retrieved his sixth can of lager of the night, evident from the five crushed empties lying scattered on the draining board.

"What the hell have you been up to?" Barnes growled pointing the can at her bandaged hand as she removed it from her coat.

"I had an accident at work." She replied suddenly feeling weary from the highs and lows of the evening. "I broke some glasses and cut myself. Maisie took me to the hospital to be stitched."

"You clumsy cow!" Barnes mocked. "You can't do anything right can you? And don't think that gets you out of doing the housework. This place needs tidying up. It's a pig sty!"

He glared at Jenny waiting for her to bite back at his words. But Jenny had no intention of being drawn into a confrontation with him. She was all too aware of the signs and knew it wouldn't take much to tip him over the edge. John's threats of reprisal or not, she was not prepared to push her luck with the drunken animal in front of her.

"Alright." She mumbled. "I'll sort it all out tomorrow."

"See that you do!" Barnes barked before adding, "You are pathetic."

"I need to go to bed." Jenny said wearily. "My hand's sore and I just want to lie down."

"Go on then." Her husband sneered. "Get yourself off to bed, poor little Jenny."

Jenny turned to go but her husband grabbed her shoulder. It was all she could do not to cringe at his touch.

"I'll be up when I've finished this beer so don't get falling asleep." He leered into her ear. "I think I might need to give you some attention."

He let go of her shoulder and rubbed his hand over her chest, clumsily fondling her. Jenny felt her skin crawl but stood still, not wanting to provoke him. He then slapped her on the rear and pushed her towards the door.

"Go on then." He leered.

Jenny climbed the stairs feeling sick to her stomach, wondering what she had ever done to be trapped in this hell. A dreamy part of her wanted nothing more than to be with Alan; safe and sound in his arms. However, the sensible part of her realised how dangerous even thinking that was. Instead, she would have to ready herself for Barnes and his insensitive advances.

Jenny woke the following morning feeling sore and dirty. Her hand had done its best to keep her awake for most of the night with its constant throbbing. She dragged herself out of bed and went downstairs in search of some painkillers.

She tried to push all thoughts of the end to the night from her mind. Barnes had never been the most subtle of lovers at the best of times but even he had surpassed himself when he had joined her in bed. He seemed to revel in the discomfort Jenny was feeling, pinning her down by her injured hand until the pain became so unbearable she had to scream. She was only too thankful that he was never able to sustain himself for long when he had been drinking. When he crawled off her, he had turned on his side without saying a word to her and was snoring loudly as soon as his head hit the pillow. Jenny had curled herself into a ball shielding her throbbing hand into her chest and fighting back her tears.

As she poured herself a glass of water to take her tablets with, she promised herself that she would change her life. She wanted no more of this shameful existence and was determined to make every effort to see that her night out with Alan, consequences or no consequences, was as enjoyable as possible.

Chapter 9

Jenny stopped half way up the path leading to the cliff top and looked at the palm of her hand. She could still make out the faint scar which she now traced with her left forefinger.

The scar was a reminder of that first touch of Alan's. She closed her eyes and tried to visualise him on that night, holding her hand. She could almost feel his touch as if he was there present with her now.

A tear dribbled from her right eye and rolled down her cheek. She made no effort to wipe it way. As it made its way down to her neck it coolness made her shiver.

Jenny opened her eyes and continued on up toward the cliff top, remembering that night when they had first gone out together.

Despite her initial fears, Jenny enjoyed the book signing the following evening immensely. Alan picked her up on time from the Red Lion and they chatted away nervously for the six mile journey into town.

Alan was wearing a smart casual jacket and trousers along with a white shirt and patterned tie. Jenny kept apologising to him that she was so under dressed compared to him. She wore a green flowery knee length dress with a rounded neckline that revealed only the slightest amount of cleavage. Draped over her shoulders hung a white cotton cardigan. Her legs were bare and she wore a pair of white open toed sandals slightly raised at the heel. She told him that he must think that she looked like a real plain Jane next to him and hoped he wouldn't be too embarrassed in front of his friends at the book launch. Alan repeatedly tried to reassure her that she looked beautiful.

Jenny explained to him that she couldn't risk coming out in anything other than what her husband would expect her to wear for her shift at the pub. If she had worn anything too fancy then he would soon have become suspicious. That being said, she informed Alan that she hadn't got much else decent to wear anyway. She had nothing in her wardrobe remotely fitting for such a sophisticated event.

Alan teased her, cheekily implying that she would no doubt look just as beautiful wearing nothing too. Far from being embarrassed by his remark Jenny couldn't help but feel strangely flattered by it.

During the journey into town Alan had plenty of time to tell Jenny a little about the author they were going to meet. Marjorie Watson was a local author who had been born and bred in the area and who was passionate about its history. She had decided a couple of years ago to use her love of this history to write a novel and tonight's book launch was the culmination of her work. The book had been tipped by the critics to be a best seller not just locally but nationally too.

"I'm surprised your wife doesn't want to be here tonight." Jenny said immediately regretting mentioning Alan's wife at all.

"Oh, in the early days Stella tried to get in with Marjorie, especially once she heard she was publishing a book. But when she realised that there was no political gain to be had from an association with Marjorie then she lost interest."

He told Jenny how up until two years previous Marjorie was a history teacher at the local high school. When her uncle died and left her a reasonable amount in his will she decided to give up work to pursue her lifelong ambition of becoming a writer. It was still a sizeable risk to take but she had taken a chance and followed her dream. It was a dream that was now on the verge of coming to fruition.

Jenny detected the pride Alan felt for Marjorie in his voice. He obviously had a fondness for the writer but Jenny couldn't help feeling a little intimidated at the thought of meeting her.

"What's she like?" She asked

"She's wonderful." Alan replied. "She has promised to donate a percentage of her royalties to the upkeep of the local museum. She says it is a *thank you* for the support it gave her while she was writing the book. Not many authors would be so generous. Another reason why my wife has no time for her. Stella doesn't agree with charity and sees the donation as a frivolous waste of money."

"She sounds like a nice woman." Jenny said.

"Marjorie, that is." She quickly clarified.

"Oh, she is." Alan said laughing. "She has no airs or graces. She is very down to earth. And she will absolutely adore you."

"Won't word get back to your wife? That you were here with another woman?"

"I wouldn't think so." Alan said reassuringly. "Marjorie has no time for my wife. And, likewise, my wife has little time for any of the other guests here tonight or she would have come herself. So don't worry about it and just try to enjoy yourself."

Jenny nodded and tried to relax. After all, if Marjorie was someone Alan was happy to know then there was no reason why Jenny should feel worried about meeting her.

The book launch was being held at the local town library and Alan parked up in a street not too far away from it. He jumped out of the car and strode around to Jenny's side to open the door for her.

"Why thank you, kind sir!" She said as Alan offered her his hand to help her out of the car.

Jenny gave him her good hand and he pulled her gently up into the warm night air. He reached down to retrieve her handbag from the foot well and then closed the door behind her. He flicked the switch on his key fob to lock the car and the indicators flashed briefly lighting up the street. Jenny placed the bag over her shoulder and waited patiently. Shyly she looped her arm through his when he offered it to her and walked by his side for the short distance to the library entrance.

When they reached the door Alan produced two tickets from his jacket pocket and presented them to the attendant. He directed them to a table filled with bubbling champagne glasses where a second attendant offered them both a complimentary drink. Alan took two glasses and passed one to Jenny. When she took her first sip the bubbles shot straight up her nose causing her to sneeze.

"Gesundheit!" Alan called out and produced a handkerchief from his top pocket.

"Thanks." Jenny replied as she dabbed her nose, smelling the faint aroma of Alan's aftershave on it as she did so.

"Keep it." Alan said as she went to hand it back to him. "I've got plenty more back at home."

"Sorry." Jenny whispered as she tucked it away inside her handbag. "I'm not used to drinking champagne."

"Stick with me, kid," Alan said giving her his best Humphrey Bogart impression, "and you'll drink nothing but champagne if you play your cards right."

Jenny laughed out loud before putting her hand over her mouth when she noticed that her laughter had attracted the attention of a number of the other guests.

"Come on." Alan said leading her gently by the arm. "Let's have a look around."

As they walked around the room Jenny was awestruck. She had never been to anything as fine as a book launch and she held tightly to Alan's arm. The library had been decorated with pictures of the author as well as posters advertising the new book. Alan guided Jenny to one of them and she read the brief plot of the book.

"It sounds a good read." Jenny whispered, suddenly self-conscious about speaking too loudly in the library.

"Would you like a copy?" Alan asked, his eyes lighting up at the idea. "I'll get you one. We can get it signed as well. Let's go find her and I'll introduce you."

Alan went to move on but Jenny held back causing him to stop.

"Are you alright?" He asked with genuine concern in his voice.

"I'm just a little nervous." Jenny admitted. "I've never met anyone famous before."

Alan laughed and then immediately apologised.

"I'm sorry. But Marjorie's not quite famous yet. Maybe once this book starts selling she will be."

He pointed to the poster in front of them as he spoke.

"Besides, she really is a lovely person. You'll love her when you meet her. And I'm positive she will like you, too."

Jenny took a deep breath and stepped forward. It had been a long time since she had trusted anyone, particularly a man, but she found Alan had a way of speaking to her that put her at ease.

They walked over to the far side of the room where they found a queue of half a dozen people waiting in line, all with book in hand, to meet the new author. Alan picked up one of the books from a table standing against the wall and then the two of them joined the queue.

Jenny watched as the grey haired lady behind the desk in front of them signed away and she knew immediately from Marjorie's smiling face that Alan was right. She was going to like her. The author was taking time to chat to each person who came up to her and was more than happy to have her photograph taken with anyone who asked. Jenny's admiration for Marjorie increased further when the young man in front of them announced that he was an aspiring author and did she have any advice she could give him.

"David?" She asked looking at the inside cover she had just signed for him.

The lad nodded.

"My advice to you, David, can be summed up in two words. *Belief and perseverance*. Believe in what you have written and persevere with it until it is published, no matter what knocks you take along the way."

The young man thanked her and moved away smiling leaving Jenny and Alan next in the queue.

"Alan!" Marjorie cried out when she looked up and recognised him. "You came!"

She rose from her seat and quickly came around the table to give him a hug.

"Of course I came, Marjorie. Do you really think I would have missed your big launch?"

Marjorie released Alan and then turned to Jenny, her face a beaming smile.

"Marjorie, this is my friend Jenny." Alan introduced the nervous woman who stood next to him.

"I'm very pleased to meet you." Marjorie announced enthusiastically, reaching out to grab Jenny's hand to shake it before noticing it was bandaged.

"Oh my dear, what have you done?" She asked with concern.

"Oh, it was just a careless accident at work." Jenny explained rolling her eyes and waving her injured hand in the air. "But it's ok now. No permanent damage. That's mainly thanks to Sir Galahad here."

She looked across at Alan with a twinkle in her eye and was pleased to see him blush a little. Marjorie looked quizzically at Alan to which he raised his hands to gesture that his part in the tending to of Jenny's hand was a small one.

"Marjorie, could I ask a big favour of you?" He asked wanting to change the subject and take some of the spotlight off himself. "I need to seek out the men's room and wondered if you could entertain Jenny for me for a few minutes or so."

"It would be a pleasure." Marjorie replied and shooed him away.

She then latched onto Jenny's arm and guided the startled girl around to the other side of the table. She located a seat for her and had her sit next to her while she signed a few books.

"He really is a darling." Marjorie announced affectionately during a slight lull in the signings. "I don't know what I would have done without him."

"Oh? Why's that?" Jenny asked with a little curiosity.

"Well, for one thing he has bankrolled this whole book launch, publicity and all. He offered to help me with it and wouldn't take *no* for an answer. Didn't he tell you?"

"No he didn't." Jenny replied looking over to where Alan had disappeared.

"That's so like him." Marjorie continued. "He is such a generous person but hates bringing attention onto himself. Not like that wife of his! I believe he had to tell her one or two little white lies to eek out the money from her for this little event."

Marjorie's face darkened at the mention of Alan's spouse.

"Can I give you some advice?" She continued, looking serious. "I don't know what your relationship is with Alan. He keeps his cards pretty close to his chest that one. But he has seemed so much happier these last few weeks and I think I can see why. He's a great man and deserves happiness. However, my advice to you is to beware his wife. Stella is a nasty piece of work and knows some very powerful people. She will do anything to win if she feels challenged. Oh, I know that she doesn't particularly want Alan but that doesn't mean she will give him up easily for anyone else either."

Marjorie broke off as an elderly lady approached the table. She exchanged pleasantries with the woman and signed the book that was placed in front of her. When she was gone, Marjorie continued.

"I can see from how he is around you that he likes you a lot. And if I may be so bold, my senses tell me you are a little fond of him too. You can be happy with him but be careful. If you want him then remember these two words.."

"*Belief and perseverance.*" Jenny said before Marjorie could get the words out.

Marjorie patted the back of Jenny's good hand as Alan arrived back at the table.

"You have a good girl here." Marjorie announced to Alan. "A good girl. Take care of her and treat her right."

Alan looked puzzlingly at the two of them while Jenny smiled back embarrassingly.

Chapter 10

Jenny reached the top of her climb and emerged onto the headland. She and Alan had loved to visit this spot on clear, starlit nights watching for shooting stars whilst the only sound to be heard would be the gentle rap of the sea breaking on the rocks below. Standing there now in the brightness of the midday sun she thought back to that first date and how, though she didn't realise it at the time, it had changed her life for good.

They had driven home in silence, each deep in their own thoughts of the worlds they were returning to after having tasted a world that might be. Alan had given her a peck on the cheek as he dropped her off back at the Red Lion and Jenny thought that up to that moment in her life, it was the most intimate feeling she had ever experienced. She stood there, outside the pub, clutching Marjorie's book in one hand and touching her cheek where Alan had kissed her with her other, bandaged hand. She watched as his taillights disappeared from view.

Jenny's emotions were mixed. Part of her felt good that she had spent a happy few hours alone with Alan but mostly she was sad that she would not finish the night with him, wanting nothing more than to fall asleep cradled protectively in his arms and to wake up in the morning next to him.

"How did it go?" Maisie's soft voice interrupted her dreams.

Jenny pulled her cardigan around herself and hugged her new book to her chest.

"It was wonderful." She replied with an anguished smile across her face, still staring after Alan's car.

Maisie placed her hand gently on Jenny's shoulder and gave it a friendly squeeze.

"You better get yourself off home." She said kindly. "You can tell me all about it when you are in on Sunday."

Jenny nodded and, taking one last glance in the direction of Alan's departure, made her way slowly home.

Barnes was sitting in front of the television watching wrestling when she got back home. He had a can of lager in one hand and the local paper in the other.

"What you got there?" Was the growl of a greeting she got from him as he pointed at the book she was carrying.

"A book Maisie has loaned me." She replied, suddenly feeling weary.

"Don't think you're sitting around all weekend reading that, lady!" Barnes barked at her. "This pigsty still needs cleaning up. You were supposed to get it sorted today. You've been letting the housework go since you started that job."

"I'm going to bed." Jenny said quietly. "It's been busy and I'm tired. I'll sort it out tomorrow"

"Make sure you do." Barnes grunted and turned back to the wrestling on screen.

Jenny trudged upstairs, her hand beginning to feel sore again. She walked into the bathroom, took two tablets for the pain and then brushed her teeth.

When she had finished she went into the bedroom and slowly got herself undressed. As she did so she couldn't resist rubbing the back of her hand gently over the spot on her cheek where Alan had kissed her. It had been a good night but as she sat half naked in front of the dressing table mirror reality began to engulf her. This was her life. Alan, as good a man as he seemed to be, would never give up what he had for her. And she had no right to expect that from him. After all, what could she offer a man like him?

The feelings she felt for him scared her especially as she knew she would never be able to build up the courage to take their relationship further.

"Relationship!" She whispered to herself. "I've spent one evening with him and listen to me."

Jenny looked across at Marjorie's book which was now lying on her bedside table.

"*Believe and persevere*." She said to herself. "That's easy enough said but how on earth do you put it into practice."

She had to face it. She was only kidding herself. She was stuck with the pitiful life she had with Barnes.

She finished getting undressed, slipped on her night dress and climbed into bed trying to clear all thoughts of Alan from her mind. As the pain from her hand began to subside Jenny gradually drifted off to sleep.

Chapter 11

Jenny woke the following day no clearer about her feelings from the previous evening than when she had fallen asleep. Her thoughts were a mixture of Alan's kiss, Marjorie's advice, and Maisie's encouragement; each one only adding to her confusion. Next to her, Barnes lay asleep snoring, the stale smell of alcohol billowing forth with every foul breath he exhaled. She was only too thankful that when he had finally come to bed he had gone straight to sleep and not bothered with her.

Jenny climbed out of bed and quickly got dressed. She had an overwhelming desire to get out of the house and away from the mean creature that had lain next to her for far too many years. She entered the bathroom, brushed her teeth and splashed her face with cold water. Looking into the bathroom mirror hanging over the sink she started to straighten her hair. In the reflection she saw a sad lonely face staring back at her and her tears began to well. Never, in all that she had been through, had she felt as lonely as she did at that moment.

Jenny wrenched her gaze away from the mirror, quickly dressed and then ran down the stairs. She slipped on her shoes, grabbed her handbag and exited the front door, not caring whether she returned to the prison that was supposedly her home again or not.

Walking briskly away from the house she felt the need to be alone so she headed in the direction of the village green. The sun was out and the birds were singing as she walked onto the grass. She found a clean, dry bench and sat on it, wondering how on earth someone could feel so low on such a beautiful day.

She felt the tears begin to well-up in her eyes so she opened her handbag to retrieve a tissue. Instead she found Alan's handkerchief from the previous night. She put it to her nose and took a deep breath. She could still smell his aftershave and, somehow, it had a calming effect on her. She dropped her hands into her lap and sat back.

Everything about Alan just seemed so right. Everything about him made her feel good.

She sat quietly for a moment taking in the start of the day. Then the thought hit her.

The handkerchief!

She couldn't keep it. If her husband found it she'd have difficulty explaining how she got it.

She looked around her and, to her relief, saw a waste bin not too far from her. She got up from the seat and, taking one last smell of the aftershave, dropped the handkerchief into it.

She sat back down onto the seat. Closing her eyes, she let the sun's warm rays land on her face. Trying to untangle her emotions she sat like this for what seemed to her like an eternity. Finally, she opened her eyes and gazed at the world around her taking in the beautiful serenity of the green.

She began to worry that she had been out longer than she could get away with so decided that she ought to make her way home. She called at the local store and bought a few provisions, not because she needed them but more to justify her disappearance from the house to her husband.

When she got back home she found him pacing up and down the lounge, Marjorie's book in one hand and the local paper in the other. The dark look on his face left Jenny under no illusion that he was fuming.

"To Jenny. Very Best Wishes. Marjorie." He read from the front page of the book. *"Very Best Wishes"* He repeated in a slow, even voice which stood the hairs on the back of her neck on end.

Jenny was frozen in place. She didn't know what to say to him. She stood there, the shopping bag hanging down by her side, staring at the man that was now in front of her waving the hard back novel at her.

"This Marjorie." He began and then looked at the cover of the book. "Marjorie Watson. This wouldn't be the same Marjorie Watson that was holding a book launch in the town library last night by any chance?"

He lowered the book to his side and then threw the local paper onto the coffee table in front of Jenny. As if taunting her it fell open on a half-page article entitled *Local Author Tipped for the Big Time!* and a smiling photograph of Marjorie stared up at her.

"You went to this book launch last night?" Jenny's husband snarled taking a menacing step towards her. "Instead of going to work?"

Jenny felt lost. She didn't know what to do or say. She daren't admit to him that she had gone for fear of him finding out that she had been with Alan and completely tipping him over the edge. She was also aware, as was he, that she was a lousy liar and that all the evidence pointed to her attending. She opened her mouth, not really knowing what was going to come out, when the phone rang.

Barnes glared at the receiver on the wall, fuming at the interruption. He looked back at Jenny and she thought for a moment that he was going to ignore it. She prepared herself for the upcoming chastisement she would receive. Instead, Barnes looked back at the telephone and stepped towards it. Still clutching Marjorie's book he snatched the receiver from its cradle.

"Hello!" He barked.

To Jenny's surprise, the anger on Barnes' face began to drain away.

"Oh yes, hello." He said suddenly becoming a little more civil.

Whoever was talking to her husband then seemed to hold a one way conversation with him.

"Yes. Yes. Ok. I'll tell her. Thanks." Was all he said before hanging up.

Jenny waited for him to continue his onslaught but for some reason his rage had now dissipated.

"That was John. The landlord from the pub." He said speaking to her as if he thought she was stupid and needed everything spelling out to her. "He rang to thank me for letting you go to the book launch with his wife last night. He said she really appreciated you stepping in at the last minute and going with her. He said he would pay you for the shift you missed and that if I want to go in tonight there will be a couple of extra pints waiting for me."

Jenny didn't know what to say. She couldn't believe that John could have rung at such an opportune moment and saved her from Barnes' wrath.

"He also asked if you can work an extra shift this lunchtime." He added. "I told him that you would."

All Jenny could do was nod at him.

Barnes seemed a little confused for a moment; as if he was unsure as to what he had been doing prior to him being interrupted by the telephone. Then he remembered the book in his hand and his face darkened again.

"Next time," he growled at her, holding the book up "don't you dare lie to me about your whereabouts!"

With that he threw it at her and marched out of the room. She caught it awkwardly with her injured hand, trying to ignore the pain that fired up her arm, and held it to her chest as though it was a shield that could protect her from the beast she had married.

She stood like this for what seemed like an age, her heart racing and her legs refusing to move. When they finally decided to oblige she tottered to the sofa and slumped down, dropping the shopping bag onto the cushion beside her. She began to shake and tears welled up in her eyes.

It took her a while to regain her composure and put her trust in her legs again. She rose and stood there for a moment making sure she had control of her balance before lifting the shopping and taking it into the kitchen. Once she had stowed it all away she slowly climbed the stairs to the bedroom to change for work, unaware that she was still clutching Marjorie's book tightly to her.

Chapter 12

Jenny arrived at the pub just before noon. She pushed the door open and walked into the empty bar looking around for either John or Maisie. She saw the landlord on the opposite side of the room rearranging stools around a low table and tidying up beer mats. He was whistling merrily away to himself unaware of her entrance.

Jenny called over to him and he turned to face her smiling. He stood up straight, letting out a short groan as, hands on his hips, he stretched his back.

"Thanks for coming in at such short notice." He said. "Maisie has had to go to the retailer's to get some supplies and I'm up to my neck sorting out the cellar. If you could cover the bar for me over the lunch period that would be a great help."

Jenny nodded and went to go behind the bar. She stopped and then turned back to John.

"How did you know to ring my husband?" She asked, looking puzzled.

The landlord raised his eyebrows.

"How did you know I would need an alibi? There? At that precise moment?" She continued when it seemed that John was not going to be forthcoming with an answer.

"Maze told me about your night out." He finally answered smiling. "She thought it might be useful for you to have some sort of story in case your husband found out about you going. Get in there first so to speak. Particularly as you brought that book back with you. I hope it helped. As for timing ...." John shrugged his shoulders.

Jenny smiled at him.

"More than you'll ever know." She said to him stepping behind the bar and starting to prepare it for the oncoming lunchtime rush.

John watched her for a while as she went through the routine of readying herself for the customers. His heart felt heavy for the poor woman in front of him. It never ceased to anger him how badly some men could treat their wives and how he would like to spend a solitary five minutes with some of these weak monsters. He didn't know exactly what Maisie was up to with Jenny but he had been with his wife long enough to realise whatever it was would have a good reason behind it.

Maisie returned from the retailers barely half an hour after Jenny had started work. She walked through the pub door carrying two large boxes of crisps and humming a tune. She saw Jenny behind the bar and smiled.

"I wasn't expecting to see you in today, my love." she chirped. "Is everything alright?"

"John rang and asked if I could cover for you while you went to the retailers and he worked in the cellar." Jenny replied looking confused.

"He did, did he?" Maisie laughed. "It was him that sent me off to the retailers in the first place when I said we didn't need anything. Insistent he was. I think I had better keep an eye on him, leaving him here alone with a pretty young barmaid."

She winked good-naturedly at Jenny who blushed a little.

"I don't think it was anything like that." Jenny said looking shocked and defensive.

"Now don't go fretting yourself, Jenny." Maisie said coming over to the bar and placing the box of crisps on top of it. "I'm only teasing. Besides, that husband of mine knows he would get what for if he started playing around."

"Like me you mean?" Jenny replied, her good mood once more deflated. "Running around with a married man."

Maisie joined Jenny behind the bar and held her arms out to the barmaid. Suddenly, the confusion of her feelings for Alan and the fear of her husband's anger that morning were too much for Jenny to bear. She fell sobbing into Maisie's arms and buried her head into the landlady's shoulder.

Maisie held her there gently patting her back until Jenny finally raised her head. Slowly, the barmaid pulled away from the landlady.

"I'm so sorry." She said battling to get herself under control. "I don't know what came over me. I seem to be a bit of an emotional wreck today. Can't think why?"

The landlady reached down to a shelf below the till and pulled out a small, stemmed glass. She filled it half full with brandy and handed it to Jenny.

"Here, drink this. Purely medicinal, you know."

Jenny hesitated accepting the glass from Maisie but the landlady persisted in holding it out in front of her, raising her eyebrows in encouragement for Jenny to take it from her. Jenny could see that Maisie was not going to take *no* for an answer so, with a resigned shrug of the shoulders, relieved the landlady of the glass. As she took a mouthful of the brandy she swallowed it a bit too quickly. She coughed and felt some of it burn her nose.

"Steady on, dear!" Maisie exclaimed. "Just sip it. That's the good stuff, you know!"

Jenny couldn't help but laugh as she wiped her mouth with the back of her hand. Once again, Maisie had managed to bring a calming air to her life. She took a smaller sip of the brandy and this time let it trickle down her throat. The warm sensation she got as it passed through her seemed to sooth her very soul.

"Thanks, Maisie." She said once the brandy had done its job of steadying her emotions. "I'm just feeling a bit mixed up, that's all. What with Alan and the book launch. And my husband finding out about it. Well, the book launch that is. Not Alan. At least, I don't think he knows I went with Alan ….."

Maisie raised her arms to stop Jenny before she managed to work herself up into a full panic again.

"Whoa! Relax!" She cried out with a gentle forcefulness that stopped Jenny dead in her tracks. "From what you've told me he only knows about the book launch and my John has sorted that out for you. So let's keep calm and not lose your head. Ok?"

Jenny nodded and took another sip of the brandy to re-calm her nerves. She let out a sigh then gave Maisie a hug.

"I'm alright now. Thanks." She whispered.

"That's good." Maisie said reaching out to hold Jenny's shoulders at arm's length. "Everything will work out for the best, you'll see."

A voice rose from below them.

"Everything alright up there?" John shouted, a slight echo in his voice.

The two women laughed.

"Everything's fine, my love." Maisie called back to him. "It's nothing to worry your pretty little head about."

They heard the sound of barrels being moved around as John went back to his work.

"Bless him." Maisie said, more to herself than to Jenny.

The barmaid saw the look of love in Maisie's eyes and found herself wishing for that same feeling in her own life.

"Right!" Maisie said slapping her left hand on the bar. "Now that that's sorted, how about helping me get the rest of this stuff we don't need out of the car. And then you can tell me all about your big night out."

For the second time that day Jenny felt her depression lift as she followed the landlady out of the pub door.

Chapter 13

When Alan came into the pub the following week, he and Jenny spent whatever moments they could manipulate together talking about the book launch and how good Marjorie's novel was. Jenny decided not to tell Alan about the episode with her husband and when she asked if his wife had said anything, Alan shook his head and told her that Stella hadn't even asked how the evening had gone.

Alan offered to take Jenny to the hospital when she was due to have her stitches removed but Jenny declined. Maisie had already badgered her into letting the landlady be the one to chauffeur her and Jenny felt this was the far safer option than being seen in Alan's car in broad daylight.

Alan also brought Jenny the good news that Marjorie's book was progressing well. Initial sales were well passed expectation and there was a good chance that it would enter the best sellers list very soon. Teasing the barmaid, he told Jenny that she may yet get to know someone famous. Jenny ignored his friendly jibes and told him how thrilled she was for Marjorie.

"That's good," He announced smiling as he scooped up the three full pint glasses Jenny had laid on the bar in front of him, "because she has invited us both to attend a *thank you* party at her house tomorrow night."

With that revelation, he turned and walked over to his golf partners.

Jenny was stunned. All the familiar feelings of dread and confusion surfaced again. The timid, submissive part of her character played on her fear of being found out by her husband. But there was a new part of her that was starting to grow in confidence; a part of her that wanted to be, no, desired to be, with Alan.

When he came back later on, she grilled him about the party.

"It's only a small house party." He informed her. "It's for one or two close friends of Marjorie's to say thank you for their support. And she has asked for you specifically"

Jenny voiced the same unconvincing arguments against not going.

"Besides, I'm having my stitches out tomorrow and may not feel up to going anywhere. Maisie has already said I don't need to work if I don't feel up to it." Jenny concluded her decline to the invite.

But Alan was in no mood to let her off the hook. He reiterated Marjorie's request that she attends and that the author would be very disappointed if Jenny did not accompany him.

While she was still deliberating one of Alan's party looked over from the table in an attempt to find out what was delaying his drink and Jenny tried to hurry Alan along.

"I'm not leaving this bar until you promise me you'll think about it." He informed her and sat at one of the high stools, arms crossed.

Jenny looked across at Alan's table where she saw both of his friends were now staring across at them.

Jenny felt flustered.

"Ok, I'll think about it." She whispered. "Now go before they suspect something."

"Them?" Alan laughed. "They would probably slap me on the back and welcome me to the club."

Jenny looked confused so Alan explained.

"They're both seeing someone else. So they are in no position to start casting stones. The last thing they want is for my wife to find out and then use it against their wives."

With that, he winked at Jenny and returned to the table.

Half way through the night Jenny saw Alan chatting to Maisie. The landlady looked across at the barmaid and then casually made her way over to the bar.

"Don't even think about starting." Jenny got in before Maisie could open her mouth, not convincing herself let alone the landlady.

"Start what?" Maisie said, trying to look innocent.

Jenny frowned and, trying not to smile, held her bosses eyes with her own.

"You should go." Maisie finally gave in whispering with excitement. "He's really keen that you accompany him."

Jenny dropped her shoulders. She knew she couldn't compete with both Alan and Maisie. Not only did she feel ill equipped to argue against them, she wasn't entirely sure she wanted to.

"But ..." She began.

Maisie cut her off before she could list all the reasons she shouldn't go.

"No *buts*. Seize the moment."

Jenny bit her lip pensively and for the second time since she had known Alan she found herself making a snap decision.

"Ok, ok..." She whispered, looking around her to make sure no one was listening. "I'll go."

Maisie clapped her hands with pleasure and looked across at Alan trying to catch his eye. When he looked over she raised her thumb discreetly and the smile on his face melted Jenny on the spot.

"Good girl!" Maisie said turning back to look at Jenny and patting her on the shoulder.

"But I have a problem." The barmaid said looking concerned. "I have nothing to wear. I can't go in what I wore to the book launch. I'd look a fool. Oh, I wish I hadn't given in so easy and said *yes* now."

"Nonsense!" Maisie replied sternly. "John and me were only saying this morning that we ought to give you a bonus for all your hard work. Let us treat you."

"I couldn't!" Jenny cried out looking horrified and feeling embarrassed.

"You can and you will." The landlady said forcefully. "And that's an end to it."

"But I can't take new clothes home." Jenny protested. "My husband would definitely suspect something was going on."

Maisie was quiet for a while and then her face lit up.

"Why don't you keep them at the pub?" She suggested. "Then you can get changed here and he will be none the wiser."

Jenny could think of a thousand and one reasons why it was not a good idea but knew Maisie wouldn't entertain one of them. So she just nodded her agreement.

"Excellent!" Maisie said and put her mind to hatching a plan.

It was agreed that they would go shopping for clothes the following day when Jenny had finished at the hospital. Maisie would bring them back to the pub and keep them there. She would ring Jenny's husband and tell him there was a party on at the pub and she would need his wife to come in a little earlier and stay a little later. Then Jenny could arrive in plenty of time to get ready and not be rushed when Alan brought her back.

Jenny had mixed emotions about the plan. Part of her felt terrified at the deception but she couldn't help but feel excitement at spending more time with Alan again. For the rest of that evening her spirit gradually lifted and she cheerfully went about her work. Maisie watched from a distance hoping against hope that the barmaid's new found happiness was the start of a better life for her.

Before Alan left that night he arranged to pick Jenny up from the pub promising her that he would have her back in time for closing time so that she wouldn't be excessively late home from work despite the groundwork Maisie was going to do with Barnes. They all agreed it was in Jenny's best interests not to push their luck too far.

After the last customer had left Jenny gathered up her coat and called across to Maisie to let the landlady know she was leaving.

"What time is your appointment tomorrow?" Maisie called over.

"Ten thirty."

"I'll pick you up at ten. Then shopping after remember?"

Jenny's heart skipped a beat when she thought about her date with Alan. She raised her hand to Maisie and then floated out of the door.

Chapter 14

Maisie was on time the following morning. She had rung Barnes first thing on the pretense of confirming her pick up time for Jenny's hospital appointment while outlining the need for the barmaid to be in work early and staying late as planned the night before. Barnes swallowed the story, even having the cheek to ask if Jenny would be getting overtime money. Maisie bit back her tongue and refrained from giving him a piece of her mind about that suggestion, not wanting to jeopardise the plan that was beginning to take shape.

She honked the horn outside the house and waited as Jenny came scurrying out. The landlady seemed happy to drive in silence to the hospital and Jenny was grateful for that. The excitement she had felt the previous evening had waned a little when she had got back to the cold reality of home. She had woken that morning feeling nervous about going to Marjorie's party and was happy to push it out of her mind for an hour or so.

Maisie dropped Jenny off at the entrance to the outpatients department and then went off in search of a parking space. By the time the landlady made it back to the waiting area Jenny had been called in. She picked up a magazine from the low table that lay between two rows of grey plastic seats, located a vacant one and sat down to read.

Maisie was half way through an interesting article on the demise of the great British pub when Jenny appeared. The stitches had been removed and she had been given a clean bill of health. She showed the scar to

Maisie who winced at the sight of it and then looped Jenny's arm around her own to lead her out to the car.

Maisie drove them into town. Despite it being market day she fortuitously found a parking space on the multi-story car park. Having paid and displayed, she suggested that they went for a coffee before they commenced their shopping spree.

Despite Maisie's protestations Jenny insisted that she pay for the coffee and pulled a battered ten pound note out of her worn purse.

"It's the least I can do to repay your kindness." Jenny explained to the landlady who was forced, for once, to give up her objection.

Jenny pocketed the change and then the two of them searched out a table. They found one tucked away at the rear of the coffee shop surrounded by two leather sofas. Though they had seen better days Jenny thought they were the grandest furniture she had ever sat upon.

Jenny was mesmerised by her surroundings. Not once in her life had she been afforded such luxury and she found herself enjoying the experience. The ambience of the place, particularly the soft background music, relaxed her. She took a sip of her coffee and had a good look around her. When she had finished surveying the room she turned to see Maisie smiling at her.

"What?" Jenny asked frowning. "Have I got froth or something on my nose?"

She grabbed a tissue from her bag and started to wipe at her face suddenly feeling self-conscious.

"No." The landlady answered laughing. "I was just looking at you and thinking how relaxed you seem. Probably the most relaxed I've ever seen you. It's nice."

Jenny felt a little embarrassed and looked down at her mug. When she peered up again Maisie looked a little more serious. Jenny sat up straight in her seat.

"Why are you being so good to me?" She asked. "Ever since I started working for you, you have been so nice to me."

"When you came to the pub that first night you looked absolutely petrified." Maisie began. "And with no wonder. I've served your husband on a number of occasions and not liked what I saw."

Jenny dropped her head again but Maisie reached across and lifted it so that the barmaid was looking into her eyes.

"Don't you ever be ashamed over that pig of a husband of yours." She said kindly. "That he is like he is, is not of your doing. You are a far better person than he will ever be. How you ever ended up with him is beyond me."

"We were sort of together at school." Jenny started to explain.

She looked across the room for a moment looking as if she was battling with herself as to whether to tell her story or not. Finally, looking back at the landlady, she took a deep breath.

Chapter 15

Jenny stood on the cliff top looking out to sea and pulled her cardigan around her. The air, though breezy, was in no way cool but thinking back on how much effort it had taken her to tell the landlady her life story sent an involuntary shiver down her spine; even after all this time.

"I was thirteen when my parents died." Jenny started, her eyes moist with emotion. "We were in a car crash on our way to the first holiday we'd had in a long time. They said I was lucky to survive. My parents were killed outright. I spent three months in hospital and no-one came to visit me. Except a social services lady. I had no other family willing to take me in so I was sent to the local children's home on the opposite side of the town. That meant I had to change school and lost all my friends.

The teaching staff were good to me there but they had a lot of kids to look after and, as I was so quiet, I sort of disappeared amongst them. I was very lonely and found it hard to make new friends because I couldn't stand the thought of losing anyone close again."

Maisie felt a lump forming in her throat.

"I'm so sorry, Jenny. I had no idea. You don't have to talk about it if you don't want to. I'll understand."

Jenny was quiet for a moment and the landlady was beginning to think that she had decided not to continue. But then she took Maisie's hands in her own and smiled.

"I've never talked to anyone about it before. But I think I want to tell you. That's if you are happy to listen."

Maisie nodded so Jenny continued.

"Well, like I said, I didn't make any new friends at the children's home or the school. I suppose I turned in on myself. I would only speak when I was spoken to and spent most of the time on my own. The other children used to pick on me; call me names; play cruel jokes on me; stuff like that. My life was miserable. And I missed my mum and dad so much."

Jenny's eyes began to fill with tears as memories of all the heartache at losing her parents flooded back.

"So I decided the best thing for me was to join them."

Maisie looked shocked.

"You thought about suicide?" She asked holding her hand to her mouth.

Jenny nodded dropping her eyes to the table.

"You poor thing!" The landlady said, feeling her own tears welling up. "You didn't try anything silly though, did you?"

Jenny laughed which took Maisie by surprise.

"When I was fifteen, I stood on a railway bridge determined to jump in front of the first train that came along. But I was too scared to do it. I closed my eyes when the train approached and when I opened them again I was still standing there. The train had passed by under me. That sort of set the tone for the rest of my life. Not having the courage to do anything that is."

Jenny suddenly realised she was squeezing the landlady's had a little too tightly. To her credit, Maisie had not complained but the barmaid loosened her grip a little anyway.

"I dragged myself back to the children's home where I found out that a new boy had been brought in. They sent him to the same school and he started hanging around me. He was a tough nut and the other kids stopped bothering me so I didn't mind.

Before long he began to refer to me as his girlfriend. At first I was happy for him to do this but then he started getting possessive. Any boy he saw talking to me he would threaten to beat up. When they backed away, which they invariably did, he would turn on me, accuse me of leading them on. I tried to break up with him a couple of times but he would get aggressive and bully me into staying with him.

"The week before I was sixteen we had a big row in my room. He had just been lined up with a job as a petrol station attendant for when he finished school and was feeling full of himself. He told me that now he was going to be earning he was going to go down to the council and get us a flat so we could live together. I was horrified. I told him I didn't want to live with him yet, if at all. He pushed me to the bed and stormed out of the room. I promised myself that no matter how angry he got with me we were finished."

Jenny stopped for a moment, took a sip of her coffee and stared into the mug she held in her hands, not daring to look at Maisie for fear of losing her composure.

"That night, when I was asleep, he crept into my room, climbed into my bed and he ..." Jenny was unable to put into words what he had done to her as even now some part of her was still trying to block it from her mind.

Maisie was horrified.

"Oh, Jenny! That's awful! Did you tell anyone?"

Jenny continued to stare at her coffee and shook her head.

"After, when he climbed out of bed, he told me I wasn't to tell anyone what we had done. He said that if I did no-one would believe me anyway and that he would tell the rest of the boys in the home what an easy lay I was. Then they would all come after me and he wouldn't lift a finger to stop them."

Jenny went quiet as she remembered how scared and dirty she felt throughout the whole experience and then lying in her bed afterwards.

"Was this boy Barnes?" The landlady said horrified. "Your husband?"

Jenny nodded.

Maisie was fuming underneath but didn't push her to continue. She waited for the barmaid to carry on in her own time. When she did start again, the more she told the landlady about Barnes in his younger days the more Maisie despised the animal Jenny was married to. What he had put the girl through during their years together was both physically and psychologically cruel.

"So I did as he said and told no-one. I was hoping against hope that that would be the end of it."

Jenny let out a sardonic laugh.

"How naïve I was. I suppose I still am really. See, he knew he had me then. By keeping quiet I gave him the green light to do whatever he wanted with me whenever he wanted to. From that point onwards he came to me most nights and took me. I tried to block it all out and withdrew even further from what little bit of the world I had been in. My school work suffered and I ended up leaving with no qualifications and no prospect of a decent job. He followed through with his promise, got a flat from the council and a month before my seventeenth birthday, with nowhere else to go, I moved in with him."

She returned her coffee mug to the table and sat back in her chair. She placed her hands in her lap and gazed down at them, not wanting to meet the landlady's eyes while she told her the next part of her story.

"Everything was alright to begin with. He treated me well and proposed to me on my birthday. Well, not exactly proposed. What he said was that he had booked the registry office and that we were getting married. When I said I didn't think I was ready for marriage he went into a rage and told me that I wouldn't get a better offer, me being *damaged goods* as he put it.

I was afraid that he was right and that I would be left on the shelf. So I agreed and not long after we were married."

"That's blackmail!" Maisie said, still not believing the depths to which the man would stoop to get his own way.

Jenny bit down on her lip fighting back the despair she felt at how she had been treated and her lack of fight against it.

"We had been living together less than a year when I fell pregnant. After the initial shock of it all I came to terms with it and started to feel excited about having a baby. But he was adamant he didn't want one. He said we couldn't afford another mouth to feed. He told me that I would have to get rid of it and made an appointment at the clinic for me. He drove me there to make sure I didn't back out but wouldn't come in with me. He left me to go through it all on my own. Afterwards, I felt so low but he wouldn't talk to me about it. The only positive thing about it was that at least he didn't go near me for the next few months."

Jenny closed her eyes. She felt ashamed and didn't want to look at Maisie for fear of what might be written on the landlady's face. But Maisie reached across and gently squeezed the barmaid's shoulder.

"Jenny. Look at me."

The barmaid forced her eyes open, waiting to see the look of contempt on Maisie's face. Instead, her gaze was full of comfort and warmth.

"My dear, you've had such a horrible time. You are such a sweet person yet this husband of yours has been nothing short of a pig to you. Don't you ever be ashamed of yourself over what that man has put you through."

Jenny sighed and breathed deeply. The compassion of the woman in front of her never ceased to amaze her. She took another deep breath and continued.

"It didn't take him long to start taking an interest in me again though and I was soon pregnant again. But this time I didn't tell him until it was too late for him to force me to do anything. By the time he found out I had gone passed the point of no return."

"What did he do when he found out?" Maisie asked fearing the answer.

"He went ballistic and smashed the flat up. But what could he do? I'd already registered with the local doctors and started ante-natal classes. He knew that if he laid a hand on me then he would be found out. Instead, he made my life a living hell. He would constantly shout and scream at me, criticising me over everything. Nothing I did was ever good enough for him."

Jenny didn't articulate that she wished now that she'd never gotten pregnant in the first place after all the sadness her son had heaped upon her. She didn't think she was ready to confide that part to Maisie yet, if ever.

She took another sip of her coffee before concluding her story.

"After our son was born he left everything to me. He wouldn't do anything. I don't think he ever changed a nappy that I can remember. He said it was all women's work anyway. It didn't help that my son was a sickly baby and wouldn't sleep at night. How I survived that period I don't know. I was completely exhausted.

"Not long after my husband got a job in the sales office at the garage. This helped out financially and enabled us to afford the rent on the house in the village. But it meant that he was out early in the morning and back late at night. It was hard but what choice did I have?"

Maisie shook her head in disbelief.

"And that's pretty much how my life has been ever since." Jenny continued, heaving a sigh of resignation.

She finished her coffee and sat back in her seat, indicating to Maisie that her story was told. The landlady knew there was more. John had shared with her his suspicions about Jenny still being abused by her husband but she didn't want to upset Jenny any further. If Jenny thought that she should stop there then Maisie didn't think it was for her to force the girl into places she wasn't comfortable going. Instead, she tried to inject an air of optimism into their conversation.

"Well, maybe your life is about to change for the good." She proclaimed. "Speaking of which, let's get out there and find you something stunning to wear. Tonight you're going to knock Alan for six."

Jenny was about to protest but Maisie rose from the table and started to move towards the exit. Not wanting to be left behind, Jenny quickly jumped up and followed her out of the coffee shop.

Chapter 16

Jenny stood in front of the mirror in John and Maisie's bedroom and couldn't believe that the woman staring back was her. The landlady had persuaded her to be more daring in her choice of dress than Jenny would ever have been herself and if there was one thing the barmaid had learned about Maisie, once she had set her mind on something she was not for turning.

Jenny had arrived at the pub just before six. She'd reminded Barnes about the party and that she needed to be in early to help Maisie set up for it. She'd been so nervous lying to him that she could barely get her words out and was a complete bag of nerves when she'd eventually left home. She'd convinced herself that Barnes would pick up on her erratic behaviour and see right through her deception. But as it was, he was too engrossed in the horse racing on the television to honour her with anything more than a grunt when she said she was leaving.

By the time she reached the pub she was shaking like a leaf and Maisie had to force a brandy into her to steady the barmaid's nerves. She joked that if Jenny kept this up then she would have to put the barmaid's name on the brandy bottle, marking it as her own personal supply. This made Jenny smile and she began to feel a little calmer.

Seizing the moment, Maisie whisked Jenny upstairs to change and, after showing her where the clothes were laid out on the bed, left her to dress in private.

Jenny stripped off and put on the new lingerie Maisie had insisted on buying for her. The set was black and consisted of a strapless bra, lace panties and silk stockings. When Jenny put them on she thought that they were the most erotic pieces of clothing she had ever worn.

She picked up the black dress that was spread across the bed and held it carefully out in front of her as if it was made of the most expensive material in creation. She studied it a while and then stepped into it. As she pulled it up over her body she felt it slide smoothly over her exposed skin causing it to break out in goose bumps. It made her feel sensual and she couldn't help stroking the skin around her shoulders as she slipped the thin straps over them. Her body felt electric and, louder than she expected, she let out a moan of pleasure. She stared at the door, half expecting Maisie to walk in catching her in this self-indulgent act. But the door remained closed and she let out a giggle. She felt like an adolescent girl discovering the sensitivity of her body for the first time.

Jenny sat down at the dressing table and began to apply a liberal amount of make up to her face and lipstick to her mouth. She pouted her lips in the mirror which brought another giggle from her. She brushed her hair until it felt smooth and straight on her bare shoulders and then stood up. Maisie had a full length mirror in the corner of the bedroom and Jenny gazed at herself in it. The woman looking back at her was a stranger. She could hardly reconcile her with the timid woman she saw every morning in her own mirror. She looked like a movie star compared to that meek, mouse-like creature that had endured the torment of a loveless marriage for too many years.

She wondered what Alan would think when he saw her.

Alan!

Suddenly, the very thought of him made her want to rip her new clothes off and get back into the drab ones she had arrived in. She felt absolutely petrified at the thought of stepping out with him dressed the way she was. She suddenly felt too exposed. The dress was far too low cut to be decent and only just about reached her knees.

As she went to free the straps from her arms to let the dress drop off her, there was a knock on the bedroom door.

"Are you decent?" The landlady called out. "Only it's nearly ten to seven and Alan will be here any moment."

Jenny called Maisie in and then sat down on the bed, worrying at her shaking hands in her lap. The landlady waddled in holding a small cardboard box and smiling. When she saw the state Jenny was in her smile dropped.

"My dear, whatever is the matter?"

Jenny looked up at the landlady with pleading eyes.

"Oh, Maisie! What am I going to do? I'm making a right fool of myself. Look at me. Dressed up like the dog's dinner and for what? A man that I've no chance of having."

Jenny felt the tears welling up in her eyes as Maisie sat down beside her.

"Hey!" The landlady said softly passing Jenny a tissue. "What's brought all this on?"

"I feel so confused, Maisie." Jenny explained. "One minute I'm scared that something will happen and we'll do something we'll both regret. Then the next, I'm scared something won't and we'll do nothing. I want him so badly but I'm afraid of the consequences."

Jenny looked up at the big round face of the landlady not believing that she had just blurted out the depth of her feelings for Alan. Maisie patted her hand and smiled.

"Jenny, whatever will be, will be is what I think. Go out and enjoy the evening with him. Have a good time and let fate take its course. If you are meant to be together, then that's all well and good. If not, I'm sure the pair of you have developed a good enough friendship to just be happy in each other's company."

"What if he wants what I can't give him?" Jenny blurted out. "What if he won't give me what I desperately need? What if ..."

Maisie place her hand on Jenny's arm to calm her and gently stroked her skin.

"Alan's a nice man. I'm sure he will take it as fast or as slow as you want to go. You look stunning in this dress and any man worth his salt would be proud just to have you on his arm. And Alan is one of those men.

Go out and enjoy yourself tonight. Don't have any expectations and then anything that does happen will be a bonus. Build up your friendship with him and then see what happens from there."

Jenny allowed herself a smile. Maisie always seemed to have the knack of putting her feelings into perspective and making her see things in a different, more positive light.

The landlady retrieved the box she had brought in with her and opened it. Inside it was a pair of black velvet high-heeled shoes.

"What do you think?" Maisie asked a wide eyed Jenny.

Jenny took them out of the box and turned them over in her hands, studying them from every conceivable angle.

"They're beautiful!" She announced before slipping them onto her feet.

They felt comfortable and complimented her new dress perfectly.

Jenny stood up and pointed her toes in numerous directions inspecting the shoes from every angle before pulling the landlady to her feet.

"I have one more thing for you." Maisie said walking over to the wardrobe and opening the door.

She rummaged about inside for a moment, mumbling to herself while Jenny stared on wondering what the landlady was up to now.

"Aha!" She exclaimed. "Here it is."

She re-emerged from the wardrobe and handed a little gold handbag to Jenny.

"This will go splendidly with that dress and those shoes."

Jenny put both her hands to her mouth and let out a gasp. Maisie passed the handbag to her and Jenny held it to her chest for a moment

"It's gorgeous." She said hugging Maisie.

She opened it and slipped her lipstick into it.

"How will I ever be able to thank you for your kindness?"

"Be happy." The landlady replied. "And enjoy yourself. You look gorgeous and you'll knock Alan for six. And don't worry about what might or might not happen. Alan's one of life's gentlemen and I'm sure he will act accordingly."

"I think that's what I'm afraid of!" She uttered before she could stop herself.

Maisie looked back at her with feigned shock before they both burst out laughing.

Alan arrived at the pub on the stroke of seven and was standing at the bar chatting to John when Jenny came downstairs following Maisie. As she emerged from behind the bar the landlord and Alan stopped talking in mid-sentence. They stared at the beautiful woman in front of them in stunned silence.

"What's the matter, boys?" Maisie said smiling. "Anyone would think that neither of you had seen a pretty lady before."

Alan was the first to break, a broad warm smile beamed across his face.

"You look absolutely stunning!"

"It's true, Jenny." John joined in as Maisie sidled up to him. "You look beautiful."

"What did I tell you?" The landlady asked.

Jenny felt a little embarrassed at the comments she was getting. She was not used to being the centre of attention and she was certainly not used to being paid so many compliments.

Alan took a step forward and offered his arm to her.

"Shall we go and party."

Jenny took his arm and, with a nervous smile, let Alan lead her out of the pub.

Chapter 17

On the journey to Marjorie's it took every ounce of Alan's will power to maintain his focus on the road ahead and not keep looking across at Jenny. Any lingering doubt that may have existed up until then had been extinguished. He was head over heels in love with the woman that was sitting next to him. There was so much that he wanted to say to her but was afraid to articulate how he felt for fear of spoiling their evening. The fact that Jenny had sat their quiet and nervous for the journey thus far didn't help so he kept what little conversation there was between them on safe, neutral ground.

"Marjorie's book is selling well. There's a real chance she might get an award for it."

Jenny nodded and felt the grip on her handbag in her lap tighten. The mere sound of Alan's voice made her feel confused, scared and excited all at the same time and in equal doses. She felt as if she was on a rollercoaster of emotions. One minute she was on a high at being with him, enthused by all his charming and caring ways. Then she would plummet to the depth of despair as the reality of what she was doing gripped her.

It had been easy in Maisie's bedroom to let the landlady's positivity sweep her along. But now, in the cold light of actually being with Alan, all her self-doubts and concerns resurfaced.

In the bedroom, she had reconciled herself with the fact that the trip to the book signing was just two friends enjoying a common interest. But, alone with him now, she felt that she had stepped way beyond that boundary. Deceiving her husband as she was doing, animal or not as Maisie was want to call him, brought home the severity of what she was doing. She began to convince herself that the new clothes she was wearing, though black, marked her out as a scarlet woman. The dress was too revealing and the lingerie was too sassy; unable to stop thinking that the underwear was chosen more for Alan's enjoyment than her own comfort.

Her underwear!

The rollercoaster took a sharp upward turn as she thought about the erotic lingerie Maisie had virtually insisted on.

In no way did she think of herself as sexually attractive. The years of being with her husband had turned her into a passive participant in their sex life and she had never got the slightest bit excited by his Neanderthal approaches. She would always switch off during the act until he rolled off her and went to sleep; his needs satisfied.

But sitting next to Alan in the car, feeling the silky touch of her underwear against her skin, she felt sensations in places she was sure she had never felt sensations before. She began to imagine Alan putting his hands on her and caressing her like all the good lovers did in the books she read. She felt his soft sensual touch; a million miles away from the harsh groping she received from her husband. She could feel his hot breath in her ear as he whispered into it and suddenly the temperature in the car ratcheted up a notch. She closed her eyes and he was there, lying next to her stroking her hair. She reached over and gently squeezed his leg.

The sharp swerve of the car snatched her back to reality. Alan quickly regained control of the steering and brought the vehicle to a stop at the kerbside. He looked across at Jenny with an astonished schoolboy-like face.   Jenny suddenly realised where her hand was and whipped it back into her lap where it gripped her handbag even tighter than before.

"I'm so sorry!" She cried out feeling flustered.

The temperature in the car had now gone from hot to sweltering and Jenny thought she was going to pass out. She kept her eyes on the handbag in her lap and didn't dare look up. Alan regained his composure and reached over to her. He placed his hand carefully behind her neck and turned her to face him. He pulled her close and gently but firmly placed his lips on hers.

At first Jenny half-heartedly resisted but the subtle smell of his aftershave coupled with the taste of his lips broke down the barriers that had been holding her back. She reached behind his head and returned his kiss passionately. Like a couple of love hungry teenagers they feasted on each other, the frustration of the preceding weeks finally breaking out.

Eventually, Jenny reluctantly pulled away from Alan and they both sat back in their seats, staring out of the windscreen in front of them as if in shock.

"Well." Alan finally said, breaking the silence between them. "Feel free to grab my leg like that at any time if that's what's going to happen."

Jenny blushed a little but gave him a shy smile.

"I don't know what came over me. Sorry."

"Don't apologise." Alan replied.

Jenny suddenly hit the depths of despair again and her shoulders began to shake as she started to sob uncontrollably.

"Is my kissing that bad?" Alan said trying to be light hearted.

"No." Jenny blurted out. "It was wonderful. I've waited so long for it and it was everything I imagined it to be. But this whole thing is so complicated! I just feel so confused. I'm sorry"

"It's me that should apologise." Alan said looking serious. "I shouldn't have kissed you like that and added to your confusion. It's my fault."

Jenny looked up from her lap and saw the concern etched on Alan's face.

"I've wanted you to kiss me for so long it seems." Jenny said battling to get her sobs under control and even managing to give Alan a weak smile. "It was just a bit of a shock when it came out of the blue like that."

Alan caressed his chin with his hand and, to his surprise, felt a little tearful himself. It was an unplanned outburst of emotion and had caught him by surprise as much as it had Jenny. He reached over and gently grasped her hand, searching for the words he wanted to say. Jenny broke the spell for him.

"We'd better get a move on or Marjorie will think we're not coming."

Alan paused for a moment before nodding. He put his hands back on the steering wheel, indicated to pull out and then set off again.

Chapter 18

For the remainder of the journey, Alan and Jenny were silent. Neither felt particularly uncomfortable but both were trying to make sense of what had just happened. They arrived at Marjorie's house just before half past seven and Jenny could see through the window that some of the other guests had already arrived.

Alan jumped out of the car and strode around to Jenny's side to perform his now customary duty of opening the door for her. As she stepped out she grasped his arm and he could feel her shaking.

"Are you alright?" He asked, staring reassuringly into her eyes.

Jenny took a deep breath and nodded, trying to mask her nervousness with a smile.

Alan led her through the gate and up the garden path to the front door. He rang the doorbell and soon a shadow was darkening the frosted glass window from the inside. The door opened and a beaming Marjorie greeted them with a glass of champagne in her hand.

"Alan! Jenny! Come in. I'm so pleased you could make it."

The author stood aside to allow them in. She closed the door behind them before pecking Alan on both cheeks and then hugging Jenny.

"You look gorgeous, Jenny." Marjorie said holding Jenny's hand and stepping back to get a better look at her. "That dress is simply divine and suits you to a T. It's very classy."

"You don't think it's a little too ....." Jenny replied wafting her hand above her cleavage.

"Oh, no!" Alan and Marjorie called out together.

Marjorie looked at Alan, who had turned a brighter shade of red, and laughed.

"I think you can say that that gives it the seal of approval." She said raising her eyebrows towards Alan. "You look stunning. Come in and meet everyone."

She grabbed Jenny by the elbow and marched her into the front room. Alan trailed along behind them, temporarily forgotten in the author's excitement to introduce Jenny to her friends.

"Everyone. This is Jenny." She announced. "A very good friend of mine."

Jenny acknowledged the salutations of the gathered throng and then allowed herself to be whisked off to the buffet table which was adorned with every type of party food imaginable. Marjorie thrust a plate into Jenny's hand and encouraged her to help herself. As she did so, Jenny looked across the room towards Alan who, slightly bemused, shrugged his shoulders and smiled. She smiled pensively back.

As Jenny reached the chicken drumsticks, the doorbell rang and Marjorie excused herself. Seizing the opportunity, Alan joined Jenny at the table. Having filled their plates, they sought a relatively quiet spot to sit and eat. Jenny was happy to remain there and watch the party unfold in front of her while Alan interspersed his conversation with her with that of a middle aged portly gentleman who had sat in a chair next to him and quizzed him on his thoughts about the England cricket team's chances of winning back the ashes over the summer. As Alan chatted away, Jenny thought that she had never been to such a grand party.

The party had been in full swing still but the closer the hands of the carriage clock on Marjorie's mantelpiece got to ten o'clock, the more fidgety Jenny became. Alan recognised her restlessness and suggested that they should maybe think of heading back home. Jenny, though sad at the thought of their evening ending, was grateful for his consideration. They located their hostess and despite her protestations to the contrary, said their goodbyes. Marjorie wouldn't let them go without a promise from them that they would visit again very soon. Alan gave his word that he would be in touch and then ushered Jenny out of the door and towards the car.

As they walked back down the garden path, Jenny suddenly felt the slight chill in the night air and shivered a little. Alan, detecting she was cold, took off his jacket and placed it over her shoulders. As he did so, Jenny looked into his eyes and smiled.

"Thank you." She said grabbing his hand and bringing it to her cheek.

"For what?"

"For being a gentleman. For bringing me here. For being such a wonderful person. For everything."

Alan smiled and pulled Jenny to him. He pushed a rogue hair that had fallen across her face back into place and then kissed her on the lips. Jenny closed her eyes and savored the moment. All too soon Alan pulled away and put his arm around her waist.

"You're welcome." He said as he guided her to the car.

He pulled the door with a bow and held it open for her while she settled herself into the passenger seat. When she was secure, he closed the door and walked around to the driver's side. Once in, he fired up the engine and drove slowly away.

At first Jenny chatted freely about the evening. But the nearer they got to the village, the quieter she became. Her thoughts began turning back to home and the husband that was waiting for her there.

Alan sensed her anxiety and pulled into a lay-by on the main road less than fifty yards from the turning to the village.

"Are you alright?" He asked reaching across to hold her hand.

Jenny couldn't hold back and grabbing him, pulled him to her, her warm tears dampening his shirt.

"Oh, Alan. What am I going to do?"

Alan stroked her hair and then kissed the top of her head.

"Hey. What's brought this on?" He said softly.

"I can't go on like this. I'm no good at all this deceitfulness. I've got to go back home and act as if nothing has happened tonight but I don't think I can. I've had such a good time."

Alan gently turned her head so that she was looking at him.

"Nothing has happened tonight that you should be ashamed of."

"We kissed! If my husband ever finds out he will kill me. You don't know what he's like!"

Jenny's sobs began to get stronger so Alan pulled her close again.

"It's alright, Jenny. He won't find out. How could he?"

"Oh, he will. Somehow he'll find out. I don't know how I'm going to hide it from him much longer."

"Hide what, Jenny? It was a kiss. Unless you tell him he'll never know."

"It's not the kiss." Jenny sobbed as she pulled away from Alan and looked him straight in the eyes. "Don't you understand? I don't know how much longer I can hide from him that I've fallen in love with another man."

Chapter 19

Alan drove Jenny back to the pub thinking on what she had just said to him. He had wanted to tell her how much he loved her too; that every waking hour without her was hell on earth and the moments they did spend together heaven. But she was having such a hard time holding herself together as it was that he felt that any such revelation would confuse her more.

Jenny had just about managed to get her emotions under control by the time Alan drove onto the pub car park. Quickly, she climbed out of the car and started towards the rear of the Red Lion. Alan caught up with her and insisted that he accompanied her to the back door to satisfy himself that she had got in safely. Jenny didn't put up a fight.

Maisie had suggested that the barmaid come in through the back entrance after Jenny had expressed concern that there might still be customers in the pub when she returned. The last thing she wanted was for them to see her enter the pub with Alan dressed the way she was. That would have been a sure fire way of getting the village gossip started and Jenny was afraid that it wouldn't be long before such gossip reached the ears of Barnes.

Maisie had left the door leading into the pub kitchen unlocked. Jenny pushed it open. She walked inside and didn't object when Alan followed her. Once safely inside and with the door shut she turned and flung her arms around him.

"Thanks for such a wonderful evening." She said and hugged him close to her.

Her eyes were watery but she managed to force aa smile which she hoped masked the torment she felt inside.

Alan turned his lips towards hers and made to kiss her but Jenny turned her head away.

"Not here, please." She whispered. "It doesn't seem right."

Alan stepped back from her feeling concerned he'd overstepped the mark again.

"It's alright." She said gently stroking his cheek with the back of her hand. "It's just that this is John and Maisie's home and I feel like a guilty schoolgirl about to get caught in the act by her parents."

Alan couldn't help but laugh and, as if on cue, Maisie bumbled into the kitchen switching on the light.

"What are you two up to in here in the dark? As if I couldn't guess."

Jenny couldn't help blushing.

"I was just thanking Alan for such a wonderful night, that's all." She stammered with embarrassment.

"Is that so?" The landlady quipped, her face beaming with pleasure. "Well, I'm glad you two had a good time. Maybe Alan would like a nightcap to finish the night off with?"

Alan saw Jenny become visibly nervous again and instinctively knew that she was thinking that she should be getting ready to go home.

"That's alright thanks, Maisie. I need to be getting off now anyway."

As he spoke Jenny's body language became an odd mixture of relief and disappointment.

"Well, if you're sure." Maisie conceded. "I'll leave you two to say goodnight then."

Jenny watched as the landlady exited and then turned back to Alan.

"She has been so good to me." She announced with a touch of warmth in her voice. "As have you."

Alan put both of his hands on Jenny's shoulders and looked into her eyes.

"And you have been good to me, too. More than you will ever know."

He bent to kiss her on the lips again and this time she didn't resist him. When he finally pulled away she grasped his right hand in both of hers.

"I meant what I said in the car, Alan. That I love you, that is."

Alan could see that the tears were beginning to form again in Jenny's eyes. He also detected the expectancy, no the need, that was also sitting behind them. He decided to honour that need.

"I love you too, Jenny. So, so much."

He kissed her on the cheek and went from the kitchen into the cool night air leaving Jenny standing there alone, tears gently flowing down her cheeks but with a warm glow in her heart.

Chapter 20

It had been two weeks since Marjorie's party and Alan had managed to manufacture a visit to the pub when Jenny was working on two more occasions. Maisie covered the bar for her while Jenny spent pressure moments chatting with Alan in the landlady's sitting room.

On the second of these visits, Alan informed Jenny that he was going away for a few days with his drinking buddies. They were going on a golfing holiday that had been organised for a while and that he had no way of getting out of. Besides, his wife was pleased to get rid of him because she had some big official function coming up and didn't want him under her feet. All told, much as he was going to miss Jenny immensely, he couldn't get out of the trip.

Jenny, though disappointed about him going, told him that it would be a good break for him and that he should go and enjoy himself. When he came to leave, she didn't want to release him from her arms. But she knew she had no choice and when he had gone, she sat on Maisie's couch and cried.

Maisie walked in and, seeing her in distress, sat down next to her and held her hand.

"Whatever is the matter, dear?" She asked kindly.

Jenny explained about Alan's trip and how, though she had told him that she was pleased for him that he was going, she was really heartbroken that she wouldn't see him again for well over a week.

"You must think I'm nothing but a silly, love struck girl acting no better than a teenager." She finished and the tears began to flow again.

Maisie shook her head and sat quiet for a moment. Then she smiled.

"How would you like to come away with me for a few days? I'm going to visit my sister on the coast next week. John has to stay here and look after the pub so it would be nice company for me if you came along. She's looking after her grand-kiddies on account of it being the school holidays and my niece and her husband being at work. I try and pay her a visit whenever I can. Besides, a change of scenery might take your mind of Alan for a while."

"I couldn't." Jenny said looking forlorn. "My husband would never let me go. There would be no-one to cook his meals for him and look after my son."

"You can and you will." Maisie said kindly but forcibly.

Jenny could tell by the look on the landlady's face that it was decided and the subject was not up for debate.

"I'll get John to ring him and let him know that you're coming with me. He seems to have a bit of a knack of getting through to your husband. We'll go down on Monday and I'll have you back for your shift in the pub Thursday night. The break will do you good."

Before Jenny could protest the landlady was up from the couch and marching out of the room. Jenny bounced up after her feeling a mixture of apprehension and intrigue in her stomach.

As the two of them walked into the bar, John looked at them with a sideways glance and folded his arms across his chest. He had just finished cashing up and was ready to turn in.

"I didn't realise I was running this pub on my own tonight." He said trying to look stern but failing miserably.

"It's good practice for you for next week, my love." Maisie replied matching his semi-serious look. "Jenny and me are going to be gone for a couple of days at our Clara's so be warned."

John gave the landlady a quizzical look and raised his eyebrows. Then he put his hand up to his mouth in a parody of concern.

"You two are going away together and leaving me to fend for myself? How on earth will I cope?"

John's eyes told them that he wasn't being entirely serious.

"That's only if my husband agrees." Jenny burst out.

"Which is where you come in, my lovely." Maisie said walking over to the bar towards her husband.

"And just what are you expecting me to do?" He asked looking warily at her.

"You, my love, are going to ring Jenny's husband and persuade him that it would be a good idea to let her come down to Clara's with me."

"I see. I am, am I?" John replied looking a little perplexed. "And if he says *no*?"

"I have every faith in your powers of persuasion." Maisie said patting him on the hand as if encouraging a small child.

John nodded his head once and then, with a resigned look on his face, moved away from behind the bar.

"I'll go and do it now then."

He winked his left eye at Jenny and then trundled off to their living quarters. Jenny looked anxious but Maisie tried to reassure her.

"It'll be fine. I have complete faith in John."

"I hope so." Jenny said uncertainly. "I really do hope so."

*

John returned to the bar fifteen minutes later looking perplexed. He walked around to the back of the bar and poured himself a double brandy. Both Jenny and Maisie watched him closely, bursting with curiosity while they waited for him to speak.

Jenny began to feel sick to her stomach the longer John delayed telling them what had been said. All kinds of crazy notions began to run through her mind as to what her husband's reaction had been to the landlord's phone call. She was beginning to work herself up into a state when finally Maisie could stand it no more.

"Well? What did he say?"

John took another swig of his drink and appeared to be considering what he was about to say. Maisie's face began to get darker as her frustration with her husband simmered. Eventually, the landlord began.

"I've spoken to your husband, Jenny, about you accompanying her to Clara's next week. And he has one major concern."

He took another sip of his brandy and then, to Maisie's infuriation, appeared to study closely the glass in his hand. Jenny's heart was like a runaway train and she was convinced that if the landlord didn't put her out of her misery soon, if would derail big style. She dreaded to think what foul mood her husband was going to be in when she arrived home.

"His main concern is," John started again, "who is going to get his meals if you are not there to make them for him?"

"Can't he make his own?" Maisie growled, her frustration at John's slow delivery boiling over into anger at the chauvinistic attitude of Jenny's husband.

"I told you he wouldn't let me." Jenny sighed, feeling deflated. "Is he angry?"

Maisie saw the fear in Jenny's eyes and her fury ratcheted up another notch. She was appalled that Jenny should be made to feel afraid at how such an innocent question might upset the beast of a man she was married to.

John smiled.

"Now, who said that he won't let you go?"

Jenny looked confused while Maisie placed her hands on her hips and pouted her lips at the jocular landlord.

"Explain!" She said in exasperation through gritted teeth.

"Well, when he said that meal times were a problem for him I offered him my services."

Both Jenny and Maisie stared across at him in disbelief.

"You're going to go and cook for him?" Maisie said, not believing her ears.

"Not as such." John began to explain. "I said he would be more than welcome to have his meals up here if he wanted. Free of charge, of course. I told him it would be company for me while you were away."

"And?" Maisie asked.

Jenny was watching the exchange between the two as if they were talking about someone else, not her and her husband.

"And he agreed." John said grinning.

"He did?" Jenny cried out astonished.

"Yes. He and your son are going to eat here with me before we open while you're away."

Jenny clasped her hand to her mouth to stop herself from shouting out with joy. She didn't know whether to laugh, cry or dance a jig. All she knew was that she would be away from her depressing household and wouldn't have to spend that time lying in bed next to Barnes while her thoughts were on Alan. Once again, Maisie had come up trumps and lightened her spirit. She skipped up to the landlady and landlord and hugged them both. Then she grabbed her coat and floated back down the hill home.

John turned to Maisie and with a serious face that contrasted his usual jovial demeanor, shook his head.

"I've got to spend time in the company of that animal. I hope whatever it is that you are planning will be worth my sacrifice."

Maisie smiled cagily.

"Oh, it will be. Mark my words. It will be!"

"Well, you owe me big time, Lady."

Maisie batted her eyelids at the landlord.

"Well, we'd better see about a down payment then, hadn't we?"

With a suggestive smile she switched the lights off and then led him by the hand up into their living quarters.

Chapter 21

Jenny woke on the Monday morning of their departure to find the sun streaming through the bedroom window. Her husband was lying with his back to her snoring and she rejoiced in the fact that for the next few mornings she wouldn't be waking up next to him but to the luxury of her own company.

Maisie had told her that they would not be staying at her sister's house which was small and lacked space. She had booked them separate rooms at one of the hotels not too far away. The rooms were cheap and cheerful and Maisie thought that the barmaid would benefit from having her own space. Jenny had offered to pay for her own accommodation but, as usual, Maisie wouldn't hear of it. As far as she was concerned she had asked Jenny to accompany her and she was going to pay. Jenny knew from past experience it was futile to argue with the landlady when she was in this mood so politely accepted.

Jenny had expected a frosty reception from her husband when she came in from the pub the night John had spoken to him. But he seemed to be only too pleased to be ridding himself of her for a few days, even highlighting the fact that he would be getting some decent food for the first time since they had been married.

Jenny refused to get drawn into an argument and let him make his cruel remarks unchallenged. She even ignored her son's twisted comments that he was happy that they were going to be free from a *miserable woman* in the house for a while. Instead, she concentrated on looking forward to getting away from the hell-hole that was her supposed family home, if only for a short period.

Her husband made it clear to Jenny that as she was going to be away from him for a number of nights he would be expecting her to be forthcoming with herself before she went. But when he did try to force himself on her that night she told him that he had picked the wrong week of the month for such demands. He soon lost interest and with a look of disgust that made Jenny feel unclean, he turned over and went to sleep.

Alan had been gone since the previous Saturday and though Jenny missed him greatly she threw all her thoughts into her impending break. She had packed her suitcase the night before and it was sitting by the door ready for when Maisie picked her up at nine o'clock. She quietly and gently got out of bed doing her level best not to wake her husband. There was still a part of her that feared he would change his mind at the last minute and would stop her going.

Her luck held as she managed to creep out of the bedroom and into the bathroom without so much as a murmur or movement from him. Also, with her son being off school for the week she could guarantee that he wouldn't be surfacing until at least lunchtime. Jenny reveled in the quietness of the house. She had hung her clothes ready the night before and after a quick wash she was dressed and ready to go. She gathered her toiletries together and tip toed down along the landing. She peered into the war zone that was her son's bedroom and found him, as expected, sound asleep spread eagled across the bed. Jenny once again thanked her lucky stars that she was spared the usual worry about getting him up for school. That said, she had long since realised that he was more than capable of looking after himself. At fifteen he had become self-sufficient to the extent that he would snarl at her if she ever tried to do anything for him. He was fast becoming a mini version of his father which depressed Jenny further. The thought of living with two such chauvinistic males had long since given her a heavy heart for her future.

Jenny stealthily negotiated the stairs and then waited impatiently in the front room, watching out the window for Maisie, praying that the landlady would arrive before there was any movement from above her. She felt as if she had been standing there waiting for an eternity when Maisie's car finally pulled up in front of the house. She gathered together her suitcase and vanity bag that were neatly lined up by the front door, grabbed her coat from the stand and then, picking up the door key, struggled out towards the car. Maisie met her halfway down the path and relieved her of her coat and vanity bag before leading her to the rear of the car. She helped Jenny lift the suitcase into the boot next to her own before rearranging the rest of the luggage.

"For someone who doesn't have many clothes that's a might heavy suitcase, dear." The landlady teased.

Jenny smiled a little nervously and shrugged her shoulders.

"I didn't know what to pack so most of my clothes are in there." She said. "I'm not that used to going away."

Maisie gave the girl a reassuring nod.

"No problem at all, dear." She said.

Once the suitcase was loaded, Maisie slammed the boot down and the two women walked to the front of the car.

Jenny was about to get in when she suddenly realised she had forgotten something.

"My handbag!" She cried out and ran back down the path.

When she reached the front door she stopped. She felt nervous about going back into the house. She was afraid that Barnes would be in there waiting for her and, even at this late stage, would put a stop to her leaving. She cursed herself for not bringing her handbag out with her. If it hadn't been for the fact it contained her purse, and hence access to what little cash she had, she would have turned around and got into the car without another thought. But she couldn't leave without her money.

Maisie watched Jenny from the driver's seat. When she saw the barmaid hesitate she leaned over the passenger side and wound the window down.

"Are you alright, dear?" She called out.

Jenny glanced across at her and gave her a faint smile. Her heart was pounding in her chest. She took a deep breath and, taking the key from her pocket, opened the door. The hallway was empty and the house was still silent. She stepped in and saw the handbag sitting on the bottom step of the stairs. Quickly she reached down and snatched it up. No sooner was it in her hands than she was back out of the door and striding to the car.

Maisie peered up out of the window at Jenny looking concerned.

"Everything alright?" She asked.

Jenny nodded.

Maisie sat back up as the barmaid jumped into the car and fastened her seat belt. The landlady started the car and as she pulled away, Jenny took a last look at the house. She had done it. She had managed to escape, if only for a little while. She sat back in the seat and suddenly all her worries began to slip away.

Chapter 22

Maisie told Jenny that the journey to the coast would probably take them the best part of three hours. As they were in no rush though, she was planning on making a couple of stops for comfort breaks and also so that she could show Jenny one or two places of interest that she was sure the barmaid would like.

They had been on the road for about an hour when Maisie suggested their first stop. They were passing through a quaint town that seemed to be blessed by row upon row of antique shops. Maisie said she knew of an *olde worlde* coffee shop which would be an ideal place to refresh themselves.

They found a small car park just off the main street, parked up and then walked back towards some black and white Tudor buildings that lined the busy through road. Jenny marveled at their architecture and was delighted when Maisie steered her into one of them. It was a modest sized coffee shop with a large glass window. Maisie chose a table which allowed them to peer out onto the street as they drank.

Jenny insisted on paying for the coffee and cake that the two women had indulged in and they sat there observing the world go by outside. They made idle chat until Maisie finally decided it was time for them to continue their journey.

As they walked back to the car, Jenny felt as if she was in another world. The village and her sad life back there seemed a distant memory as she truly felt herself starting to relax and unwind. Even the heartache of being apart from Alan seemed so much easier to bear.

Sitting in the car as they continued on their journey, Jenny decided to ask Maisie a question that had been buzzing in her head for a while.

"Why have you and John been so good to me?" She asked as Maisie indicated to pull out of the town onto the main ring road. "Not that I'm complaining, you know. It's just that I often wonder why it is that you have been so kind to me."

Maisie stared through the windscreen for a moment as if gathering her thoughts before starting to speak.

"When me and John had been married a couple of years I became pregnant and we had a daughter. Emily was her name. Prettiest girl you've ever seen. Well, we thought so anyway but then we were biased. She was the apple of John's eye and as much as I loved her, he absolutely doted on her."

"I didn't know you had a daughter." Jenny said, sitting up in her seat intrigued. "You've never mentioned her before."

Maisie's face became sad and Jenny started to sense she had managed to inadvertently open old wounds.

"We don't talk about her much these days." Maisie continued. "She died when she was seventeen. Leukemia it was. She was a brave girl. Fought it to the end and never complained. John took it hard and doesn't like to talk about it even now."

Jenny could see the tears welling in Maisie's eyes and she reached over and placed her hand on top of the landlady's as she gripped the steering wheel. She felt guilty at raking up the heartache for this woman that had done so much for her.

"I'm so sorry, Maisie. I didn't know. How insensitive of me."

Maisie smiled and brushed the tears from her eyes with her free hand.

"It's alright, my dear. You weren't to know. Besides, I'm pleased you asked. You see, she would've been not far off your age had she still been alive."

Jenny felt a lump in her throat and her own tears began to collect in the corner of her eyes.

"Having you around is a bit like having our Emily back." Maisie confided. "Don't get me wrong though. Me and John don't think of you as a substitute for Emily or anything weird like that. That wouldn't be fair on her or you. It's just that helping you out seems the right thing to do. Besides, when you said you'd lost your parents it seemed like we could relate to how you feel, you losing your family like we have. Not that we would ever consider ourselves replacements for them either."

For the first time since Jenny had known her, Maisie seemed a little flustered.

"That's alright." She said reassuringly to the landlady. "I'm sure they would have been very grateful for the way you have treated me. You and John have been the nearest thing to a loving family that I have had since I lost them. My home life isn't exactly a picture of family bliss, what with having a tyrant of a husband and a teenage son who treats me like dirt. You and John have treated me with nothing but kindness from the moment I met you and I will always love you for that."

Jenny could see that the landlady was starting to well up again so she decided to change the subject.

"Tell me about your sister. Is she anything like you?"

"Oh yes, dear!" Maisie said brushing the accumulating tears from her eyes and smiling gratefully at the barmaid. "Me and Clara are like peas in a pod. I think you'll like her. And I know she will adore you."

With that Maisie burst into childhood stories of the antics she and her sister used to get up to. Jenny sat back in her seat and listened intently to the landlady's tales, feeling a warm glow inside. For the rest of the journey to the coast the two women were giggling like schoolgirls.

Chapter 23

The sound of seagulls broke into Jenny's daydreams as she stood at the top of the cliff. She felt the breeze on her face gently massaging her skin. If it was at all possible, the sad tale of Maisie's lost daughter had somehow bought the two women even closer together that day. Knowing they shared a common grief washed away any confusion Jenny may have had about the motives of John and Maisie towards her.

Jenny moved over to the bench that she and Alan had shared so many times during their time together and sat down. She placed her the rucksack carefully on the ground beside her and stared out over the glistening sea feeling the familiar conflicting pangs that she got whenever she made her pilgrimage to the cliff top since Alan's death. Nowhere else did she feel as close to him as she did there. Cruelly, however, nowhere else did she feel so far away from him. She missed him so much. She longed for his touch so much.

The sea breeze gently rustled the heather behind the bench and she caught the sweet, earthy smell of it on the wind. Somehow it reminded her of Alan's cologne. She closed her eyes again and concentrated her very being on that smell.

Maisie pulled up at the hotel and Jenny jumped out. The car park overlooked the sea front and Jenny felt like a little girl who was seeing the magic of the ocean for the first time. She had vague recollections of her parents taking her to the seaside when she was very young but these, along with most of her memories of them, were sadly clouded at best.

Maisie let Jenny take in the sights and sounds of the seafront before suggesting that they go inside to check in. She helped Jenny retrieve her luggage from the boot of the car and informed her that she would retrieve her own once they had got Jenny settled into her room.

They walked into the entrance lobby of the hotel and Jenny was immediately enthralled by its quaintness. The walls were bedecked with old photographs of the town and modestly-clad bathers from a bygone age. Interspersed with them were more modern pictures of headland views and coastal profiles.

Maisie dealt with the formal process of checking in and then escorted Jenny to her first floor room. She placed the key card into the slot under the door handle and waited for the tell-tale click of the lock releasing. She pushed the door and stood back to let Jenny in.

Jenny let out a squeal of delight as she entered the room. Smiling, Maisie followed her in. She closed the door behind her and when she turned back, she found Jenny had stopped about a half dozen steps into the room and was now staring transfixed.

So much was running through Jenny's mind. The room was spacious, light and airy. To the right there was a king sized doubled bed flanked by two small mahogany cabinets. Further into the room there was a writing desk on top of which lay a number of local interest brochures. On the opposite side to the bed, just below ceiling height, protruded a small portable television secured to the wall.

But what had grabbed Jenny's attention the most was the large bay window that overlooked the sea front and on down to the ocean. There was an armchair and small table set up in front of it that the barmaid was already imagining eating her breakfast at.

"What do you think?" Maisie asked unable to stop herself from feeling excited for Jenny.

"It's wonderful." Jenny replied almost skipping over to the window.

"I thought you might like it." Maisie said placing Jenny's luggage on the bed. "I asked for the sea view especially for you."

"I love it! Thank you so much!" Jenny said walking back over to the landlady and hugging her.

Maisie handed her the key and then turned to go.

"Wait." Jenny cried out. "I'll come and give you a hand with your bags."

"No you won't." The landlady said kindly. "You stay here and enjoy the view. After humping beer barrels around for most of my life I'm sure I can manage a suitcase. Settle yourself in and I'll meet you downstairs for afternoon tea later."

Jenny knew better than to argue with Maisie so skipped across the room to give her another hug. The landlady kissed the top of Jenny's head and then made her way out. Jenny stood and watched the door click shut behind her.

Suddenly, she felt conscious of being alone but curiosity soon took over. As she turned to go back to the bay window she heard a soft rap on the door. Laughing to herself she skipped excitedly over to open it.

"Change your mind?" She beamed as she pulled the door towards her.

"As a matter of fact I did!" Alan said as Jenny stood staring open mouthed at him, holding tightly on to the door handle. "Sometimes you realise that there are far more important things in life than golf!"

Chapter 24

Time seemed frozen as Jenny stood looking at Alan. Her heart was racing and her legs felt leaden, rooting her to the spot. In her wildest dreams she could not have expected Alan to be standing there in the doorway. She tried to speak but no words would come out.

"Aren't you going to invite me in?" Alan asked smiling.

Jenny closed her eyes and shook her head. When she reopened them she expected Alan to have disappeared. But he was still there.

Alan frowned a little and then glanced into the room, still waiting for an invitation. Trance-like, Jenny opened the door fully and stood aside so he could enter. As he passed her, she caught the faint aroma of his aftershave which added to the surreal direction her world had now taken. It was all she could do not to go weak at the knees and crumble to the floor behind him.

She closed the door and then, grasping the door handle with both hands behind her, leaned back against it for support. She turned to face Alan.

"What...what are you doing here?" She managed to force out, still in a state of shock.

"I decide not to go on my golfing trip after all." Alan said as if that explained everything.

"But what are you doing HERE?" Jenny asked again, slowly beginning to emerge from her hazy shock. "How did you now I would be here with Maisie? We only decided to come after you had left."

Alan let out a nervous laugh and smiled innocently.

"I arrived yesterday. We thought it would be best if I got here the day before you. It would be less conspicuous."

A large penny dropped in Jenny's head.

"You set this up." She blurted out and placed her hands firmly on her hips. "You got Maisie to bring me down here. You arranged it all."

"Me?" Alan said pointing to himself and feigning offence.

"Don't give me that little boy innocent look." Jenny growled. "You don't expect me to believe that this is all just one big coincidence, do you?"

She took a step forward and Alan took a reciprocal step backwards, thrusting his hands out in front of him in a parody of defense.

"Now, Jenny! Let's not get too overexcited."

"Overexcited?" Jenny cried out half laughing in disbelief. "You turn up here out of the blue and then tell me not to get *overexcited*"

She gently thrust her chin towards him to emphasise her words, a motion that Alan found strangely enchanting and captivating. He cleared his thoughts and concentrated on the situation at hand.

Jenny took another step towards Alan who obligingly took another away from her. He felt the back of his knees come into contact with something solid but springy. He half turned to see that he was now trapped against the mattress on the bed. As he turned back to face Jenny he was just in time to see her dive towards him. Her momentum caught him off guard and he fell backwards, ending up prone on the bed. Jenny landed on top of him and pinned his arms above his head. She straddled his chest and secured him between her knees. He made no attempt to resist her.

Amazed at her own self-confidence, Jenny gazed at the man she now had trapped beneath her and grinned down at him.

"Now then! What's going on? How did you get Maisie to play along with your little game?"

"Has anyone told you how sexy you are when you're being dominant?" Alan said as he gazed directly into his assailant's eyes.

Jenny felt a tingle in her stomach then shook her head.

"Oh no you don't!" She said, pushing Alan's hands deeper into the bed spread. "You're not going to sweet talk yourself out of this so easily."

Alan tried to look serious for a moment but then burst out laughing. Jenny raised her eyebrows and then dropped her face close to his.

"Tell me! How did you persuade Maisie to bring me here?"

"Me? Persuade Maisie?" Alan replied grinning. "Jenny, she was the one who thought this all up. It was her idea!"

Alan felt Jenny's grip relax slightly and raised his head so that his lips covered hers. That was all it took for her to completely release him and in one swift movement, he rolled her off him and onto her back, their lips never once parting. Jenny threw her arms around his neck and pulled his mouth harder onto hers, relishing the feel of him above her.

When they finally pulled apart, Alan lay on his back and stared at the ceiling.

"Wow." He murmured dreamily. "That's was definitely worth waiting for. For a moment I wasn't that sure you were pleased to see me but after that ...."

Jenny turned onto her side and looked down at him smiling. She reached out and started playing with his hair.

"It was just a surprise to see you standing there." Jenny explained. "You were the last person I expected to see here. I thought it was Maisie returning."

Jenny frowned.

"Maisie! She put you up to this? Why?"

Alan laughed and reached out to stroke Jenny's face with the back of her hand.

"I think she has made it her mission in life to bring us closer together. Not that I took much persuading, you understand."

"Yes, and she can be very persistent." Jenny sighed. "I might have to have a few words with her when I call for her later."

Alan gave out a hearty laugh.

"What?" Jenny said looking confused.

"I suppose she hasn't told you about that either, has she?"

"Told me what?"

"She's gone to her sister's. She's staying there not here. She thought it would be better for us to spend some time alone."

Jenny sat up concerned.

"She's left me here on my own?"

Alan raised himself up next to her and gently squeezed her shoulder.

"It's alright, Jenny. You're not on your own. I'm staying here."

Jenny's concern turned to panic.

"You're staying here? With me?"

Alan took hold of her other shoulder and turned her to him.

"No, Jenny. I have my own room. Not even Maisie would be that bold."

Jenny stared out of the window onto the seascape behind Alan.

"Your own room? Yes, I suppose that's alright. That shouldn't be a problem."

Alan stayed quiet for a moment, allowing Jenny to compose herself. Then he stood up and offered his hand to her. She looked up to him looking confused again.

"Come on." He said. "There's something I want to show you!"

With that, he pulled her towards the door.

Chapter 25

Twenty minutes later, Jenny and Alan stood hand in hand barely five feet away from the edge of the cliff looking out to sea. The late afternoon sun was shimmering on the gently rippling surface and the sound of the waves gently caressing the rocks below was brought up to them on the fresh sea breeze generated by the turn of the tide.

Alan had swiftly guided Jenny up the pathway leading up to the cliff top, happily explaining to her that while he was waiting for her arrival the previous day he had found what he thought must be the most perfect place in the world.

Jenny felt herself caught up in Alan's enthusiasm and was exhilarated to find that he had not over exaggerated the beauty of the view. She fell in love with it the moment she saw it. The sky was clear and she imagined that she could see all the way to the very end of the world itself. Standing there, gazing out over the ocean, she finally felt as if she had found some peace. For the first time that she could remember the grief she had felt for her parents and the painful fear of her home life seemed to melt away.

"It's wonderful." She whispered just loud enough for Alan to hear, not daring to take her eyes off the sea for fear of it dissolving from sight. "It's the most beautiful sight I have ever seen."

"Am I forgiven then?" Alan asked staring ahead of him, his eyes closed as he let the sea breeze brush over his face.

Jenny reached for his hand.

"Oh, yes! Yes! Yes!"

Alan's heart seemed to expand tenfold inside his chest. There were so many things he wanted to say to Jenny but held back for fear that he would spoil the moment for her. Instead, he led her further down the cliff top path that ran parallel to its edge. A short distance along they came to a wooden bench where, taking out his handkerchief and exaggerating a cleaning motion across the seating area, he invited Jenny to sit. With a giggle she did so and Alan dropped down next to her.

Acting like a love struck teenager, Alan draped his arm along the back of the bench behind Jenny. The greater part of him wanted to wrap her in his arms and protect her for the rest of her life. But there was a part of him that was holding back for fear she would pull away from him. He needn't have worried.

Sensing Alan's arm behind her Jenny turned her head to look at him. She smiled before moving closer and nestling into his side. Alan dropped his arm around her and gently pulled her into him.

Any nerves Jenny had had while she was in Alan's presence completed evaporated in that moment. As she sat with his strong arms around her, she was left feeling as safe as she had ever been. She placed her head on his shoulder and closed her eyes. She could hear the sea and feel the breeze on her face. It was as close to heaven as she could ever have imagined.

With his free hand, Alan began to run his fingers through Jenny's hair. It sent excited goose bumps down her neck.

"Mm... That's nice!" She murmured. "I could sit here like this for the rest of my life."

She felt Alan heave a small sigh. She looked up into his eyes, being careful not to cause him to stop playing with her hair, and frowned a little.

"What?"

Alan looked serious for a moment and then smiled.

"I was just thinking about how you are the most wonderful, beautiful, caring woman I have ever known."

Jenny dropped her chin a little and blushed, still unused to being paid any kind of compliment. Alan lifted her chin back up so that he was looking directly into her eyes.

"I love you, Jenny!" He whispered.

Jenny turned placed her hands gently either side of his head lifted it and turned it towards her.

"I love you too, Alan." She said before pulling his mouth firmly to hers.

For the next few moments their lips were inseparable. The controlled passion of their kiss underlined their need for one another. As they parted, Jenny held Alan's cheeks softly in both hands. Suddenly, it all seemed so clear to her. She knew what she needed to do.

"Let's go back." She said with a steely look of seriousness in her eyes. "I want you to make love to me."

Alan went to say something but Jenny placed her finger on his lips motioning for him to be quiet.

"Don't say anything. Not here. Not now. I don't want anything to give me a reason to change my mind."

Alan closed his eyes for a moment and swallowed deeply. Then he stood up, reached down to Jenny and pulled her to her feet. Hand in hand, they followed the cliff path back down to the town and on to the hotel.

Chapter 26

As they walked through the hotel entrance Jenny felt giddy with excitement and anticipation. All thoughts of home and her horrid life there were temporarily buried away in the darker reaches of her mind. She could no longer fight the need in her for Alan and as he led her through the hotel corridors she felt as alive inside as she had ever been in her sad lonely life.

When they reached the door to her room Alan stopped and reached out for the key card. Jenny took it from her jacket pocket and passed it over to him. As he took it from her their fingers touched and a tiny spark of static jumped between them. Jenny let out a squeal of surprise and then, holding her hand to her mouth, giggled at her own reaction.

Alan stood their mesmerised, turning the key card over and over in his hand.

"What?" Jenny asked smiling at him in bemusement.

"You are so beautiful." He replied with a wide boyish grin.

"Hurry up and open the door." Jenny said pointing at it. "Before I change my mind."

"Yes, ma'am." Alan said exaggerating a bow before slipping the card into the lock turning the small light on it from red to green.

There was a soft click as the lock released and Alan depressed the handle. As if to indicate her impatience Jenny put her hand on the door and pushed it open, quickly nudging Alan inside as she did so. With surprise plastered across his face he stumbled into the room. Jenny followed him in and closed the door firmly behind her. She flicked the catch over to lock it and then stood there for a moment, her back resting against it, staring at Alan.

Alan quickly regained his balance and turned to face Jenny. He was about to speak when Jenny launched herself across the room and into his arms. Her mouth was on his before he could utter anything and her hands were clasped firmly behind his head. Giving in to her, Alan matched her passion and pulled her tightly into him.

Jenny's tongue began to explore the inside of Alan's mouth which he returned with interest. As they devoured each other Jenny gently steered Alan towards the bed. Without breaking contact with his mouth she sat him on the edge. She slipped her hands into his jacket and swiftly removed it from him. Once it was off she pushed him onto the bed and stared down to him. Alan wriggled himself up the duvet until only his feet were dangling over the edge. In two quick movements he flicked his shoes off and looked up at her, desire unashamedly etched across his face.

Throwing her cardigan haphazardly across a nearby chair Jenny crawled up onto the bed and, lifting her skirt above her knees, straddled him so that she was now kneeling over him and sitting across his thighs. Alan felt himself beginning to grow as the first pangs of physical need began to course through him.

Jenny began to undo the buttons on his shirt while he returned the compliment and started to undo her blouse. As he slipped it from her shoulders the sight of her breasts tight in her white lace bra filled him with a desire so strong he quietly moaned. He slipped his hands under the cotton and pushed it up to release her. Her breasts were firm; her skin was soft and her nipples stood erect and hard betraying Jenny's own excitement. Squeezing her breasts gently he caressed them between his thumb and forefinger. Jenny groaned with ecstasy and Alan felt himself grow further.

Jenny peeled back Alan's shirt to reveal his bare chest and leant forward to place her mouth over his own right nipple. With vigour she ran her tongue back and forth across it.

Jenny could feel him straining between her thighs and removed her mouth from his chest. She reached down and undid the button to his trousers before lowering the zip to reveal the expectant bulge in his now exposed boxer shorts.

"My! My!" She uttered cheekily running her finger over the cotton, teasing him.

As Jenny pulled back the elastic waist band to expose him, Alan felt the cool room air on his now extra sensitive skin. That and the feeling of freedom he now had caused him to grow harder.

Alan began to sit up but Jenny shook her head before gently pushing him back down onto the bed. Lifting up on her knees she raised herself over him, slipped her left hand under her skirt, took him and, slipping her panties aside, guided him into her.

They both groaned with pleasure as they finally joined. Alan thrust in time to Jenny's motion as she raised and lowered herself onto him. She felt good around him and he could not help but quicken his rhythm as he reached up to caress her breasts. Jenny matched his speed and before long they were both panting with the exertion. They reached a crescendo and both exploded in a sea of ecstasy.

Jenny dropped beside him and laid her head on Alan chest. He placed his arms around her, feeling the quickness of her heart against him. Playing with her hair he felt a wave of emotion flood over him. All the months of waiting had ended and he was finally with the woman he wanted.

As if reading his mind Jenny looked up at him and smiled.

"I love you!" She said, her eyes glistening. "And I want to be with you forever."

Alan felt a lump develop in his throat. He had never felt so happy. As they both drifted off into sleep he promised himself that whatever it took, he would make her wish come true.

Chapter 27

Jenny couldn't help smiling as she stood there on the cliff top. That afternoon with Alan had been the most erotic, sensitive, loving experience of her life. It had been as if all the barriers she had built up around her life until then – the death of her parents and her brutal marriage – had suddenly been swept away by the tsunami that was Alan's love.

And even though they had made love many times since that day, it was that first time that Jenny would always think of with fondness. It was not the most sensitive of lovemaking but the raw passion they reached that day was something they never managed to achieve again. It not only saw the awakening of her inner sensuality but was also the prelude to the dawning of a new life.

Now, being here on the cliff top, that moment seemed a lifetime away. And in truth it was. A whole new life that neither of them could have dreamed would happen. But happen it did. And now Jenny's heart ached in the knowledge that what had been found that day had been taken away from her again.

Sitting on the bench she imagined she could still feel Alan's arms around her, and smell the sex they had shared, as she had woken up next to him that first time.

Jenny woke to find that she was under the duvet, her naked body warm against Alan's. At some point after their lovemaking they must have both finished undressing and crawled into bed but she could remember little more than the thrill of his hands on her and him being in her.

She could feel Alan's skin against hers as they lay on their sides curled together. Jenny's back was cradled against Alan's chest and stomach and his arms held her tightly against him. She could feel him, flaccid now, resting against the back of her thighs and her body let out an involuntary shudder of pleasure at its touch.

It was still light outside and a beam of late afternoon sun shone through the window onto the bed where they lay.

Jenny sighed as she submerged herself tighter into Alan's embrace. His strong arms around her made Jenny feel safe and secure and she truly believed that nothing in the world could ever hurt her again.

Alan stirred and slowly stretched his feet down the back of Jenny's calves. The touch of his skin against hers made her tingle with excitement. Releasing herself from his grip she rolled onto her back. As she stared up at him Alan raised himself up on his left elbow and rested his head on his hand. Jenny reached up and pulled his lips to hers. She felt Alan's reaction against her skin and she pulled him gently on top of her. Without a word, he slowly made love to her again.

When they had finished, Alan rolled onto his back panting with the exertion. A thin film of sweat covered his chest. Jenny couldn't resist the urge to reach over and run her finger down it before leaning over and kissing his lips. When she eventually pulled away from him she saw a tear begin to form in the corner of his right eye.

"Hey." She said softly, wiping the tear away before it could roll down his cheek. "What's the matter?"

Alan took her hand quickly in his and planted a kiss on it.

"I've wanted you from the moment I first laid eyes on you." He said smiling. "And now I can't believe that we are here now, together, like this. I am so happy."

Jenny ran the fingers of her free hand through his hair.

"I know." She said, now beginning to feel herself welling up. "And I meant what I said about us being together. I don't know how we will do it but all I know is that it's right. I don't want to waste any more of my life being lonely."

"My wife won't give in easy." Alan said. "She may not want me but that doesn't mean that she will let me go without a fight. And a nasty one at that."

Jenny thought back to Marjorie's prophetic words at the book signing. A battle with Stella for Alan would not be a pleasant one. But if she wanted him, it was one she had to be prepared for. Besides, she realised she was facing a bigger problem than Alan's wife.

"I think she could be the least of our worries." She said biting her bottom lip. "When my husband finds out he will probably kill us both."

Alan let out a tentative laugh. But both of them knew that Jenny's words were not necessarily in jest!

Chapter 28

Alan and Jenny tried to put any future problems they may have with their spouses aside for a while in an attempt to enjoy the moments they now had together. Their lovemaking exploits had left them both hungry and Jenny, in particular, felt ravenous; a feeling she couldn't remember having in a very long time.

By the time they had showered together and dressed, the sun was slowly beginning to set towards the sea. Jenny put on the same dress that she had worn to Marjorie's book signing, continually apologising to Alan for the fact that she had nothing else fancy to wear. She hadn't packed the black dress she had worn to the party for the simple fact that she didn't think it would have been appropriate attire for anywhere she may have gone out to with Maisie and her sister. Thinking about it now, it was not lost on Jenny that Maisie had tried to persuade her to take it but not pushed too hard for the obvious reason of not wanting to give the game away about Alan. Jenny realised she should have suspected something was afoot then. Again, she bemoaned her own naivety.

Alan, for his part, made numerous attempts to reassure her that she looked beautiful and when she finally allowed herself to accept that he was sincere found that his words made her feel warm inside.

As they strolled along into town holding hands Jenny was content to let Alan chat away. She was just happy to feel her hand inside his and take comfort from him being by her side.

Walking along the seafront the day was beginning to lose the heat of the sun. At one point a ripple of cool air blew over her and she shivered. Alan promptly put his arm around her waist and pulled her close into him. Jenny reveled in the new found feelings of warmth and security he gave to her.

They reached the town and strolled along the quietened streets that exist in the twilight zone between the hustle and bustle of the daytime holiday town, and the busy night time of holiday makers out to enjoy the nightlife on offer.

Eventually they stumbled upon an expensive looking seafood restaurant.

"Let's try here." Alan said reaching for the door.

Jenny quickly grabbed his hand to stop him. Alan turned and looked at her quizzically.

"Can we go somewhere else?" Jenny said biting her bottom lip.

"You don't like seafood?" Alan said looking a little perplexed.

"I don't know. I've never really tried it much." Jenny said shaking her head.

"Then let's change that." Alan said smiling as he turned to reach for the door again.

"No!" Jenny cried out pulling Alan's hand from the door handle again. "It's not that. It looks very posh. I'll look out of place and everyone will stare at me. Plus the prices are way too expensive."

Alan reached up and gently took Jenny's head in his hands. He pulled her to him and kissed her lips.

"Jenny, you will not look out of place in there." He said trying to reassure her. "You look gorgeous and deserve to be taken to the best restaurants in the world. And if I have my way then that is exactly where I'm going to take you."

Jenny went to speak but Alan placed his finger on her lips.

"Let's eat." He declared and taking her hand firmly in his, led her into the restaurant.

*

Despite feeling nervous when she first walked into the restaurant, Jenny soon began to relax when she saw that it was populated by couples too engrossed in their own romantic evening together to be worried about how she looked.

A waiter met them just inside and warmly welcomed them. Having confirmed a table for two with Alan he then led them across the room to the far side of the restaurant before taking them up a flight of stairs to a second dining area. Jenny was delighted when the waiter led them over to a table near the window and asked them if it would be suitable for them. Jenny gazed open mouthed through the window which overlooked the harbour below. The lights were just starting to come on making it look magical.

"I think this will be fine." Alan said to the waiter who promptly pulled out Jenny's chair to allow her to sit.

Jenny sat without taking her eyes of the harbour below. Smiling, Alan took his seat.

Jenny was in a world of her own. She was so engrossed that it took three attempts for the waiter to attract her attention and ask her what she would like to drink.

"Can I just have a glass of water, please?" She requested when she finally re-emerged into the room.

Alan shook his head and smiled.

"We'll have two gin and tonics." He said to the waiter who nodded, placed two menus in front of them and left the table.

Alan looked at Jenny questioningly.

"I didn't know what to ask for." She answered his gaze. "I'm not used to this. I don't normally get to go to a restaurant let alone one as fancy as this. Sorry."

Alan reached over and took her hand.

"You don't have to keep apologising." He said trying to reassure her. "When I've finished with you you'll be bored with all this fine cuisine and long for the days of fish and chips."

Jenny laughed and Alan's heart melted at the beauty of it.

"I've never had gin and tonic before." Jenny said sitting upright and placing her hands in her lap. "I hope I like it."

"I'm sure you will." Alan said sitting back into his own chair. "Just think of it as another first in a day of firsts."

He winked at her mischievously.

Jenny smiled coyly back at him and felt a warm glow inside as Alan reached over to stroke her cheek. She raised her hand from her lap and place it over his, holding it firmly to her. Turning her head, she kissed the back of it.

The waiter returned with their drinks and laid them on the table. Alan made no attempt to remove his hand and sat staring into her eyes, almost mesmerised. Having delivered the drinks the waiter took out his notepad to take their order. He explained that the dish of the day was freshly caught lobster.

Realising that they hadn't even looked at the menu both Jenny and Alan quickly opened them and started to scan the dishes on offer. Immediately Jenny was thrown into a state of confusion. Having never been more adventurous than cod from the local chip shop, she felt totally bemused. Half the dishes on the menu she did not recognise as seafood let alone know which one she might find edible.

Picking up on her hesitation the waiter asked if they wanted more time. Alan nodded.

"Need some help there?" Alan asked.

Jenny nodded; her face a state of total bewilderment.

"What type of fish do you like?" Alan asked.

Jenny began to blush.

"Cod and Tuna." She replied realising that she must look like the complete novice she was to Alan. "Oh, and salmon."

"Thought so." Alan nodded knowingly. "I think it's time we expanded your horizons."

Jenny gave Alan a puzzled look but he took the situation in hand. He indicated to the waiter that they were ready to order who then made his way briskly back to the table.

"We'll both have the prawn cocktail starters and lobster to follow." He announced. "Oh, and a bottle of Chardonnay too."

Jenny gazed down at the menu and her eyes widened.

"But, Alan, the price ...." She started to speak.

Alan raised his hand up to cut her short.

"It's a special occasion and we deserve the best."

Jenny sat back in her chair.

"You'll love it." He added softly to reassure her.

The waiter relieved them of the menus and disappeared towards the kitchen. Jenny sipped her drink, found that she quite liked the taste and then took more adventurous swigs of it. Alan followed suit.

After a short time the waiter returned with the wine. He uncorked it, poured a little into Jenny's glass and waited while she tried it. With a giggle she nodded her head and the waiter proceeded to fill both glasses. He placed the bottle in a bucket of ice next to the table and then left.

Alan raised his glass to Jenny in a toast.

"To us." He declared.

Jenny lifted her own glass and tapped it slightly against Alan's.

"To us." She replied happily.

As she sipped the wine she could not help but wonder what she had done to deserve such happiness and how long it could possibly last. But she was determined to make the most of it and enjoy whatever time she had with Alan.

On the cliff top, Jenny sat thinking back to that first romantic meal she and Alan had had together. By the time the main meals had arrived they had already worked their way down their first bottle of Chardonnay and Alan had ordered a second. The wine had brought her to a state of complete relaxation and she had been happy to chat away to him about everything and nothing.

And he had been right. The lobster had been exquisite. Never had she tasted anything like it. The evening was probably the most perfect one she had ever spent in her entire life leading up to that point, and arguably since. Unknown to them both, from that night onwards their lives would take another twist that would push them to the limits of their new found love.

Chapter 29

Alan and Jenny were the last ones left in the restaurant. They sat and talked all night, oblivious to anyone or anything around them. Occasionally they would glance out of the window to gaze upon the harbour lights below them.

Jenny enjoyed listening to Alan's stories of his adventures abroad. She was amazed at the variety of places he had visited and cultures he had experienced. She knew that these must have been lonely times for him, abandoned by his wife while she followed her own holiday agenda but not once did Alan bring any bitterness toward her in his tales. In fact, in their conversations they managed to successfully skirt around any mention of their respective spouses. Both Alan and Jenny seemed aware that the mere mention of either of them would poison the magic of the moment.

Over coffee Alan explained to Jenny how he and Maisie had conspired to ensure that he would be able to spend time alone with her. Jenny, for her part, could only marvel at how naïve she had been. Alan asked her whether, if she had known about the landlady's devious plan, she would have come along. Jenny shook her head vigorously and told him that she would never have been so brave.

When the waiters began to tidy the tables around them in obvious preparation them for the next day's trade, Alan suggested that they pay the bill and make their way back to the hotel.

Jenny reached for her handbag, pulled out her purse and began to take out her money. As she did so her library card fell out unseen onto the carpet beneath the table.

Alan gently placed his hand on her arm and shook his head.

"This is my treat." He said. "I persuaded you to come into this restaurant so I can't expect you to pay anything. Besides, you can call it penance for getting you down here on false pretenses if you like."

Jenny did her best to object but Alan remained insistent. He motioned for the bill to the nearest waiter who, eager to get home, gladly disappeared toward the till. Jenny placed her purse back into her handbag and reached up to cradle Alan's face in her hand. He nestled into it rejoicing in the feel of her touch.

"Thank you." She whispered. "Thank you so much."

"You are welcome." Alan replied smiling. "If a man can't buy a beautiful lady a meal then what is the world coming to?"

"Not just the meal." Jenny said. "Thank you for everything. For making me laugh again. For making me feel like a woman again. For just being you."

Jenny felt her eyes beginning to well up. Alan noticed and reached over and wiped away a tear forming in the corner of her eye with his thumb.

"Hey, don't be upset." He said softly.

"I'm not upset." She replied. "I've never felt so happy."

The couple stared into each other's' eyes, the moment only broken with the arrival of the waiter with the bill which he passed to Alan. Alan casually studied it to check that it was correct and then produced his credit card from out of his wallet. While he was doing so, Jenny took the napkin from her lap and dabbed her eyes with it before placing it on the table completely unaware that she had now covered her purse.

The waiter disappeared for a moment before returning with the card machine. Alan inserted his card, authorised the transaction then slipped a healthy tip to the grateful waiter. He stood to leave and the waiter hastily placed the card machine on the table and positioned himself to pull Jenny's chair from under her as she stood. It was a simple gesture but it made her feel special and, feeling a little light-headed from the alcohol she'd consumed, couldn't help but giggle.

The waiter escorted them back downstairs to the main door, shook their hands and wished them a pleasant evening as they exited the restaurant. Jenny snuggled into Alan as they walked down the main street and then on down to the sea front.

Jenny found the walk back to the hotel magical. A full moon hung brightly in the clear sky; its reflection extending across the calm bay like a pathway to the horizon; a pathway Jenny would have dearly loved to walk along.

When they arrived back at the hotel they had a quick nightcap in the bar before retiring to Jenny's room; all thoughts of staying in separate rooms gone from their minds. Very soon they were fast asleep cradling each other in their arms.

Jenny woke the following morning to the *click* of the kettle switching itself off. She reached over to where Alan had been lying but found it empty. Propping herself up on her elbow she glanced around the room. Alan was nowhere to be seen.

As she sat up the door opened and a fully dressed Alan entered.

"Good morning." He called across with a cheerful grin. "I popped downstairs to see if they had a paper and luckily they had a few spare."

As he announced this he waggled a copy of The Times in the air in front of him.

"What time is it?" Jenny asked scanning the room for a clock.

"Eight Thirty." Alan replied walking toward the kettle perched on the desktop. "Breakfast is served until ten so we have plenty of time. Tea?"

Jenny nodded.

Alan pointed at a tray of assorted drinks packets.

"We have English Breakfast, Darjeeling, Earl Grey, Green, or a selection of fruit teas?"

Jenny looked confused.

"Is there any ordinary tea?" She asked screwing her face up.

Alan rummaged around and pulled out a packet with a green and red logo on it.

"Voila!" He cried out as if he had just pulled a rabbit out of a top hat.

Jenny looked relieved as Alan dropped the enclosed teabag into a pottery teapot before drenching it with the hot water from the kettle. He arranged the cups on their saucers and then extracted two cartons of milk. He held one up and shook it in the air while he looked quizzically at Jenny. Jenny nodded and he poured the contents into the cups. He repeated the action with a sachet of sugar but this time he got a shake of the head in response. With an exaggerated flourish he tossed it back amongst the rest on the tray.

Having deemed that the tea had stood long enough he poured it into the two cups. Picking both up he walked over to Jenny's side of the bed and placed hers on the cabinet beside her. He then took his over to the chair in the window, sat down and took a sip.

"I think I could get used to you bringing me tea in bed every morning." Jenny said with a cheeky grin.

"It would be my pleasure." Alan replied with an equally cheeky grin of his own.

For the next half hour they sat and chatted about what they should do that day. Alan offered to drive her up the coast so that they could explore the surrounding area. However, Jenny said she would be just as happy to walk back into the town and explore the harbour in daylight; maybe taking in a coffee somewhere.

"Then what I would really love to do," she said once they'd agreed on the morning itinerary, "is take a picnic up to the cliff top."

"Then what the lady wants the lady shall have." Alan replied.

Jenny giggled and jumped out of bed. She threw her arms around him, kissed him full on the lips and then disappeared into the bathroom to shower.

Chapter 30

The day could not have been more glorious if they had put in a request to Mother Nature herself. The sky was cloudless and the sun radiated sufficient heat for Jenny to forgo her cardigan and venture out in a light cotton knee length dress that was tied at the shoulders with thin fabric straps.

Alan, for his part, was dressed in a pair of stylish three quarter length shorts and a short sleeved collared t-shirt.

Halfway into town they stopped at a refreshments kiosk on the promenade. Alan asked if Jenny would like an ice-cream. With a child-like grin she requested a cone complete with chocolate flakes and finished off with strawberry sauce.

Alan disappeared to get them while Jenny wandered over to the wall segregating the beach from the promenade. It was low enough for her to lever herself onto so that when Alan returned he found her sitting facing the sea, gently swinging her crossed legs out towards the beach and then back again.

He passed her the two ice cream cones and climbed onto the wall next to her. He relieved her of one of the cones, drizzled with chocolate sauce rather than the straw berry Jenny was daintily licking from her own cone, and dangled his legs next to hers so that their thighs were touching.

Even this slight contact gave Jenny goose bumps. She wriggled up closer to him and Alan, transferring the cone from his left to right hand, put his arm around her.

"This place is beautiful." Jenny sighed between licks. "I could stay here forever."

"There's something magical about the sea." Alan said staring out at the distant waves as they rippled serenely across the ocean. "It seems to go on forever yet you feel as if you can reach out and touch the horizon."

Jenny took a bite of the flake leaving a fleck of chocolate in the corner of her mouth. Alan reached up and brushed it away with his finger which made Jenny giggle.

They sat on the wall until they had finished their ice creams; neither feeling the need to speak; both of them comfortable just being close to one another. As Jenny popped the last remnants of the cone in her mouth Alan eased himself up.

"Come on then." He said with authority. "I do believe it's time for coffee."

He swung his legs back to the promenade side of the wall and dropped down onto the path. Jenny turned and allowed Alan to lift her by the waist before gently placing her onto the pathway. She gave into the urge and gave him a quick peck on his lips before, hand in hand, they carried on towards town.

Alan and Jenny strolled slowly towards town; the sun warm on their faces. They followed the promenade right down into the harbour where they stood gazing down at the boats bobbing on the incoming tide and watching dads and their children sitting on the edge trying to catch crabs with baited lines.

Jenny remembered the serene silent beauty of the night time harbour from the evening before and how that contrasted to the bustling functional efficiency of its daytime counterpart. Seamen from all walks of life were tending to their boats; some preparing for departure on pleasure cruises around the bay while others were loaded with expectant amateur fishermen off to haul in the catch of a lifetime. Intermingled with these were the veteran seadogs washing down their vessels and stowing equipment having unloaded and dispatched their bounty from their trawler exploits of the previous night.

Alan suggested to Jenny that they maybe postpone their picnic in preference of one of the excursions but she declined on the grounds that she would be petrified of being on such a big ocean in such a small boat. Besides, she had set her heart on revisiting the cliff top and that was what she wanted to do.

Across the road from the harbour railing they found a coffee shop with outdoor seating. As luck would have it, there was a spare table and Alan drew out one of the chairs facing out across the harbour before indicating to Jenny for her to sit down.

"Thank you, kind Sir!" She said as she took the seat.

Alan took the seat next to Jenny so that they could both enjoy the view.

"This is just so perfect." Jenny said closing her eyes and feeling the sun on her face.

Alan nodded and took hold of her hand. He raised it to his mouth and kissed the back of it before lowering it onto his lap without letting go. Jenny turned to him and smiled.

"I'm so pleased you're here." She said. "I thought I was going to have a marvelous few days with Maisie but this is even better."

Alan raised his eyebrows and gave her a cheeky grin.

"Not just because of that!" Jenny said rolling her eyes and giving him a playful thump on the shoulder. "This place is so beautiful and it's such a perfect day. I can't think of anyone else I would rather spend it with. It's not something... something I'm used to."

Jenny went quiet and looked thoughtful before looking at Alan and continuing.

"But it's something I could quite easily get used to."

Alan gazed back into Jenny's eyes and for a moment neither could bare to look away. Eventually, it was Jenny that broke the spell.

"Shall we order coffee then?" She said picking up one of the menus from the holder in the middle of the table and concentrating on what was on offer.

They sat drinking their coffee for the next half an hour and watched the world go by. Every so often one of them would quietly comment on the attire of one of the holidaymakers that passed by or the beauty of the scenery in front of them but both felt comfortable with each other not to spoil the magic of the moment with too much chatter.

When it came to settling the bill, Jenny reached down to her handbag but Alan placed his hand on hers.

"This is my treat." He said.

Jenny opened her mouth to protest but Alan gently placed his finger across her lips.

"No arguments." He continued. "I want to spoil you. Please let me."

Jenny couldn't resist the warmth that that simple gesture gave her inside. Never in her life since her parents had died had anyone wanted to spoil her the way first Maisie, and now Alan, had. They had a way of making her feel very special indeed.

"Ok." She replied. "

"It's so difficult for me to do it back at the village. But here; here I can treat you like the lady you deserve. You've made me so happy and I want to show you how grateful I am for that in any way possible."

Jenny leaned over and kissed him on the cheek.

"It's me that should be spoiling you." She said. "I feel like you're bringing me back to life again and I will always be grateful to you for that."

Alan cupped her face in his hand and caressed it. Jenny let him do so for a while before sitting up straight in her chair.

"Right." She said. "What about this picnic you promised me?"

Chapter 31

Though they had frequented that coffee shop on many occasions after they had finally moved down to the coast, since Alan's death Jenny had been back there only the once. She had hoped to feel his spirit with her but, in contrast to the cliff top, all she had felt was a deep despair at his passing.

There were numerous places around their adopted home town that reminded her of him but none that made her feel as close to him as when she was high above the waves on the headland. Sometimes it made her happy; other times, like now, she wanted to push it to the back of her mind.

All she wanted to think about now was that first perfect day together and how their picnic had seemed like a banquet.

They had found the local supermarket at the top end of town and filled a basket with all sorts of food stuff. Conscious that whatever they bought they would have to carry up to the cliff top they concentrated on buying lightly packaged foods, the exception being a bottle of Chardonnay which they made sure had a screw top.

Being a holiday town supermarket they were also able to get plastic cutlery and glasses as well as a reasonably large plastic backed green tartan picnic rug. By the time they reached the checkout till Jenny felt like an excitable schoolgirl as she looked forward to sharing the afternoon with Alan on the cliff top.

They had managed to fill four plastic carrier bags with provisions and, after having distributed the weight evenly between these, Alan and Jenny set off for the cliff top path. At Alan's insistence he carried the bags whilst Jenny took responsibility for the picnic rug.

By the time they reached the top of the cliff Alan felt as if his arms were going to drop off. Though he continually refused Jenny's offers to lighten the load for him he was glad when they arrived at the seat and their planned picnic site. He sat down with a sigh and was ordered to rest while Jenny organised the blanket, laying the food out neatly along the top of it.

Once she had finished, she kicked off her sandals and sat down on the blanket. Alan joined her and shuffled up to her. Holding her close, they both gazed out over the cliff edge and beyond to the sea.

"It's so beautiful up here." Jenny said. "I don't think there could be a more perfect spot in the whole of the country to have a picnic."

Alan squeezed her to him and then reached for the wine bottle.

"We had better start drinking this before it warms up." He said.

As he unscrewed the top Jenny picked up the glasses. She held them out in front of her so that Alan could fill them. Replacing the top he put the bottle in the shade of the seat and took one of the glasses from Jenny.

"To you, Jenny." He said. "The most beautiful lady I have ever met."

Jenny shook her head as if humouring him and tapped her glass against his. She took a sip and then repaid the compliment.

"To you, Alan. The most kind, generous man I've ever met."

Alan saluted her with his raised glass.

"Let's eat." He said grinning. "All of a sudden I'm starving."

As they tucked into their feast they chatted away enjoying their new found freedom however brief it might turn out to be. After they had had enough to eat, Jenny packed away what was left. To her amazement they now only had one bag of food to carry down when they returned. Alan lay on his back with his hands behind his head. Jenny lay down by his side and rested her head on his chest. Alan put his arm around her to cradle her to him and began running his fingers through her hair.

"I want to stay here like this forever." He said with a contented smile on his face.

"Yes please." Jenny sighed. "That would be wonderful."

Lying next to Alan with the heat of the afternoon on her face, a full stomach and feeling the safety of his arms around her she began to feel drowsy. To the rhythmic beat of his heart pounding against her ear she closed her eyes and dozed off.

Jenny woke with a start. For a moment she felt disorientated. Slowly, she began to focus back on where she was and with whom. She raised her head and looked up at Alan. He was peering back down at her smiling.

"What?" She asked frowning.

"I've been watching you. You're so cute when you're asleep. I couldn't take my eyes off you."

Jenny blushed a little and gave him a playful poke in the ribs with her finger.

"I wasn't snoring was I?" She said biting her lip.

Alan shook his head.

"No. You were the picture of peacefulness." He said.

Jenny smiled up at him.

Suddenly Alan's smile disappeared and he began to look serious.

"What's wrong?" Jenny asked feeling perplexed at Alan's seemingly change in mood.

"I don't ever want to give you back." He said. "I want to keep you with me forever. I want to spend the rest of my life with you. I want to fall asleep next to you every night and wake up next to you every morning. I want to …."

Alan's speech was quickening so Jenny reached up and placed her finger on his lips. Alan took her hand and kissed it. He kissed her fingers; her hand; her arm before pulling her to him to kiss her lips. Jenny followed his lead and kissed him back as passionately. By the time they broke away from each other they were both panting.

"I love you, Jenny." Alan whispered in her ear. "And I want you to be mine forever."

Chapter 32

Jenny sat in silence for a moment absorbing the power of Alan's words. As scary as they seemed, deep down she knew they only echoed the way she was feeling about him. Alan had not only ignited the passion within her but also a zest for life she had never experienced before. It began to dawn on her that her life had now changed; that she wouldn't be able to return to her home and be the subservient brow beaten wife and mother that she had been for all those dark years. Alan made her feel good about herself and after all the heartache she had been through she finally realised it was a feeling she deserved.

Mistaking the true meaning of Jenny's silence, Alan cursed himself for exposing the depth of his feelings so soon in their relationship. He was now worried that he had scared Jenny to the point where he would lose her.

"I'm sorry, Jenny." He said, a slight tremor in his voice.

Jenny looked at him in confusion.

"Sorry for what?"

"I'm sorry for getting carried away and saying all those things." Alan explained.

"So, are you saying that you don't mean any of it?" Jenny frowned.

"Of course I do." Alan quickly replied. "I mean every heartfelt word of them. I just don't want you to feel pressured by what I said. I don't want to risk scaring you away from me."

Jenny reached for Alan's hand and grasped it in hers.

"You haven't scared me." She said. "You haven't scared me at all. You have just made me realise that I want you too. Ever since we met all you've done is made me feel alive. When I thought my life was lost to me you gave me back my dignity. I thought I was worthless but you've showed me I'm not. But most of all you've shown me how to love when I thought I could never love again."

Jenny looked Alan in the eyes before she continued.

"I meant it when I said you were the most wonderful, kind, generous man I've ever known. And the only thing that scares me is that I don't have the courage to be where I want to be; with you."

Alan pulled her to him and held her like he was never going to let her go. Jenny could feel his heart beating fast against her and tears began to well in her eyes.

"I love you so much." She said, her words muffled as she spoke against his chest before continuing in a near panicked voice. "I don't want to go back to him. I can't bear to be near him or have him touch me. He makes my skin crawl. Oh, Alan! What can I do to get away from him?"

The emotion became unbearable for her and her body shook with the power of her sobs as the tears fell. Alan pulled her closer into him and tried to soothe her.

"Hey! It's alright." He said as reassuringly as he could.

"My husband ... Your wife... My son... It all seems so complicated." She blurted out.

"We'll work something out. I promise you." He said gently lifting her face to look at him. "I promise."

He brushed a strand of hair back across her forehead that had fallen across her damp eyes.

"I'm going to do my very best to make sure no-one or no-thing will make you unhappy ever again." He said cradling her chin in his hand. "Somehow we'll find a way for you to leave your husband and then he won't be able to hurt you again."

He kissed her forehead as he held her cheek to his chest. Jenny began to feel calmer, lying there in his arms, and fought back her tears. She tried hard to believe what he was saying to her when he said it would all work out for the best. All she needed to do was to have the courage and dare to believe; believe she could move on to a happier life; a life she knew, in her heart of hearts, was destined to be with Alan.

Chapter 33

The sun was starting to make its way down towards the horizon as Jenny stood there alone. The heat of the day was still evident and she knew that the evening was going to develop into one of those barmy ones that she and Alan used to sit out in until way passed dark, talking about everything and nothing, both being content just to be in one another's company.

She stared at the rucksack next to her. The time was drawing near and she knew what needed to be done. She just hope that, when the time came, she would have the courage to do it.

However, for now she was more than happy to stand there, alone with her memories of how much this particular place was instrumental in turning around the fortunes of her life.

Jenny lay against Alan taking comfort in his closeness. Neither of them spoke for a while; she lost in her thoughts about daring to believe she could be happy with Alan for the rest of her life; he musing on how he could help this wonderful woman he held in his arms throw of the shackles of her loveless and menacing marriage.

It was Jenny that broke the silence first.

"I'm going to ask Maisie if she will let me move into the pub. I don't like imposing on her but her and John are the only friends I have I can turn to. Do you think she would mind?"

Alan stared at her in disbelief, not believing what he'd just heard her say. Then he laughed.

Jenny looked concerned.

"You think it's a bad idea then?" She said biting her lower lip.

Alan shook his head and smiled.

"Do you really think she would let you live anywhere else once she finds out you're leaving your husband? Don't forget who was instrumental in setting this up in the first place. Who it was that did her best to throw us together. I'm sure she would love to have you stay with her. Besides, it would only be until we can find somewhere of our own."

Jenny stared open mouthed at Alan. It took her a few moments to gather her thoughts before speaking.

"You're planning that we live together?" She finally uttered.

"Well, yes." Alan replied quickly. "That's what I was thinking of doing. It is what you want isn't it?"

Alan began to look a little perplexed thinking again that he had misread the situation.

"Oh yes! I want that more than anything else in the world." Jenny said with enthusiasm.

Alan puffed out his cheeks in relief as Jenny continued.

"That's alright then." He said scrunching his eyebrows together. "I thought I'd been a little too presumptuous there for a moment."

Jenny smiled and shook her head. Her smile quickly changed to a frown.

"But how is that going to be possible? I have no money of my own to buy clothes let alone a property. And it would take me a lifetime to save up for a home on the wages I get from the pub. My husband has no money so I won't be walking away with a big payout from him."

Alan could see that Jenny was starting to look downhearted again so he took hold of her hands and smiled at her.

"I have a little money tucked away for a rainy day." He winked at her. "Money I saved from the sale of my garage as well as some that Stella has so *generously* given to me. I'm sure we will have enough to get by on until I can find some sort of employment. I've been getting bored with all this time on my hands anyway and have been wanting to work for a long time but Stella wouldn't let me. I'm sure it won't be long before I get something. In fact Marjorie has been badgering me to go and work for her on the publicity side but I fancy getting back to being a mechanic again. Besides, it will probably take a while to find somewhere we like so we have plenty of time to find the necessary money. The most important thing at the moment is to get you away from that husband of yours."

Jenny opened her mouth to counter his argument but Alan held his hand up to indicate that the subject was closed and no longer up for discussion. Jenny let herself get caught up in Alan's enthusiasm and decided not to push the matter any further.

As the afternoon moved into early evening Alan and Jenny began to feel the grass beneath them grow damp. They decided to gather up their things and move over to the seat, draping the picnic blanket over it or added comfort. There they sat watching the sun slowly melt into the sea, marveling at the colour of the sky as it changed from bright blue to fiery orange to deep violet. Eventually, as the last slither of sun disappeared beyond the horizon they decided to make their way back to the hotel.

By the time they had returned to their room they were both shattered. A combination of the heat, sea air and the emotions of the afternoon finally caught up with them and it wasn't long before they had crawled into bed and were both fast asleep curled up in each other's arms.

Chapter 34

Jenny was woken by the early morning sun streaming into the room. From the feel of the warmth already emanating from it she thought that it promised to be another beautiful day.

She reached over to Alan's side of bed wanting to feel the touch of his body but was disappointed to find that yet again it was empty. Sleepily she sat up and glanced quickly around the room. She found him standing by the window, his back to her and gazing out onto the sea below.

Sensing that she was awake he turned to her, smiling.

"Good morning." He said as he came over and sat down on the edge of the bed beside her.

Jenny pulled him to her and planted her lips on his.

"Good morning to you, too." She replied as she withdrew from the kiss. "Are you alright? How long have you been awake?"

Alan shrugged his shoulders.

"About an hour." He said casually. "Once the daylight woke me up I couldn't get back to sleep again. And you looked so peaceful I didn't want to wake you."

Alan reached up and cupped her chin. Jenny closed her eyes and let the gentle stroke of his thumb across her cheek soothe her.

Alan raised her face to his so that when she opened her eyes she was staring straight into his.

"I've been standing here thinking." He said with an earnest look on his face. "About what we do about living together."

Jenny sat up straight and gave him her full attention.

"When we do find our own home, what would you think about moving out of the village?" He continued.

Jenny looked thoughtful for a moment before answering.

"I suppose once I've left my husband there won't be much there for me to stay for." She said. "And I'm sure if I did stay then he'd still find a way of making my life hell."

"What about your son? I'm happy for him to come with us if that's what you want."

Jenny thought about it for a while and then shook her head.

"I don't think so. It's not even as if we're close. He's too much like his father. Besides, he's old enough now to look after himself." Jenny said looking perplexed before adding "Does that make me sound too hard hearted? A bad mother?"

She turned her eyes away from Alan but he grasped her hand and brought it to his lips.

"Nothing you can say or do will convince me there is an ounce of hard heartedness or badness in you." He said rubbing the back of her hand against his cheek. "I just don't want you to feel you have to leave everything behind."

"I am pretty sure if it wasn't for meal times he wouldn't know I was there." Jenny sighed. "Besides he's made it pretty clear that as soon as he's old enough he's leaving home."

Alan nodded sadly. The more he heard of Jenny's family the more determined he was to take her away from the misery and give her the life he felt she deserved.

"And the pub? Your job?" He said.

Jenny's eyes dropped.

"I would miss not working there. John and Maisie have been so good to me. But the one thing they have given me above all is confidence in myself. I think it would be hard but if I had to I know I would be able to find bar work somewhere else."

"So a move out of the village would not necessarily be out of the question then?" Alan probed.

Jenny shook her head.

Alan nodded slowly with a knowing look on his face. Jenny narrowed her eyes and frowned at him before speaking.

"What have you been plotting while I was asleep?"

Alan laughed and turned to look at Jenny.

"Hear me out before you say anything." He said. "What if we were to move to a place like this?"

Excitedly he gesticulated with his hands through the air, a gesture that encompassed the room.

"Move into a hotel room?" Jenny said shaking her head and looking bemused.

"No." Alan said pulling a face that indicated that he thought such an idea was crazy. "I don't mean a hotel room. I mean a town like this. By the seaside. In fact, not a town like this but actually this town."

Jenny laughed as in his enthusiasm to explain Alan's speech had quickened so that he was getting himself a little tongue-tied.

"Stop teasing me." She said, her eyes glowing and giving him a friendly punch on the shoulder.

Alan stared back at her smiling without saying a word. Jenny stopped laughing and stared back at him.

"You're not teasing, are you?" She said biting her lip and looking confused. "You're really serious about this aren't you?"

Alan nodded slowly running his tongue behind his bottom teeth and raising his eyebrows.

"Wouldn't you like to live by the sea?" He said. "Stroll along the beach every day? Have picnics up on the cliff top and watch the sunset whenever you wanted?"

"Yes, but ..." Jenny started to speak but found herself lost for words.

"We have one more day here together before Maisie picks you up tomorrow." Alan continued excitedly. "Let's spend it looking around the place and seeing what's on offer. It can't hurt to look can it?"

Alan's eyes were almost pleading with Jenny to say *yes*. And before she knew it that strange ability of his to make her acquiesce had her saying exactly what he wanted to hear.

"No, I suppose not. It wouldn't hurt to look."

Alan hugged her to him and kissed her before breaking away.

"I'm going to get showered and then I'm going to treat you to a delicious cooked breakfast in the harbour." He said jumping from the bed. "And then we are going to go to the estate agents and see what's available."

With that he disappeared into the bathroom.

Jenny lay in bed listening to him whistling as he prepared for his shower. Caught up in his enthusiasm she couldn't help thinking she must be living in a dream. She knew it was probably a dream that would very soon end. But for now, she was going to enjoy the moments she shared with Alan and push everything else to the back of her mind.

She sighed contentedly and thought about how much her life had changed since she had met Alan. The old Jenny would have run a mile at the merest hint of living with another man. But here was the new Jenny off to look at houses with one. It may be just a wild idea – a whim even – but Jenny couldn't suppress the excitement she felt inside. If nothing else, for one glorious day they could act like any other love struck couple planning their future life together

She couldn't help smiling to herself when she thought about her new found confidence. Alan had made her the happiest woman on the planet and she was determined that she would spend whatever time they had together repaying him for that.

She dived out of the bed and joined him in the shower.

Chapter 35

Alan and Jenny spent the morning driving around the town and its surrounding area looking at properties that were on the market there. They had selected four and by lunchtime had seen three – a one bedroomed flat on the promenade leading into the town; a well-kept bungalow in the next village down the coast and a mid-terraced house that had the hills protecting the town to the rear as its backdrop. Though they all had their merits, none of them pulled in any way to either of them.

By lunchtime both Alan and Jenny were ravenous. They had an hour or so to kill before their next appointment, a cottage just outside the town, so they stopped off at a quaint pub by a river for some lunch. They managed to find a table on a balcony that overlooked the river where they sat and ate while looking at the details of the cottage.

Neither would admit it to the other but both had been looking forward to seeing this property more than the others. Jenny loved the way the photograph on the flyer portrayed an almost fairy tale looking cottage. It's four square windows, two up; two down, were bisected by a large wooden door giving it an enchanted look which was particularly enhanced by the front face being festooned with ivy.

Alan, for his part, was taken by the small but well stocked garden. The photograph had been taken on a beautiful summer's day and the colours of the flowers in bloom were as vibrant as he could wish for. Secretly he could imagine himself lost amongst them for hours.

The price of the cottage was a great deal more than any of the other properties they had looked at but Jenny couldn't help but dream of one day living in a cottage such as this. She was under no illusions that they would be able to afford anything as beautiful as this but she was determined to enjoy the experience.

Five minutes before their allotted appointment time they pulled up outside the cottage. The photograph did not do it justice. It was more beautiful than Jenny could have imagined and she fell instantly in love with it.

As they walked up the path to the door their senses were overloaded with the sight of the colours of the blooms, their scent and the sound of bees busily going about their business. Jenny grabbed Alan's arm and pulled him to her.

"It's beautiful!" She whispered.

Alan nodded back in reply.

They rattled the brass door knob and were warmly greeted by a silver haired lady who looked as if she might be in her mid to late sixties. She invited them in and took them on a tour of the cottage. Jenny was taken by the deceptive size of the rooms and how beautifully it was laid out. She began to imagine how she might like to lay it out to her own taste.

At the end of the tour the old lady invited them to take afternoon tea and cake with her in the back garden. Alan and Jenny half-heartedly declined but the old lady insisted. So with no further viewings planned, they let themselves be guided out onto the garden patio where they were left at a mahogany picnic table while their hostess disappeared to make the tea, turning down Alan's gallant offer of help.

Alan and Jenny sat there giggling like a couple of teenagers, marveling at the beauty of the garden around them. Before long, the old lady returned with a silver service tea set, china cups and the largest Victoria sponge Jenny had ever set eyes on.

Having indulged in two generous slices of cake at the insistence of their hostess, Jenny closed her eyes and let the sun warm her face; listening to Alan and the old lady chatting away. She tried to imagine what it would be like to live there, just her and Alan, away from the stresses of the outside world. She found herself wishing they were in a position to buy the cottage. She would gladly move there than have to face whatever lay ahead for them back in their own village.

This final thought darkened her mood and, with a sigh, she began to feel a wave of melancholy seep into her. As much as she wanted to stay positive she began to think of all the reasons why a cottage such as this would never be theirs.

As if to reinforce her morose thoughts a cloud passed over the sun temporarily removing the heat from the day causing her to shiver back into reality. Alan seemed to be rounding off his conversation with the old lady so Jenny prepared herself to leave, trying to distance herself from her previous thoughts of an idyllic life.

The old lady walked with them down the path to Alan's car and waved to them as they pulled away. Jenny let the sadness take over and began to weep. Alan pulled the car over into a layby and switched the engine off. He reached over and cradled her to him, running his fingers through her hair and trying to soothe her.

"It's such a beautiful place." Jenny said as her sobs finally began to subside. "In fact, it's perfect."

Alan smiled sadly in agreement and brushed the tears from her cheek.

"But we'll never be able to live somewhere like that." Jenny continued. "And even if we were, I don't deserve to live anywhere as beautiful as that."

Jenny felt as if all the new found confidence she had been feeling earlier was now draining away from her.

"Of course you deserve somewhere that beautiful." Alan whispered in her ear. "You deserve to be surrounded by such beauty wherever you go."

Jenny looked up at Alan, her eyes wide and glistening from her tears.

"If anyone doesn't deserve anything it's me." Alan said putting his head against Jenny's. "Here I am dragging you around houses and raising your expectations. I've done nothing but rush you into things against your will since the moment we met. No wonder you're so confused and upset."

Jenny pulled away from Alan a little and looked directly into his eyes.

"You have done nothing to upset or confuse me at all." She said with a determined steady voice that belied the emotion she was feeling. "Everything I have done I have done willingly. It's my fault I let myself get carried away with the magic of the moment. Tomorrow I am going back to the village and leaving my husband for you. I'm doing that because you are the most beautiful man I have ever met and I want to spend the rest of my life with you. But I am under no illusion that this fairy tale life we are dreaming up for ourselves is just wishful thinking. I've had a taste of what life could have been and that's nice. But I know that, as of tomorrow, my life is going to be anything but magical. What's important to me is that I love you. That's what will see me through the tough times ahead. And if we end up having to live in a bedsit without two pennies to rub together then I will still be happy. I will be happy because we will be together. That's what matters to me."

When she had finished talking Jenny bent over and kissed Alan. She held the kiss until she was giddy with lack of oxygen and had to part to breathe.

"Now let's go." She said. "Let's spend this last night together making each other happy. Because after tonight, who knows when we will get the chance again.

Chapter 36

Jenny and Alan spent that evening alone in their room. They did not crave the company of anyone else, determined to make the most of what time was left to them. They lay on the bed holding each other close, talking about all the things that interested them, thereby learning new things about each other as they did so. They avoided the topic of returning to the village both knowing that this was a reality that hung over them like a black cloud and that it would dominate their lives in the coming weeks and months. For that last night, they put it to the back of their minds and concentrated on happier things.

They made love with a passion, again not knowing when they would be able to share their love. Just after midnight they fell asleep in each other's arms, exhausted not only from their exertions but also the emotions of the day.

The following morning it was Alan's turn to wake up to find he was alone in bed. Jenny was sitting on the chair near the window wearing one of Alan's t-shirts. She had her knees tucked tightly up to her chest tucked into it and she was hugging them close to her. She was staring intently out of the window.

"Hey, you ok?" He called out gently across the room.

Jenny turned to look at him and smiled.

"Yes, I think so." She replied.

"Second thoughts?" Alan asked looking concerned.

"No." Jenny replied slowly shaking her head.

"I'm just not looking forward to going home and facing my husband." She admitted.

Alan got out of bed and joined her at the chair. Taking hold of her hands he knelt down in front of her.

"Do you want me to come with you when you tell him?" He asked looking concerned.

Jenny shook her head.

"No, it's ok." She replied. "I think you're presence might just antagonise him even more. He's going to be angry enough as it is."

"Please be careful." Alan said holding her hand to his face. "I don't like the thought of you and him alone together when you tell him. I don't want him to hurt you. I would never forgive myself if he did."

"I will." She reassured him. "I'm going to ask John if he'll come with me. He seems to have some sway with my husband and I'm sure he won't do anything stupid while John is around. Besides, you have your own problems to deal with."

Alan took a deep breath and then puffed air out between his lips.

"True enough." He said. "I must admit I'm not looking forward to breaking the news to Stella either but it'll be worth it in the end. You'll see."

Jenny closed her eyes momentarily before returning her gaze back through the window. Both sat in silence contemplating what was ahead for them.

Jenny smiled to herself. That day after their first time alone together was destined to become probably the most traumatic day in her life. And when she thought about her experiences up to that moment it was not a statement she made lightly.

But in the grand scheme of things it could also be looked upon as being the best day of her life because despite the dark days that followed in the immediate aftermath of their announcements to their respective spouses, it proved to be the day when her life finally moved on to the path of true happiness.

Chapter 37

Maisie arrived at the hotel just after eleven that morning. She greeted Jenny and Alan in the lobby acting as if she had in no way played a part, or even been aware of, the deceit that had taken place to get Jenny down there in the first place.

Alan insisted on helping Jenny place her suitcase in the boot of the car while Maisie made herself scarce citing the need to powder her nose so that they could say their good byes to each other.

Jenny nestled into Alan's chest and gently wept. He consoled her as much as he could and tried to reassure her that everything would work out alright and that they would be together soon. He told her he would keep in touch with Maisie and as soon as Jenny was settled at the pub he would come to see her. Jenny reminded him that as yet she hadn't asked Maisie if she could stay and that they should not assume that the land lady would be agreeable. Alan couldn't help laughing and told her that if Maisie did refuse to take her in then he would drink lager at the pub for a whole month instead of his beloved ale. The serious manner in which he delivered this promise made Jenny smile and when Maisie returned the pair of them were giggling like a couple of teenagers.

"There's no need for me to ask if you two have had a good time." The landlady said as she stood with her hands on her hips shaking her head and nodding in Jenny's direction. "I haven't seen anyone with a smile that wide since my John had two barrels of Paddy's delivered and he was only invoiced for one!"

"I suppose you're going to deny all knowledge of having anything to do with this." Jenny called across to Maisie from under Alan's protective arm trying to look serious but failing miserably.

"I have absolutely no idea what you are talking about, my dear." Maisie replied walking around to the driver side door. "Anyway, it's time we were making a move. Come on. Put him down and let's get cracking."

Alan drew Jenny to him and kissed her lips.

"Be brave." He whispered in her ear. "It won't be long now until we're together permanently."

Jenny held him close before reluctantly pulling away from him. She held onto his hand for as long as possible until she was finally forced to release him. She hurried around to the passenger side door and jumped into the car.

Alan remained where he was as Maisie started up the car. Neither he nor Jenny could take their eyes of each other, even as the car pulled away. Their longing look was only broken when, having exited the hotel car park, Maisie drove down a side street that ran away to the main road.

Jenny settled back into the seat and stared ahead. Maisie left her alone with her thoughts for a while before breaking the silence.

"Are you alright, sweetie?" She said.

Jenny turned to look at her and though she had tears in her eyes she nodded and smiled.

"Don't be sad." The landlady said without even trying to hide the pleasure in her voice. "Things are definitely on the up for you."

"And that's all down to you." Jenny said reaching over and squeezing Maisie's arm. "You've made it possible and I'll never be able to thank you for that."

Maisie felt a lump growing in her throat. It took her a moment to compose herself and speak.

"You know I would do anything to help you find happiness." She finally said. "Anything at all. You only have to ask."

"Really?" Jenny asked with the slightest hint of a tease in her voice.

Maisie nodded.

"Well," Jenny continued, "it's funny you should say that because I have a really big favour to ask."

Jenny proceeded to outline the plans to Maisie that she and Alan had made together. The landlady sat transfixed behind the wheel, glancing alternatively at the road then across to Jenny until in the end she had to pull over into a layby so that she could give Jenny her full attention.

"So," Jenny said biting her lip nervously, "the upshot is that when we get back to the village I am going to leave my husband and wondered if you could put me up at the pub. Only temporary until we find somewhere to share."

Maisie's face lit up.

"Of course you can, my dear." She burst out. "You can stay as long as you want. It would be a pleasure."

"I'll pay you rent." Jenny quickly added. "And I won't be a burden."

"You'll do no such thing." Maisie said. "It will be good to have a bit of female company around the place for a while. As much as I love my John, he's not always the most scintillating conversationalist in the world."

"Will he mind?" Jenny asked.

"Of course not." Maisie said as if the very thought was preposterous. "I won't allow him to!"

With that, they both burst out laughing.

Chapter 38

The journey home was uneventful and despite a couple of brief stops for comfort breaks they made good time. Maisie told Jenny that she wanted to get back in time to help John open up the pub for the evening session. Though she didn't admit to it, and Jenny thought never would, she got the impression from the tone of the landlady's voice that she had missed her husband. Jenny was not fooled by the brusque nature of the conversations Maisie had with John, understanding fully that here were two people who could not exist without each other.

As they travelled, Jenny recounted with enthusiasm all that she and Alan had done over the past few days together, deliberately skimming over their more intimate moments with an embarrassed glance down at her hands which were clasped on her lap.

Maisie's eyes widened when Jenny told her about their excursions around the area searching for suitable properties and how they were both particularly taken by the cottage.

"It was so beautiful." Jenny said looking a little forlorn. "But I can't see us being in a position to buy anything like that for a very long time; if ever."

Maisie was quiet for a while after Jenny had finished talking, so much so that Jenny mistook her silence for disapproval.

"You think we're mad, don't you?" She said turning to look out of the side window. "All this talk about buying somewhere together and moving away from the village when we hardly know each other. Come to think of it, when you say it out loud it does sound crazy."

"I most certainly do not think you are mad." Maisie said sternly. "I think that it's wonderful that you are planning a life together. And moving away from the village is probably the most sensible idea."

Jenny turned back to look at the landlady.

"Oh, don't get me wrong." Maisie continued. "I will be very sad to see you leave and miss you like crazy. But knowing both your spouses as I do, I think a complete clean break from the village would be highly preferable for both of you. Make no mistake, Alan's wife will not take his leaving lying down but as long as you and he stay true to each other, I know you will win through."

Jenny sat quietly letting Maisie's words sink in. She couldn't stop herself from chastising herself when she realised how selfish she'd been. In all her thoughts and worries about how she was going to approach leaving her husband, and the ramifications that was going to heap on her, she had hardly considered what the consequences of Alan leaving his wife would be for him. She remembered Marjorie's warning at the book signing about being wary of Stella and that she would not give Alan up at all easily. Alan's wife would not take lightly the embarrassment that his leaving would bring upon her.

All these thoughts were circulating in Jenny's head as Maisie turned off the main road and headed towards the village. She began to feel light-headed and nauseous.

"Stop the car quick!" She shouted out in a panic.

"What's the m...?" Maisie began but Jenny's desperate voice interrupted her.

"Please, pull over now."

Responding to the urgency in Jenny's voice Maisie did as she was asked.

The car had barely come to a stop when Jenny launched herself out of it and up to the hedgerow running alongside the road. Bending over and dropping her hands to her knees she was violently sick in the drainage ditch.

Maisie flicked on the car's hazard lights and hurriedly joined Jenny at the roadside. Silently she stood by the side of her gently rubbing the girls back as she threw up for a second time.

"My dear, whatever is the matter?" Maisie asked as Jenny stood upright.

"Oh, Maisie! What am I doing?" Jenny said suddenly feeling cold and shaking.

Tears began to stream down her cheek.

The landlady pulled Jenny into her and held her tight, whispering words of comfort to her. She stroked the stricken girl's hair gradually soothing away the trembling.

"I'm so afraid." Jenny finally said. "I don't know if I can go through with this."

Maisie pushed her gently but firmly away from her to arm's length.

"You can and you will." She said her face full of compassion for the terrified girl she held. "It's your only option for happiness. If you stay with that brute of a husband and selfish son of yours your life will continue to be miserable. Likewise for Alan if he stays with his wife. Is that what you really want?"

Jenny turned her moist eyes to Maisie and slowly shook her head.

"Then take control of your destiny." The landlady continued. "You have the opportunity to have a happy life with Alan. Granted it won't be easy to begin with but then nothing worth having ever is. But you have a good man in him who will support you all the way. And I've already told you John and me will do everything in our power to help you. So be brave."

Maisie took a tissue from the sleeve of her cardigan and dabbed the corner of Jenny's mouth with it.

"You deserve happiness." She reiterated. "Go out and grab it."

"*Belief and perseverance.*" Jenny muttered.

"What's that, dear?" Maisie asked looking puzzled.

"*Belief and perseverance.*" Jenny repeated. "It's what Marjorie's always saying."

"She sounds like a very wise woman." The landlady said. "Take heed of what she says and take this opportunity."

Jenny gave the landlady a half-hearted smile and nodded.

"Good girl." Maisie said returning the smile. "Now let's get back and find out what state that husband of *mine* has got the pub into!"

With that she led Jenny back to the car.

Chapter 39

On the cliff top, Jenny felt a shiver run down her spine. Even after all these years she could still remember the feelings of fear and dread she had had as she was being sick by the roadside; particularly the fear of facing up to Barnes and telling him she was leaving him. Never once in their whole relationship had she had the nerve to even contradict him. And thee she was about to confront him and tell him their marriage was over.

Added to this was her concern for Alan breaking the same news to Stella. It was no wonder she had felt sick to her stomach. She had never been able to deal with confrontation and there she was, inviting it into her life.

If it hadn't been for the solid support of John and Maisie, and her deepening love for Alan, she was pretty sure she would've caved in there and then and not gone through with walking out on Barnes.

As it was, she had taken a deep breath and steadied herself; ready to face up to him

It was mid-afternoon when Maisie pulled up on the car park. The pub was already closed up. Jenny had begged the landlady to take her there first before she went home so that she could try to pull herself together. The last thing she wanted was for Barnes to see her in the fragile state she was in. She told Maisie that she needed time to compose herself before facing her husband.

When they walked into the pub, they found John standing in front of the bar tapping his hand nervously on the bar stool next to him. He looked agitated and a little nervous. Maisie walked over to him and gave him a peck on his cheek.

"Are you alright, my love?" She asked looking concerned. "You look a bit out of sorts."

The landlord took a deep breath and exhaled slowly.

"Barnes has been on the telephone four times today asking if you and Jenny were back yet. I told him you weren't and that I wasn't sure what time you were due back. Then he started ranting on about making sure Jenny went straight home as soon as you arrived. I'm sorry Jenny but he didn't sound in a good mood at all. Each time he rang the angrier he sounded. The last time he virtually accused me of lying to him and that I was keeping you here away from him."

Jenny felt the nausea returning and began to feel light headed again. Maisie strode across the room and, taking her by the arm, guided her to one of the benches by the window.

"Brandy!" She called across to John but the landlord was one step ahead of her, decanting a large measure from the now familiar bottle on the back shelf.

Jenny tried to pull herself free of Maisie's embrace.

"I've got to go." She mumbled more to herself than Maisie or John, her breathing becoming rapid. "He'll just get angrier if I don't."

"You're not going anywhere yet." Maisie said firmly as John passed the girl the brandy. "Not until you've drunk this."

Jenny took the drink from the landlord and took a sip. She went to pass it back to him but he nodded at her to encourage her to drink some more. She obliged and then, holding it in both hands, held the glass tight to her chest as Maisie sidled up to her on the bench.

Jenny laid her head on the landlady's shoulder and closed her eyes.

"He knows. He must know." She kept repeating in an almost mesmeric whisper.

"Knows what?" John asked but didn't push it when Maisie shook her head at him signaling that he should leave the subject.

Jenny went quiet and sat staring into space thinking. Slowly her breathing began to return to normal. With a concerted effort she emerged from her trance, looked down at the glass and then finished off the contents. She turned to look at Maisie and, with a steely look on her face the landlady didn't recognise, she stood up.

"Right. I'm ready." She said

Maisie and John exchanged concerned glances. Maisie was the first to speak.

"You don't have to go rushing down and do it now." She said. "Give yourself a little longer before you do."

John opened his mouth to say something then decided against it. He knew better than to interfere with anything once Maisie had taken charge.

"No." Jenny said with a determined look. "I need to do it now or else I may never do it. I'll find a million and one reasons not to if I don't."

"Are you sure, dear?" Maisie said looking concerned and holding Jenny's hand.

Jenny nodded.

"Alright then." The landlady continued. "But take John with you just in case."

John nodded though obviously didn't know what he was agreeing to.

"Get your things and then come straight back here." The landlady said firmly glancing across at John hoping he was finally understanding what was going on. He raised his eyebrows but continued to keep quiet. Finally, from the resolve that developed on his face Maisie knew that John had tuned in to what was happening.

"Ok." Jenny said trembling despite the bravado she was trying to portray. "But this is something I have to do myself. I have to face him and tell him it's over. I have to learn to fight my own battles."

Maisie felt herself well up inside as she watched Jenny take a deep breath and walk resolutely towards the door. She wanted to grab her and keep her safe from Barnes but knew that if Jenny was to find happiness in her new life she had to throw off the shackles of her old one.

As John went to follow Jenny out the door Maisie pulled him to her and hugged him tight.

"Bring her back safe." She pleaded and with a cold, hard look on his face, John nodded.

Chapter 40

John pulled up outside Jenny's house and switched off the engine. The blinds across the front room window twitched and Jenny knew that her husband had been watching, waiting for them to arrive. As she went to get out of the car John gently grasped her arm.

"Are you sure you don't want me to come in with you?" He said looking concerned.

Jenny shook her head.

"I need to do this myself." She said. "I can't spend my life being afraid of him. I've lived with that fear for as long as I care to remember and it has to stop now. If I don't stand up to him now that I have a reason to fight I never will."

"At least let me walk you to the door," John pleaded, "if it's only for my own peace of mind."

Jenny smiled at the landlord, leaned over to kiss him on the cheek and nodded. They exited the car and walked up the pathway, John a couple of paces behind her. When they reached the front door it was already slightly ajar. Jenny reached out to push it open and then stopped. She closed her eyes and took a deep breath as she summoned up the courage to enter. John gave her shoulder a gentle squeeze.

"I can still come in with you if you've changed your mind." He said.

Jenny forced herself to stand tall and shook her head.

"Ok." John conceded. "But I'll be right here listening for the slightest hint of trouble. Call out if you need me."

Without turning Jenny nodded and entered the house.

As she walked down the hallway she could hear Barnes in the lounge muttering to himself. Her heart was beating fast and she felt sick to her stomach. But somehow she managed to find the conviction to put one foot in front of the other despite having an overwhelming desire to turn tail and run.

The lounge door was open and she tentatively entered the room. Barnes was standing with his back to the hearth, swaying a little. His mouth turned up in a sneer as he looked across at her with a mixture of aggression and contempt. He had obviously been drinking heavily which was evident from the remains of a twelve-pack littering the lounge carpet.

"Well, well, well!" He growled, his voice slurred. "Look who's finally decided to come home! It's that slut of a woman I married."

Jenny stood in the doorway trying not to be intimidated by Barnes' aggressive stance. Her mouth was dry and her tongue felt as though it was paralysed so depriving her of the ability to speak. She tried to focus her thoughts on Alan and the reason why she was about to do what she was going to do.

"You're a conniving whore!" Barnes spat out. "A lying, cheating whore. Pretending that you're going away with that bitch of a landlady when all along you were planning to go screwing around with some other bloke."

He glared at Jenny, his look confrontational just daring her to contradict him.

Jenny was stung by the venom in Barnes' words. She had been on the end of his vicious tongue on many occasions before but never had it delivered them with the level of hatred he was now lashing her with. She felt rooted to the spot and, with her mind in turmoil, couldn't map out the words she wanted to say. When she didn't respond Barnes took a couple of steps towards her.

"You know how I know you've been a slag and cheating on me?" He asked through gritted teeth, pointing aggressively at her to accentuate his point. "How I know you've been whoring with another man?"

He took another step forward and it took every ounce of Jenny's courage not to take a step away from him. She knew she had to stand up to him, no matter what the cost, because backing down to him now would give him the power to keep her there forever. So, despite the fact she was shaking uncontrollably, she stood firm.

"I'll tell you why, shall I?" Barnes continued not giving her the chance to answer even if she had been able to. "I had a telephone call this morning. It was from the manager of the restaurant you went to the other night. Apparently you dropped your library card there. He got your name and number from the local librarian and then rang me. He said one of the waiters found it under the table when he was clearing up after the two of us."

Jenny's husband stopped for a moment and looked up at the ceiling. When he looked back down his eyes were glaring.

"THE TWO OF US!" He growled before continuing in a scarily reasonable tone. "I told him he must have be mistaken because I wasn't there with you; that you were on holiday with another woman and if you had been to his restaurant it would have been with her."

Barnes' voice was gaining in volume the more he told the story.

"But he assured me that you were definitely there with a man. Who is he?" He continued. "Who is this mystery man you were with?"

Jenny was still unable to speak which agitated Barnes further and added fuel to his rage.

"WHO...IS...HE?!" He screamed as he finally snapped reaching for her throat with his left hand and thrusting her violently against the wall. "Who is this man you've been screwing around with?"

Jenny's head smacked against the plasterboard and her vision blurred. The room began to spin as Barnes' grip tightened. He started banging the back of her head against the wall as he repeatedly asked for Alan's name. Jenny felt as if her very life force was being shaken out of her but try as she might she could not find the strength to struggle free of his grip. His rage filled assault was too much for her to counter.

Jenny tried to kick out at him but to no effect. He had her held so tightly against the wall that she couldn't get enough power in her legs to dent his onslaught. In a moment of knowing clarity she finally realised that she had been a fool to think that standing up to him could end in any other way. She had been stupid to think that he would let her just walk away from him.

Deprived of oxygen, Jenny gradually began to feel consciousness slipping away from her and through a haze saw Barnes draw back his right hand. She knew he was about to punch her full force in the face and tears filled her eyes as she closed them. Using what remained of her strength she tried to turn her head away from the blow. It was a futile attempt. He had her gripped firmly by the throat. With an eerily calm resignation she waited for the impact.

Finally there was the sound of fist on bone and Jenny waited for oblivion to take her. In the seconds after, she thought she must be dead or at least unconscious as the pain that she was expecting to feel from the blow didn't materialise. Instead she found that suddenly she could breathe again and that she was no longer in Barnes' grasp. She slowly slid down the wall stroking her throat and gasping for air.

Jenny kept her eyes closed while she tried to fathom out what was happening. Suddenly, two strong hands grabbed her under the arms and she screamed. She started flailing her arms about her in an attempt to keep Barnes off her but when she opened her eyes she saw John standing in front of her. Despite her struggles he was trying to lift her from the floor. To the right of him Barnes lay groaning and curled up in a ball holding his arms over his head.

"Are you alright?" The landlord asked, his face full of concern.

Jenny nodded trying her best to reassure him before bursting out crying. John pulled her to him and tried to soothe her. He carefully inspected her throat and, satisfied there was no permanent damage, eased her onto the arm of one of the chairs. As he did so, Jenny caught sight of the bruise that was beginning to form on his knuckles.

"Thank you." She whispered finally realising that John had come to her rescue.

Her throat felt like it was full of broken glass as each of those two simple words grated. She stood up on shaking legs and threw her arms around the landlord, nestling her head into his chest.

"You're welcome." John said letting her take as much comfort as she needed. "Everything will be alright now. We'll get your things and then you can get out of here. You'll never have to put up with this animal again."

Barnes lay on the floor and seemed reluctant to move. Jenny thought she could hear him sobbing but she had no sympathy for him. She finally saw him for the sniveling coward that he really was.

"I'll be alright now." She said holding her throat as she peeled away from John and took a step towards the door.

The landlord went to follow her but she stopped. Breathing a little less heavily she turned and walked over to the prone Barnes. Still dazed, he mistook her for John coming over to beat up on him some more so he curled up tighter into a ball, whimpering.

Jenny bent down and put her mouth next to his ear.

"I'm leaving you." She whispered. "If you ever, ever, come anywhere near me and lay a finger on me again I'll go straight to the police and tell them all the things you've ever done to me. I have a witness now too so don't think that I wouldn't."

She stood up and looked thoughtful for a moment. Then, pulling her leg back, she kicked Barnes between the legs. He let out a cry of agony and lay sobbing on the floor.

"That's for all the times you took me whether I agreed or not." She growled through gritted teeth.

Jenny pulled her leg back and kicked him again.

"And that's for being a complete and utter bastard to me for all these years." She said through gritted teeth.

John looked across at her in amazement.

"Do you feel better for that?" He asked, smiling at her.

"Oh yes." Jenny replied looking serious. "You will never know how much better that makes me feel."

She lifted her head and walked back towards the landlord. As she did so her son came running into the room.

"Dad! Dad!" He cried as he passed Jenny before dropping to the floor and hugging Barnes.

"What have you done to my dad, you bitch?" He turned and hissed at Jenny with a look of hatred on his face.

"Don't you speak to your mother like that!" John growled angrily as he stepped towards the teenager.

Stuart cowered away from the menacing big man in front of him.

Jenny moved in front of John and gently placed her hand on his chest, shaking her head to indicate that he should leave it.

"He got what he deserved." Jenny said looking at her son before calmly turning to John. "I'm going to pack my things."

She placed her hand on his forearm and smiled.

"Then we can go." She continued swallowing hard as she felt her throat tightening from the bruising. "There's nothing left for me here now."

John patted her hand and then stood, arms folded, blocking the doorway while Jenny went upstairs to pack up the meagre belongings that defined her wretched existence with Barnes.

When she returned downstairs carrying a single battered suitcase neither Barnes nor her son made any attempt to stop her leaving. Despite the soreness in her throat Jenny walked out of the front door with her head held high for the very last time.

Chapter 41

When John and Jenny arrived back at the pub they found Maisie prowling up and down behind the bar. She had a tea towel in her hands and was working off her nervous energy by polishing as many of the drinking glasses in sight as possible. She was in mid polish when they walked in. She took one look at Jenny before hurriedly placing the glass on the bar and, throwing the towel over the till, marching around to her.

"Oh, my dear." She cried out when she saw the developing bruising around Jenny's neck. "What has that animal done to you?"

Before Jenny could answer the landlady had swiftly guided her over to one of the window alcoves and forced her to sit down. She ordered John to fetch some more brandies and before long the three of them were sipping from their glasses. The first sip stung Jenny's throat but after that she found it having a soothing effect against the pain.

Assured that the barmaid was alright Maisie made her recount the whole experience. When she came to the part where Barnes had grabbed her by the throat the landlady put her hand to her mouth and jumped to her feet. She made to move away from the table.

"Where are you going?" John asked.

"I'm going to notify the police so that they can arrest and lock that beast away." She replied.

Jenny grabbed her hand.

"No, Maisie, please!" She pleaded. "Please don't do that. It'll only make things worse."

"But he can't be allowed to get away with this." Maisie said horrified and confused. "Surely you're not going to let him? He could've killed you."

"Maisie, please sit down." John joined in placing a loving hand on her arm. "Let Jenny finish the story before you go barreling into anything."

The landlady stood there for a moment before sighing and then sitting back down next to Jenny.

Jenny continued with the story.

As she told Maisie about how John had come to her rescue and knocked her husband to the ground she watched as the landlady looked opened mouthed across at him. Jenny felt a lump in her throat as Maisie's look of amazement morphed into one of pure love. She couldn't help but think that if she and Alan could have half of what Maisie and John had in their marriage then they would be more than happy for the rest of their lives.

"My hero!" Maisie said staring at John and breaking into Jenny's dreaminess.

"MY Hero!" Jenny corrected her with a smile.

John, overwhelmed with embarrassment, suggested they have another brandy and disappeared quickly to the bar.

When he came back and was handing out the fresh glasses, Maisie noticed the damage to his knuckles. She had been so concerned about Jenny's welfare that it hadn't even crossed her mind that John might have gotten himself hurt too. She took his injured hand and began to gently massage the wounded area. John winced but allowed her to continue making a fuss of him.

"My poor baby!" She said pulling a sad face and looking at him wide eyed.

"If it hadn't been for John I don't know what would have happened." Jenny said looking adoringly at the landlord. "I think he might just have saved my life."

This started Maisie off again about going to the police but Jenny would still not entertain the idea. She finished the story by telling the landlady about the threat she had made against Barnes.

"I don't think he'll dare come anywhere near me now." She concluded. "I think I left him in no doubt about the fact that I meant every word of it."

John and Jenny looked at each other and laughed like they had a shared secret. Maisie looked at them puzzled and then badgered them to tell her just exactly what had happened. When John finally explained about Jenny's parting present to Barnes Maisie clapped her hands with glee and hugged the girl.

"That's been a long time coming but good for you, dear!" She pronounced.

"Like I said, I don't think he'll come anywhere near me again." Jenny reiterated. "Plus he's always been a little scared of John and now he has even more reason to be."

John raised his injured hand in the air and waggled it about in confirmation.

"Well, good riddance is what I say." Maisie proclaimed raising her glass. "Here's to a bright and beautiful new future for you and Alan."

John and Jenny raised their glasses and joined the landlady in her toast. All three downed the remainder of the brandy in one.

"Now, my dear." Maisie said standing up and winking at Jenny. "Let's get you settled into your room and then I can inspect what damage John here has inflicted on the pub in my absence."

Jenny laughed as John groaned, his new found hero status short lived as he fell back into his time honoured position of second-in-command in the pecking order of their marriage.

Chapter 42

Jenny stood thinking back to the drama of that day. As Maisie helped her get settled into the spare room at the pub, chattering away about how much fun they were going to have being under the same roof, Jenny remembered how, for the first time in her life since her parents had died, she had felt free. She was no longer tied to the brutality and slavery of her marriage. She was no longer at the beck and call of her tyrant husband and unappreciative son. She was finally getting to live her life the way she wanted to.

Though she had escaped the clutches of her husband she had been naïve at the time in thinking that she and Alan were now free to start building their life together. Jenny may have managed to shake off her husband but Alan being able to leave his wife? That had brought its own problems.

John and Maisie had given Jenny time off so that she could acclimatise to her new surroundings as well as get over her confrontation with Barnes. However, by the end of the week Jenny was begging the landlady to let her return to work to relieve her boredom. Maisie finally relented and allowed her to come back to work.

As she was getting herself ready for work Jenny felt quite excited. Although it had only been a week or so since she had last been behind the bar, so much had happened that that week had felt like a lifetime. From now on she was going to be working for the benefit of herself and not to finance Barnes' drinking habits.

She took special care with her appearance spending a lot of time on her make-up and hair, as well as choosing the prettiest, though functional, dress she owned. By the time she had finished and was ready to go downstairs she felt ecstatic.

Maisie was replenishing the shelves of bottled mixers and John was pulling through the next ale when Jenny came through into the bar. They both stopped what they were doing and stared at the new woman in front of them.

"You look wonderful, dear!" Maisie announced smiling.

"I thought I'd make an effort." Jenny replied looking a little bashful. "I thought I would make this the first day of the new me. Sort of throw of the shackles of the old life."

"You look splendid!" John added. "If I was ten years younger …"

"You'd still be ten years too old for her!" Maisie said giving him a friendly glare before joining Jenny.

John held his hands up in surrender and grinned.

Maisie held the girl's hands and stood back admiring her.

"Good for you." She said. "Take the world by the scruff of its neck and make it yours."

"I thought I would feel a bit self-conscious dolled up like this." Jenny continued. "But the truth is, I actually feel really good."

"Well, I'm sure that the customers will appreciate the effort." Maisie said smiling. "Particularly a certain customer if he comes in."

Jenny smiled as she hoped against hope that Alan would be able to find a way to come to her at the pub that night.

*

To Jenny's disappointment the bar was quiet; quiet enough for John and Maisie to comment that they hadn't seen it so dead in a long time. As the time got closer and closer to eleven, Jenny could feel her spirits getting lower and lower. By the time John told her it was time to close up all the positivity she had felt earlier in the day had seeped away.

John locked the doors and disappeared down into the cellar. Maisie began to tidy the tables as Jenny busied herself cleaning down the bar and rinsing out the pump nozzles. She was just screwing them back onto the pumps when there was a knock at the door. Jenny looked at Maisie who returned a puzzled look. The landlady ventured over to one of the windows, peeled back the curtain and peered out. She couldn't see who was standing in the porch but she recognised the car on the car park.

"I think you might want to get the door." She called across to Jenny, smiling.

Jenny looked questioningly at the landlady who just nodded and gestured with her head that Jenny should go to the door. With her heart suddenly beating fast, Jenny skipped from around the bar and over to the door. She reached for the key in the lock but hesitated for a moment. She stood back, smoothed down her dress and then finger-combed her hair. Satisfied that she looked her best she unlocked the door and opened it. Her smiling face took the full force of an open-handed slap across her left cheek; the force of which caused her to stumble back into the pub.

"Stay away from my husband, you little slut!"

Alan's wife stood in the doorway hatred burning in her eyes.

Jenny was too stunned to speak and could only stare at the woman in front of her.

"If you know what's good for you, you'll keep away from him." Stella snarled before turning and marching across the car park to Alan's car. Without looking back she got inside, slammed the door and, with a screech of tyres, sped away.

Jenny stood in the door way, bewildered, as her eyes began to fill with tears. She felt numb from the neck down, as if her body was no longer her own. All she could do was stare out to the spot where Alan's car had been parked.

Maisie was quickly at her side throwing her arms around her. She closed the door and guided Jenny to a seat where she slowly sat her down.

Drawn by the commotion above, John's head peered out from the cellar door. Seeing the distressed state Jenny was in and the look of concern on his wife's face he strode across the room to join them.

"What's happened?" He asked looking first at Jenny and then at Maisie.

Neither seemed capable of answering him.

"Maisie, what has happened?" He asked again.

The commanding tone of her husband's voice seemed to jolt the landlady out of her trance and she quickly explained what Alan's wife had said and done.

John sat down beside Jenny and took her hand in his. Gently he massaged the back of it.

"I'm so, so sorry!" Maisie said, her voice beginning to crack with emotion and tears welling up in her eyes. "This is all my fault."

Jenny slowly turned her head to the landlady and looked at her with a puzzled expression.

"Why on earth is this your fault?" She whispered, genuinely confused.

"I saw the car and assumed it was Alan. I should have checked first" The landlady began, her tears escalating into sobs. "Ever since you started work here I've encouraged you to be with Alan. I've pushed you and Alan together for all my own selfish reasons as well as because I thought you would be happy together. But all I've caused you is pain; first your husband and now this. I'm just a selfish, interfering old busy body."

Maisie's body shook as she sobbed.

Jenny had never seen Maisie so distraught. Retrieving her hand from John's grasp she stood up and walked over to the landlady. This time it was she that did the consoling. She threw her arms around Maisie and pulled her to her.

"No, no, no!" Jenny whispered into the landlady's ear trying to soothe her. "None of this is your fault. I'm old enough to make my own decisions and this is what I want. All you have done is to help me try to find happiness and I will always love you for that."

She gave the landlady a gentle squeeze before continuing.

"I love Alan and will do anything it takes to be with him. I'm not going to give him up just because I'm afraid of his wife. I've done the being afraid bit all my life but not anymore. I've finally stood up to my husband so I'm sure I can take whatever Stella has to throw at me."

Jenny released Maisie a little and held her hands before her as she finished.

"I will never, ever be able to thank you enough for what you have done for me and I never, ever want to hear you apologise to me for it again. You understand?"

Maisie smiled at Jenny and nodded.

"When did you suddenly become so tough?" She said laughing through a sob and releasing her hand so she could gently thump Jenny on the shoulder.

"It must be the company I keep." Jenny said laughing before embracing Maisie again.

Maisie held onto Jenny for a moment before letting her go.

"Look at me!" She said a little embarrassed. "I'm blubbering like a baby. I haven't had a good cry like that since, well... since..."

Her eyes darkened again and her face filled with pain.

"... since I lost my little angel."

The sobs returned and John stood up. He took his wife in his arms and, despite her initial half-hearted attempts to wriggle free, he held her close.

"My angel." She sobbed into his chest. "My poor, poor angel."

Jenny felt herself welling up again and stepped back from the grieving couple. She was just contemplating leaving them to their grief and going up to her room when there was another loud knock at the door.

Maisie and John broke from their embrace and the three of them looked at each of with trepidation. As John walked over to the door Jenny took a deep breath and braced herself for another onslaught.

Chapter 43

John opened the door to a somber faced Alan and when the landlord was satisfied that he was on his own, stood aside to let him in. Alan rushed passed him to Jenny and pulled her tightly to him. The landlord took a wary look outside, scanned the car park and then closed the door, making sure he locked it behind him.

"Oh Jenny, I'm so sorry." Alan said as he released her and saw the red mark left by his wife's hand still decorating her face. "I should have been here to protect you from her."

He reached over to gently stroke her injured cheek with the back of his hand.

"Everyone seems to be sorry tonight." Jenny said half smiling at him.

She looked over at Maisie and winked at the landlady, sharing the joke. Maisie forced a smile back at her.

Alan looked confused but Jenny just laughed.

"It doesn't matter." She said.

Now that Alan was there with her she really did feel as if nothing else in the world mattered. She felt safe and secure tucked into his arms.

"Why are you here so late?" She finally asked him, more in puzzlement than accusation.

"Stella told me she had been to see you and I needed to make sure you were alright." Alan replied.

"I'm fine." Jenny tried to reassure him. "A little shaken up but I'll live."

"That woman is certifiable." Maisie chipped in. "Why, if I had my way…"

"Now don't go getting all het up again." John intervened causing the landlady to huff in frustration.

Alan suddenly noticed the bruising around Jenny's throat.

"My God!" He groaned. "Did she do that?"

Jenny shook her head.

"No, that was a parting gift from my husband."

Alan could feel his temper boil up but Jenny put a soothing hand on his shoulder.

"It's alright. John sorted him out. I don't think he'll be laying a hand on me again in a hurry."

John flushed with embarrassment but stayed silent.

"Looks like you've had a horrendous few days." Alan said shaking his head. "Makes mine look like a walk in the park."

"Tell me what's been going on." Jenny said leading Alan to the window seat. "How did you're wife react to you telling her?"

Jenny sat down and Alan took his place by her side. John glanced over at Maisie and nodded towards the stairway, trying to indicate that they should leave the pair alone. The landlady deliberately ignored him; standing with her arms folded across her chest waiting to listen to what Alan had got to say. John abandoned his subtlety.

"Well, I think Maisie and me will get ourselves off to bed now and leave you two lovebirds to chat alone." He said gently grasping the landlady by the arm and steering her towards the stairway. "Besides, it's been a long day and we need to be up early tomorrow. The man from the brewery's paying us a surprise visit so we want to be at our best when he gets here. You two help yourself to a drink. I think you both need one."

Maisie frowned but didn't resist. She said goodnight and then disappeared with John upstairs muttering her protests quietly in his ear. Finally alone, Alan fetched them a drink and then began to tell Jenny what had been happening between him and his wife in the time since they had parted at the hotel.

"As soon as I got back I told Stella that I was leaving her. At first she just laughed and went off to her parish council meeting as usual. But when she came back she was in a foul mood."

Alan took a quick swig of his drink.

"Apparently Stella confided in one of the other women on the council about my saying I was leaving her. She told the woman that she'd never heard such a pathetic excuse of a statement, even by my standards. Unfortunately, the woman is the wife of one of my drinking buddies and he'd told her a while ago, half in jest mind you, that he thought I was having an affair with a barmaid."

Jenny couldn't help but feel a wave of guilt flow through her, a feeling not helped when Alan nodded at her to indicate that it was her that his friend had meant.

"Anyway, it appears that his wife had been holding this nugget of gossip waiting for the right moment to reveal it to Stella. Well, she decided last night was that moment."

Alan lifted his glass and studied its contents before taking another sip. He placed it back down on the table and held it in both hands before continuing.

"Stella came storming back home and we had a blazing row. She wanted to know who you were and where you lived. I told her it was none of her business and that it was over between her and me. The more I wouldn't tell her the angrier she got until she stormed off to bed screaming that there was no way she would let me leave her."

In truth, Stella had told him that there was no way she was going to let him humiliate her by leaving her for a slut of a barmaid. However, Alan wanted to spare Jenny's feelings.

"I spent a sleepless night listening out for her in case she did something stupid." He continued.

"You don't think she's suicidal do you?" Jenny said horrified and looking concerned.

Alan couldn't help but laugh before immediately apologising when he saw that Jenny was serious.

"Oh no!" He said trying to alleviate her fears. "Stella is far too unfeeling to be suicidal over me leaving. She doesn't want me but she'll be damned if she'll let me go to someone else. That would be far too embarrassing for her. No, I was more afraid that she might come and seek you out in the middle of the night. I wanted to be ready to stop her."

Jenny sat up straight. She was horrified at the thought that Stella might have turned up in the early hours of the morning and maybe catching her alone. Tonight had been bad enough and she had been with Maisie then.

"Anyway, obviously she didn't." Alan continued. "In fact, when she came downstairs this morning she acted as if there was nothing wrong."

Alan saw Jenny looking puzzled.

"Oh, don't get me wrong. She was frosty with me and never spoke. But that was no different than she normally is. The unnerving thing was she never spoke about us at all. It was as if what had happened the previous night had not... well... had not happened at all. When she did speak to me she told me she had some business in town to see to and that she wouldn't be home until late this evening. I told her not to expect me to be there when she did return but she didn't bite and left without saying anything else."

Alan raised his glass for another sip. By now Jenny was hanging on to his every word.

"I spent the rest of the day packing up what belongings I wanted to take with me. I can tell you, that wasn't a pleasant experience. It's not nice when you come to the sad conclusion that, for all the years Stella and I had been together, not much of what we had was mine. Most of what we owned was Stella's."

Jenny nodded in agreement, painfully aware of her own meagre belongings.

Alan shook his head sadly before continuing.

"Anyway, I rang Marjorie and asked if I could crash at hers for a couple of days; just while I decided what I was going to do. She was more than happy to put me up but said she was not going to be in until gone ten tonight as she was off promoting her book. She told me I was welcome to go around any time after that. I decided to pack my stuff into the car and then come up here to see you while I waited for her to come home. But when I went to my car it had gone. Stella had taken it to stop me going anywhere while she was out. I was left high and dry so that all I could do was to sit and wait until she came back. I should have known she was coming here. Jenny, I'm so, so sorry."

Alan turned to Jenny and held her hands; his eyes pleading for forgiveness. Jenny obliged with a smile.

"When she finally came in about half an hour ago she taunted me with the car keys and asked me if I'd lost something. Then she mentioned you and she had a smirk on her face that told me she had been to visit you and done something. I got scared for you and when I asked her what she'd done she laughed. She said she'd been to see you and sorted you out. She said she told you to stay away from me and that she was sure that after her little short, sharp, shock that you would never want to see me again. I could tell by the way that she was rubbing her hand while she spoke that she must have struck you or something."

Alan took a moment to compose himself as he recalled the emotional turmoil he had been feeling while Stella had been standing there laughing about what she'd done.

"I was so worried that she'd really hurt you that I lost my temper with her. I snatched my keys from her hand and pushed her out of my way. I got here as fast as I could.

"Do you think she will follow you back here?" Jenny asked suddenly feeling fearful.

Alan shook his head.

"I don't think so." He said. "As I was getting into the car she was standing in the doorway laughing and calling me a *pathetic love-struck teenager*. She told me I wouldn't be able to stay away and I'd soon be straight back to her."

"But you won't will you?" Jenny said smiling and resting her head on his shoulder. "Now you've left her you'll never have to go back again. I'm the one you're with now."

"I wish it was that simple." Alan said nervously. "I'm going to have to go back."

Jenny looked at him horrified as her heart sank.

"You're going back? To her?" She said almost hysterically. "But you said you wanted to be with me!"

Alan looked sheepish.

"I'm going to have to go back tomorrow." He said with a sad look of resignation on his face. "I'm going to have to go back because I left in such a hurry that I forgot to pack my things into the car!"

Jenny didn't know whether to laugh or cry. Instead she chose to thump him on the arm in a mixture of relief and anger!

Chapter 44

Jenny asked Alan to stay the night but he refused on the grounds that Marjorie had been kind enough to offer him a place to stay and he did not want to take that kindness for granted. Besides, he was also mindful that Jenny was a guest of John and Maisie and didn't want to push their generosity to the limit either. He promised Jenny that they would soon be together permanently and that they just had to be patient while he sorted things out. Once they had found a place of their own there would never be a need for them to be apart again.

Alan suggested that Jenny should get some sleep and that he would call on her the following day after he had hopefully retrieved his belongings. Despite feeling tired after the trauma of the evening Jenny tried to persuade Alan to stay longer but in the end he told her he really needed to go as Marjorie would be waiting up for him to let him in. Jenny grudgingly gave in.

Alan checked out of the window to make sure Stella wasn't lying in wait for them and when he confirmed the coast was clear she unlocked the door to let him out. They stood in the porch embraced in a goodnight kiss which Jenny didn't want to end. Alan then made her go inside and lock the door behind her before he would leave. She stood at the window and watched him walk across the car park, get into his car and then drive away.

She gathered up their glasses from the table and took them behind the bar. After swilling them under the tap, she put them in the glass washer ready for a proper clean in the morning. With a last glance around the pub she armed the burglar alarm, switched off the lights and went up to her room. By the time she had brushed her teeth, got into her night dress and slid under the duvet she felt totally exhausted. However, despite the events of the week she felt a warm glow inside. She had no reason to doubt Alan's promise of them being together soon and the thought of falling asleep in his arms every night for the rest of her life lifted her spirits. She vowed to herself that she would try to stay positive for however long it took them to find a home together.

With the soreness in her face beginning to recede it wasn't long before she was fast asleep.

When she woke the following morning the sun was already out. Despite having the curtains drawn the room was bright and the warmth of the rays gave promise to a gloriously beautiful day outside.

Jenny stayed tucked under the duvet, the drama of the previous night slowly started to feel like a bad dream as she lay there feeling warm and cosy. Her cheek seemed to be fully recovered and even the bruising around her throat seemed to be less problematic. She stretched her arms up over her head and grasped the pillow, pulling it down around her ears feeling comfort in the way it hugged her face. She let it go and lay staring at the ceiling for a few moments. She glanced across at the alarm clock sitting on the bedside table. It read nine thirty.

Jenny couldn't remember the last time she'd stayed in bed this late. At home she was expected to be up by seven thirty at the latest to make sure her son was awake and ready for school. Briefly she wondered how he was getting on without her to cajole him but then she remembered that look of hatred on his face when he'd found his father curled up on the floor and pushed all thought of him from her mind. As wrong as it would probably seem to the outside world, she felt nothing but numbness towards both her husband and son. Neither had ever showed her an ounce of warmth or compassion in all the time she was with them and she wasn't going to lose a minute's sleep over how they were going to fare without her. For now she was going to dwell in the luxury of being able to sleep in.

To her dismay, she found that she didn't take naturally to just lying around in bed so by ten o'clock she was sitting reading Marjorie's book. By ten thirty she was starting to feel guilty and restless about still being in bed, particularly as she could hear John and Maisie moving about downstairs. She slid out from under the duvet and made her way to the bathroom where she treated herself to a long, hot shower.

When she'd finished she wrapped a large towel around her body, a smaller one around her hair, scooped up her night clothes and returned to her room. As she moved across the landing she could hear the muffled voices of John and Maisie downstairs in discussion with a third voice. Remembering that the landlord had mentioned about a meeting with the man from the brewery she assumed that was who it was.

Jenny took her time getting dressed; not wanting to go downstairs into the pub until the meeting had finished. She made her bed and then, still hearing voices below, lay on it with her back against the headboard. She picked up Marjorie's novel again and continued to read it. When she finally heard the voices cease and the pub door open and close, she laid the book down on the bedside table and ventured downstairs.

She entered the bar area eagerly, wanting to share the happiness she was feeling with John and Maisie but came to a sudden stop when she was greeted by the landlady in floods of tears. She was being comforted by John. Seeing Maisie in such a state for the second time in such a short period unnerved Jenny and she couldn't help but get a very bad feeling that something wasn't right.

"What's wrong?" She asked as she hurried over to them. "Has something happened?"

John shook his head looking shell-shocked and upset. Maisie, for her part, seemed unable to speak. She was sobbing heavily into the landlord's chest as he held her tightly to him.

"Please tell me what's wrong!" Jenny pleaded; unable to shake the feeling of dread that was beginning to take hold of her.

John didn't say a word but guided Maisie over to the window seat that Alan and Jenny had been sitting at the previous evening. He indicated that they should all sit. Even then he seemed at a loss as to where to start.

"We've just received some bad news." He finally said looking bewildered. "We've been told that we're no longer needed here. We're no longer needed to run the pub."

Jenny sat open mouthed, not able to comprehend what John was saying. The landlord sat up straight and placed his hands on the table in front of him before continuing.

"The brewery has decided that the pub's not profitable enough under our tenure and they want to put a younger couple in to freshen it up and modernise it."

Jenny shook her head unable to believe that this could be happening to her friends. She was beginning to feel as if every time she was on the point of some sort of happiness in her life something else was sent along to knock her down.

"Surely they can't do that?" She said, still finding it difficult to take it all in.

"They can do what they like." John replied trying not to sound bitter but failing. "After all, it is their pub. We just manage it."

"But it's your home too. Surely they can't just evict you."

"They can and they are." Maisie finally spoke, blowing her nose into a tissue. "All they are obliged to do is give us notice and then we have to go. That's what this surprise visit was all about this morning."

Jenny was astounded. She was no expert at running a pub but she still couldn't understand why the brewery would come to such a decision. She knew from the short time that she had been working there that it wasn't the busiest pub around but they always seemed to have enough customers to make it a viable business. And the customers they did get always commented on how quaint the pub was and how good it was to have a traditional village pub in their midst. Not once had she heard anyone say that the pub was old fashioned and in need of modernisation. In fact, on many occasions she had heard the opposite. Customers had commented to her that there were too many characterless pubs around these days; pubs that had lost their identity.

"I can't believe the brewery would do this to us." John said putting his elbows on the table and placing his head in his hands. "We've always had such a good relationship with them. We've always met our targets and we've never given them cause for concern over anything. So why are they treating us like this now? And to do it with no warning. I just don't understand it."

The landlord stared down at the table disconsolately. Maisie reached her arm around her husband's shoulders and gave him a squeeze.

"I don't know, my love." She said doing her best to comfort him. "I really don't know. But I do know this. As long as we're together then nothing else in this world matters; no matter where we are or what we do, as long as we have each other we will be fine."

"When do you have to go?" Jenny said feeling a lump coming to her throat as she looked at how crest-fallen John was.

"We're on three months' notice." Maisie replied. "But the brewery has said they would like us out as soon as possible; even if that means having to pay us off."

"Aye, but we're to keep the pub *operational* in the meantime." John said with a hint of sarcasm in his voice.

Jenny felt tears beginning to well up in her eyes as the gravity of the situation began to sink in. Try as she might she still couldn't get to grips with what it all meant. John and Maisie had devoted their life to making the pub a success. They were proud people and she couldn't imagine how they must be feeling to have it all taken away from them like this on what seemed like a whim.

"Where will you go?" She asked.

"I don't know yet." Maisie replied. "We've not really had time to think about it. My sister's maybe. At least in the short term until we can sort ourselves out. John has a brother in the Midlands but he has a large family so I don't know if he'd have room for us too."

The landlady shook her head.

"Oh Maisie!" Jenny said as she wiped the tears from her own face. "Surely there is something you can do. Is there no-one you can speak to who can help you fight this?"

The landlady shook her head.

"It's all in the contract." She explained. "As long as they give us notice they can get rid of us whenever they like and there's nothing we can do about it. We've always known that but never really believed they would have need of doing it."

Jenny reached over and held Maisie's hand, unable to find the right words to comfort her. She felt inadequate. All the times the landlady had been able to soothe her worries and now, when she needed to reciprocate, she couldn't think what to say. It was Maisie that spoke next.

"So what will you do now?"

Jenny looked at the landlady with puzzlement and confusion.

"Me?"

"Yes, dear." The landlady said. "Where will you go now?"

Until that moment, and to her credit, Jenny could honestly say that she hadn't grasped the full implications of what was happening to John and Maisie. In her concern for her two friends Jenny had failed to consider the fact that she would be homeless too. She sat back in her seat trying desperately to fight off the wave of nausea and panic that was starting to sweep over her.

"I'm so sorry." She heard Maisie say through a haze. ""I'm so, so sorry."

Jenny took a deep breath and tried to pull herself together. She tried to return herself to the happy place she had been in before she had come downstairs. She focused on her pledge to stay positive and thought about Alan.

"It's not your fault." She said to the landlady, a look of serious determination on her face. "I'll sort something out so don't you worry about me. I'm sure Alan can help me find somewhere. You concentrate on finding someplace for you."

Jenny hoped she sounded convincing to Maisie and John. Though she was directing the words at them deep down she knew she was doing her best to convince herself.

The three sat there in silence, each trying to come to terms with this new twist of fate that had been forced on them. The silence was broken by a tap at the window. They turned as one to see a middle-aged man staring in at them and tapping the watch on his wrist.

"Are you open yet?" He called through the glass.

John looked across at the clock above the bar to see that it was showing twelve o'clock. He turned back to the window and nodded at the man before slowly getting up to open the door. While he did so, Maisie and Jenny moved over to the bar to prepare to serve.

With an effort, they all put a smile on their face determined not to be miserable in front of the customers.

Chapter 45

Jenny stood on the cliff top thinking back to that horrendous day when they realised that they would have to leave the pub. Even to this day, she could still not believe that the brewery had treated Maisie and John so badly. They had been the only people in her wretched life to that point, Alan excluded, that had shown her any kindness and they hadn't deserved to have the pub taken away from them like that.

It was also a testament to their character that when the real reason for them being removed was made clear they stood by her. The strength of their love for her was immense. But the aftermath of that day was something that was to test Jenny's resolve to stay with Alan to breaking point.

During that lunchtime shift John, Maisie and Jenny seemed to come to an unspoken pact to put their plight to one side and concentrate on serving their customers. Thankfully, they were surprisingly busy so they didn't have much time to dwell on their predicament.

Normally, John would have closed the pub at its usual time of three in the afternoon but due to the glorious weather he decided to stay open. They had a number of customers in the beer garden enjoying the sun and a few inside now making the most of the extended drinking time.

Halfway through the afternoon Alan walked into the bar.

"I was going to come in tonight to see you." He said to Jenny who had come from behind the bar to kiss him. "But when I drove past and saw you were still open I thought why wait."

He gave Jenny his cheeky school boy grin which she returned with a half-hearted smile. Straight away he knew something was wrong.

"Are you alright?" He asked looking concerned. "My wife's not been in causing any more trouble has she?"

Jenny shook her head and returned behind the bar to pull Alan's favourite pint.

"What is it then?" He asked starting to feel worried.

Jenny looked across at Maisie who nodded at her.

"Why don't you take your break, dear, and go sit outside in the sun with your man." The landlady kindly suggested to Jenny.

Jenny nodded and re-joined Alan. Maisie poured her a half of cider and passed it over the bar to her. Alan went to get his wallet but Maisie shook her head.

"These are on the house." She said smiling sadly.

Alan thanked Maisie and then led Jenny outside into the beer garden. They found a secluded table and sat down opposite each other. The afternoon sun was still strong so Alan opened up the umbrella piercing the centre of the slatted table so that it provided some welcome shade. Jenny kicked off her shoes and stretched her legs along the seat. She could feel the warmth massaging her bare feet, throbbing from her shift behind the bar but now seemingly rejoicing in their new found freedom

"It's such a beautiful day." She said sounding morose. "How can anyone possibly have problems on a day like today?"

Alan took a sip of his beer and reached across the table to hold Jenny's hand.

"Are you going to tell me what's going on now?" He asked sounding concerned.

Jenny sighed and looked across at Alan, sadness painted across her face. Tears began to well up in her eyes again as she told him about the visit from the brewery and how Maisie and John were being turned out of their own home.

"It's just not fair!" She said. "Why would the brewery do such a thing to them? After all that they've done for the pub. This is their home and their life. Why would they take it away from them?"

Alan was quiet and looked pensive. Jenny stared at him for a moment before speaking.

"What?" She asked realising Alan was holding something back. "What are you thinking?"

Alan took a large gulp of his beer before answering.

"Stella's part of many committees around here," he began, "one of which, I think, is the licensing committee. It's quite possible that when she went out yesterday after our argument she may have been in touch with them. It's the sort of low-down underhanded trick she would do. It's the only thing that I can think of that makes any sense."

Jenny looked horrified.

"She wouldn't do something like that, would she?" She said mortified at the suggestion. "Surely she wouldn't take her anger at you and me out on John and Maisie?"

"Stella will do anything she thinks fit if it gets her what she wants." Alan replied nodding his head and sighing. "She's not a person to be crossed. She likes to win and will achieve it in any way possible."

"But the brewery?" Jenny said trying desperately to hold back her tears. "They wouldn't let her do this to them. They know how good John and Maisie are, and how hard they work. Surely they wouldn't turn their back on them just because Stella says so?"

Alan shrugged his shoulders.

"Unfortunately Stella has great amount of influence in many circles. If she tells the licensing committee there's a problem then they will act. The brewery, in turn, won't want problems with their license so will do whatever they are told to do."

"But that's not right." Jenny said wiping her eyes with the back of her hand. "If Stella wants to get back at me then why doesn't she do that and leave John and Maisie out of it. Her fight is with me not them."

"She doesn't think like that." Alan replied. "As far as she's concerned they've given you a place to stay; given you the opportunity to be with me; even encouraged it. If she can get at them then that's a bonus. Unfair? Yes. But I've lived with her long enough to know that that is how she works. Besides, while she's getting them out of the pub she's getting you out of here too."

Jenny stood up; a look of determined resignation on her face.

"Then I can't do this." She cried, finally giving in to her tears. "I can't sacrifice my friends for my own happiness."

"What are you saying?" Alan said looking up at the stricken woman above him, concern etched on his face.

"I think we should stop seeing each other." Jenny sobbed. "Too many people are getting hurt and I can't live with that."

Alan tried to intervene but Jenny held her hand up to stop him.

"No, I've made up my mind." She said trying to stay calm though she could feel her very soul crumbling inside her. "Go back and tell Stella she's won. I'll leave the village and stay away from you. Just tell her to leave John and Maisie alone and let them keep the pub."

With that Jenny ran barefoot across the beer garden and into the pub, leaving Alan behind to be stared at by the remaining bemused customers.

Chapter 46

Alan sat for a while and finished his beer. With the brief commotion over he was no longer the centre of attention in the beer garden and the rest of the customers returned to their own conversations. He couldn't believe that his relationship with Jenny had taken such a turn for the worse and the happy, positive mood that he'd arrived at the pub in had completely dissipated.

Alan was well aware of Stella's propensity for getting her own way but he'd honestly thought that he and Jenny would ride out whatever his wife could throw at them. But this was a different situation altogether. By including John and Maisie in her revenge, and to such devastating effect, Alan feared that there was a very good chance that he wouldn't be able to hold on to Jenny. He knew how much Jenny thought of the couple and how difficult it would now be to see them turned out of their home in this way.

It was John that came out to him to find out what had upset Jenny so much.

"She blames herself for you and Maisie being thrown out of the pub." Alan explained to the landlord as he sat down.

"That's rubbish!" John said frowning. "It's not her fault at all. Why on earth would she think that?"

Alan explained his theory about Stella, the licensing committee and the brewery. When he had finished John took a moment to let it sink in.

"You really think this is what's happened?" He asked. "Seriously? Your wife has that much influence?"

Alan nodded his head.

"It's the only thing that makes any sense." He said. "You've never had any problems with the brewery before, have you?"

John shook his head.

"Then it's either a very big coincidence or Stella's behind it." Alan continued. "And to be honest, I don't believe in coincidence. Do you?"

The landlord shook his head again.

"But that still doesn't make it Jenny's fault." John finally said.

Alan shrugged his shoulders.

"It's what she feels though." He explained. "And now she thinks the only way to remedy the situation is to leave me, leave the village and get Stella to get you the pub back."

"But that's just crazy!" The landlord said not even trying to hide the incredulity in his voice. "She can't just give up like that; not after all she's been through to get this far."

He forcefully pointed towards the pub.

"Go and tell her everything will be alright. Tell her that John says me and Maisie will be just fine and this is not what we want for her. I'd rather lose the pub and her be happy than get it back and know she's sacrificed her future for us."

The landlord gathered up Alan's empty pint glass and Jenny's unfinished cider. He turned to go and then stopped.

"Jenny has never had anyone stick up for her before. If you bow to her wishes and let her leave you then she'll never trust anyone again. You are her last hope at love and happiness. Don't let it slip away from her."

Deciding he had said his piece John went off around the other tables to collect as many empty glasses as he could carry, chatting to those that were responsive to him before returning inside the pub.

Alan sat for a moment gathering his thoughts. He decided he would be damned if he was going to let Jenny push him out of her life on some misguided guilt trip brought about by his wife's actions. He wanted nothing more than to be with her for the rest of his life and, one way or another; he was going to make sure that happened.

With a renewed sense of purpose he stood up from the picnic table, scooped up Jenny's discarded shoes and followed the landlord into the pub.

Chapter 47

As Jenny ran barefoot and crying through the pub to get to her room, she passed John and Maisie standing by the bar. Maisie looked worriedly at John to which the landlord indicated with a nod of his head towards the stairs that his wife should follow the stricken girl. By the time the landlady got to Jenny's room the girl was lying face down on her bed sobbing violently into her pillow.

"What on earth is the matter, dear?" Maisie asked kindly as she perched herself on the edge of the bed and began to stroke the back of Jenny's head. "Is this about us having to move out? If so, don't fret yourself about it. We'll all be fine. You'll see."

If it was Maisie's intention to ease Jenny's concerns then she was unsuccessful. If anything her words just served to add fuel to Jenny's sobs. Her body shook on the bed as the emotion of everything that had happened to her over the last few days finally came bursting out.

Maisie was unsure what to say or do next so she decided to let Jenny cry herself out; content to just comfort her by stroking her hair and holding her hand. Slowly Jenny's sobs subsided. As they did so, her muffled voice came from behind her pillow.

"I'm sorry, Maisie." She wept. "It's all my fault."

"What is dear?" The landlady replied soothingly.

"Everything!" Jenny continued still ensconced in her pillow.

"Oh, everything is it?" Maisie said with a slight hint of tease in her voice. "So you're to blame for everything are you?"

As she spoke the landlady gently turned Jenny over so that she was now lying on her back. Jenny's eyes were puffy and the make-up she had so carefully, and happily, applied that morning was now streaked down her cheeks."

"So. Please tell me all these bad things that you think you've done then." The landlady said jokingly raising her eyebrows. "All these bad things that you feel you have to take full responsibility for."

Jenny sat up and blurted out all that Alan had told her he suspected. Maisie listened intently and without interruption. When Jenny had finished the landlady held her arms out.

"Is that everything then?" She asked, her calm exterior not betraying the anger she felt inside towards Stella.

"Isn't that enough?" Jenny said bemused. "I've lost you your pub and your home. It's because of me that you've got to leave."

Maisie pulled Jenny to her and hugged her tight to her chest. She felt the spasmodic shudder of the girl's grief and felt an ache in her heart for Jenny's plight.

"You haven't done any such thing." The landlady said running her fingers through Jenny's hair. "If anyone has done these things then it's Stella, not you. You can't be responsible for the wickedness of other people."

"But if it wasn't for me …" Jenny started but she was cut off by Maisie.

"Now stop thinking that way because that will make me angry with you." Maisie said sternly. "This is exactly the kind of reaction that evil woman wants from you. Don't give her the satisfaction. What's done is done but you stand firm and make sure she doesn't win. Alan loves you, not her, so don't you lose sight of that. He's a good man and you do whatever it takes to keep hold of him."

Jenny bit her lip and looked pensive. Maisie held her away from her looking puzzled.

"What is it?" The landlady asked. "What have you gone and done?"

Jenny closed her eyes and let out a deep sigh.

"I told Alan to forget all about me and tell Stella to ask the brewery to give you the pub back."

"You did what?" Maisie cried out with incredulity.

Jenny opened her eyes but had to gaze away from the landlady as she was unable to meet her eyes.

"I told Alan to tell Stella that she'd won; that I'd stay away from him and that I'd leave the village." Jenny said looking crestfallen. "But only if she made the brewery keep you here."

Maisie raised her hand to her mouth; a picture of shock.

"I don't want you to lose all of this because of me." Jenny continued trying to hold back her tears but knowing she wouldn't succeed.

Maisie lowered her hand and tried to gather her thoughts. It was a moment before she could speak but when she did, she battled hard to keep the anger from her voice.

"What does Alan have to say about all of this?" She asked through gritted teeth.

"I didn't give him a chance to speak." Jenny replied raising her eyes to the ceiling and sniffed deeply in an effort to control her emotions.

"Then you get right back out there and tell him you're sorry and that you were wrong. " Maisie said with a sternness in her voice that Jenny had not heard before. "I will not have you throw away your happiness because of the selfish actions of that … that …"

Maisie's anger had now welled up so much that she was struggling to get her words out.

"… that WITCH!" She finally managed to finish.

Jenny was shocked by the vehemence in Maisie's voice. She was just about to argue back when Alan came bursting into her room, red faced and also angry.

"I will not allow you to throw away our relationship on that … that …" He began, obviously having his own problems in articulating himself.

"Witch?" Jenny suggested through her tears though she was unable to suppress a little smile when she said it.

"Yes, WITCH!" Alan continued unaware that Jenny's face was now starting to lighten a little and that Maisie was staring at him with a mixture of shock and respect.

"You mean too much to me for me to let you walk out like this. I love you and I am not going to lose you." Alan decreed having found his own stern-edged voice which, in truth, Jenny actually found strangely sexy.

"And I won't stand by and let you throw away this future you can have with Alan." Maisie contributed. "I won't hear of it?"

Jenny looked from Maisie to Alan and then back again. She was just about to speak when a third voice piped up from behind Alan.

"And nor will I!"

Maisie and Alan turned in the direction of the voice and found John standing calmly in the doorway polishing a pint glass with a towel.

Jenny felt a strange sensation in the pit of her stomach. Suddenly she felt her throat begin to contract and just when she thought she was must be going to vomit, she began to giggle. She started thinking about Alan and Maisie's anger towards her and the giggles got stronger. Then she looked at John standing there, a picture of calmness against all the rage of the other two and her giggles turned into full blown hysterical laughter.

Alan, Maisie and John looked at each other in turn, their puzzled faces betraying their thoughts of confusion.

Jenny threw her hands up defensively in front of her.

"Ok! Ok!" She bellowed between sobs; sobs now of laughter. "I get the message."

"So you're not going to leave me then?" Alan asked, his face now full of hope and expectation.

Jenny shook her head.

"No, I'm not." She said smiling; her laughter slowly dying down. "How can I possibly compete when it's three against one?"

Maisie smiled at John who, as unflappable as ever, just nodded in satisfaction back at her. Maisie reached out her hand to him and, with a little bit of juggling of glass and towel, he took it.

"Thank you." She mouthed to the landlord, her back to Jenny so that the girl was unaware of the words that were spoken.

"Well, that's that sorted then." Alan said sitting down on the edge of the bed next to Jenny, looking exhausted.

John looked across at Maisie and then indicated with his eyes that they should leave the room so Alan and Jenny could talk in private. The landlady nodded and turned to hug Jenny.

"What am I going to do with you, dear?" She said shaking her head and squeezing the girl.

"More to the point," Jenny responded, closing her eyes as she accepted the hug. "What am I going to do *without* you?"

"You have Alan now." The landlady said breaking from the hug, holding Jenny at arm's length and smiling. "He's what you need from now on. He'll look after you."

Maisie glanced across at Alan with a look that told him that the landlady now held him solely responsible for Jenny's happiness. Alan answered with a nod and Maisie looked satisfied.

"Right!" She said releasing Jenny and standing up. "We'll leave you two lovebirds to chat. I'm sure you have plenty you need to say to each other. Meanwhile, I'd better get downstairs and make sure the customers are not helping themselves to the takings seeing as the landlord is neglecting his duties up here."

John rolled his eyes playfully and turned to leave.

"Thank you." Jenny said speaking to the landlord's back. "Thank you both for being there for me when I needed you. I couldn't have done any of this without your strength and I want you to know how much I love you both."

John hesitated in the doorway for a moment. Jenny was pretty certain that, despite having his back to her, she heard him let out a small sniff before continuing on his way.

"We love you too, dear." Maisie said sadly smiling before turning to leave too.

"What *am* I going to do without them?" Jenny said staring forlornly after them.

Alan reached out and gently squeezed Jenny's hand.

"You'll be fine." He said with a smile that warmed Jenny's aching heart. "I'll make sure of that. You'll see."

Jenny pulled his hand to her face and caressed it against her cheek.

"I love you, Alan." She murmured as she guided his hand into the neckline of her dress. "I love you so much."

Without breaking contact with her Alan reached over and pushed the door closed. Jenny wriggled across the bed making room for him beside her. Alan obliged and joined her. As he lay by her side he pulled her to him and placed his lips on hers.

Jenny let all her anxiety escape and, never needing him as much as she did at that moment, slowly began to undress him.

Chapter 48

Now, even after all these years, Jenny's heart still ached when she thought back to that afternoon and how she very nearly pushed Alan away. She also knew that it was a turning point in their relationship and that she was going to be with Alan whatever the cost.

Standing on the cliff, she smiled to herself as she remembered how the three people she had ever loved in her grown-up life made her see sense that afternoon and how their love for her had stopped her making the second biggest mistake of her life. It also proved to be the catalyst to the most loving period in her life, despite Stella's continued attempts to break her relationship with Alan.

When Jenny woke later she found herself lying naked next to Alan. They had made love and fallen asleep in each other's arms. Alan was still asleep, his breathing shallow and rhythmical, almost hypnotic. His bare chest was above the duvet and Jenny couldn't resist leaning up on her elbow and running the fingers of her free hand across his skin. He murmured slightly in his sleep causing her to stop and remove her hand for fear of waking him. She contented herself with lying their watching him sleep.

While she lay there, watching every movement of his chest as he soundly slept, Jenny tried to clear her mind of the problems that surrounded her. Gazing down at the beautiful man in front of her she found the bleakness she had felt earlier in the day melt away. Alan had proved himself to be the most caring man she had ever met and, even after knowing him for so little time, knew that she trusted him implicitly. If he said that things would turn out fine for them then she was willing to place her faith in him.

Jenny glanced at the clock. It read six thirty. Maisie and John would be opening the pub in half an hour and Jenny was determined to be at their side when they did so.

She carefully raised herself out of bed, tip toed across the room, slipped on her dressing gown and gathered up some fresh clothes. She made her way down the corridor and into the bathroom where she reveled in a hot shower, symbolically letting the warm water wash away any remaining worries about the future she may have. When she returned to her bedroom clothed and refreshed she found that Alan was still fast asleep having turned on his side and now facing away from her.

Jenny quietly sat down at the dressing table and re-applied her makeup. Her mood was good. However, the child-like excitement that she had been filled with on her previous visit to the dressing table was now replaced with a more mature, understated self-confidence as she readied herself to face the public.

She looked into the mirror, nodded with satisfaction at the image of the woman staring back at her and left the bedroom; gently pulling the door behind her. When she emerged into the bar area she found John unlocking the external door and Maisie re-stocking the tables with fresh beer mats. They both looked across at Jenny, the unspoken question about her welfare in their eyes. Jenny smiled and nodded back reassuringly at them so they continued with their tasks as Jenny readied the bar. The tables fully stocked, Maisie joined

Jenny behind the bar as John disappeared down into the cellar for one last check that all was as it should be.

Maisie looked across at the barmaid and nodded once more. Indicating that she was ready Jenny returned the nod and the two of them turned their gaze to the pub door, awaiting the first customer of the evening.

The warm weather of the afternoon had continued into the evening bringing with it a steady stream of customers out to spend a rare barmy evening drinking in the beer garden. Jenny and Maisie were kept sufficiently busy not to have time to dwell on the drama of the afternoon and both took it in turns to take advantage of the beautiful evening as they alternated going into the beer garden to collect empty glasses. It was from one of these forages that Maisie returned looking a little flustered. She deposited the empty glasses on the bar and wordlessly set off to locate John down in the cellar. Jenny, frowning, watched the landlord, with Maisie following him as far as the bar, disappear outside looking concerned. Jenny came from behind the bar and stood next to the landlady.

"What's wrong?" She asked. "Has something happened out there?"

"I just can't believe the bare-faced cheek of some people." The landlady replied shaking her head to accentuate her disbelief.

"Why? What is it?" Jenny pushed.

"Not *what* but *who*!" Maisie said cryptically without explaining further.

"Then *who* is it?" Jenny said feeling a little frustrated with Maisie's lack of detail.

"Stella! That's *who!*" The landlady said finally. "Sitting out there, bold as brass with a friend, drinking a bottle of wine; acting as if she owns the place."

Jenny couldn't help but let out a little giggle catching Maisie off guard.

"What's so funny?" The landlady asked. "I would have thought this would be the last thing you would find amusing."

"After all this alleged business with the brewery," Jenny explained between giggles, "she probably thinks she does.

"Not yet she doesn't!" Maisie growled. "John's still the landlord here and he has every right to evict people from the premises as he sees fit. And after her little escapade with you the other night he has more than enough reason to do so."

Jenny shrugged her shoulders and returned behind the bar to serve a customer who had just walked in. By the time she had finished with him, John had returned.

"Well?" Maisie asked. "Have you got rid of her?"

John shook his head.

"She says that she has every right to be here and that if I want her to leave then I'll have to get the police involved." The landlord said barely able to contain his rage.

"Then do it!" Maisie said reaching for the telephone and holding the handset out for John to take.

John made no attempt to take the phone from his wife.

"She also reminded me that she is big buddies with the Chief Inspector and that I should think very carefully before I even contemplated such an action, especially as she has recently been doing a lot of charity work for him."

"Why that ...." Maisie began before sensing a presence in the doorway.

"Well, well, well!" Stella said looking at Jenny mockingly as she moved into the bar area. "Look who we have here. I'd have thought you would have been evicted by now."

Her eyes were full of hatred as she stood staring at Jenny.

"What do you want, Stella?" Jenny said with an outward calmness that belied the turmoil she was feeling inside.

"The mouse speaks!" Stella said feigning surprise.

"Haven't you caused enough trouble for Maisie and John without coming here to make a scene?" Jenny replied ignoring Stella's taunt.

Stella raised her eyebrows as she took in a defiant Jenny.

"And what exactly do you mean by that?" She said in a voice designed to intimidate Jenny.

"Come on, Stella." Jenny replied. "We're not stupid. We know you're behind Maisie and John losing the pub. You couldn't get at me through Alan so you thought you'd ruin their lives. And why? Just so you can frighten me off and get a man back that you don't even want?"

Stella seemed genuinely taken aback by Jenny taking a stand against her. It took her a moment to regain her composure.

"I think you credit me with having too much influence over people." She said narrowing her eyes.

"You shouldn't believe everything people say about me."

Maisie opened her mouth to speak but John gave her a look that told her, in no uncertain terms, that she should suppress whatever it was that she was about to say. The strength of his look was enough for the landlady to obey his wish for once.

"Stella, what do you want?" Jenny asked again.

"I want my husband back." Stella replied sternly. "He belongs to me and I won't have some dreary barmaid take him away from me."

Jenny laughed surprising not only Stella, Maisie, and John but herself too.

"Oh, please Stella!" She heard herself saying. "He doesn't *belong* to you. He doesn't *belong* to anyone. He's a human being with feelings not an ornament or piece of furniture for you to display as and when you choose. Besides, he loves me not you. And you certainly don't love him. You just can't stand the thought of him wanting someone else. Well, get used to it because it's me he wants to be with and I certainly want to be with him. Nothing, not any of your underhanded tricks, is going to keep us apart. Just learn to live with it and leave him… us… alone."

Something in Jenny's determined, even voice left Stella momentarily speechless. When she did finally speak there was a slight quiver in her voice and, despite her veiled threat, she didn't sound so domineering.

"You'll regret crossing me." She said through gritted teeth.

"Yeah! Yeah!" Jenny replied almost mocking Stella. "Change your tune. You're wearing this one out."

Jenny steeled herself for a tirade of abuse from Stella but Alan's ex-wife just glared at her before turning to storm out the door.

John and Maisie stood in silence staring at Jenny; unable to comprehend what they had just seen and, more importantly, heard.

"What?" Jenny said in response to their puzzled gazes.

"You stood up to her." Maisie said shaking her head in disbelief.

"Yes." Jenny said slowly, frowning. "I did, didn't I?"

"You were magnificent." John said grinning, his face a picture of pride.

Jenny blushed.

"You were amazing!" A voice called out from the stairway behind them all.

The three turned to see Alan standing there, his face beaming. He hurried around the bar and took Jenny in his arms. Only then did she allow herself to start trembling.

Chapter 49

John and Maisie gave Jenny the rest of the night off allowing Alan to propose that they went out for a meal. When asked where she wanted to go she told him that, despite the heat of the day, she would very much like to go to an authentic Indian restaurant. Throughout her life with Barnes the extent of her experience of Indian cuisine had solely been from take-aways. Alan said he knew of a local restaurant that fitted the bill so suggested they should go there.

Jenny's altercation with Stella had left her feeling surprisingly hungry. She had expected to crumble into a heap when Alan had put his arms around her but once the trembling had stopped, she found that she actually felt as good about herself as she had ever done. Never before had she had the confidence to stand up to anyone as she had done to Stella. She could only put this down to the new found belief in herself instilled into her by Maisie, John and, especially, Alan.

Alan took her to one of his favourite restaurants situated in an old renovated pub in one of the nearby villages. Jenny walked in and instantly fell in love with the quaint intimacy of the place. The reception area was neat and tidy and had ample seating for at least a dozen people.

They were greeted by a smiling waiter who guided them to a seat in the reception area before offering them the menus and taking their drinks order. Jenny remembered how much she had liked the gin and tonic she had had at the seafood restaurant so ordered one of those.

By the time the waiter came back with their drinks they were ready to order. Having written it all down and confirmed it all back to them he took them through to an intimate table for two towards the back of the restaurant overlooking a small indoor goldfish pond. He then disappeared into the kitchen.

Jenny sat back and surveyed the room. There were about ten tables of varying sizes spread around. Other than their own, three others were populated with diners at varying stages in their meals. In one corner sat an Asian family happily eating and chatting. Alan told Jenny that this was a sign that the food was particularly good.

It was obvious from the way they spoke to Alan that the staff there knew him. One-by-one they greeted him as they passed the table. Each, in turn, was introduced to Jenny and she made a conscious effort to remember their names. Throughout the evening whenever they passed by they would smile at her making her feel special.

Half way through their main course an older man appeared at the table and asked if everything was to their satisfaction. He commented on how lovely Jenny was looking and that he was pleased to see Alan in the restaurant again after what seemed a long time. Alan introduced him as Raziq, the manager and owner of the restaurant. Raziq bent down and whispered to Jenny, though loud enough for Alan to hear, that he was pleased to see Alan looking so happy and not to be dining alone as he usually did. Jenny looked across at Alan and queried this with her eyes. Alan's reply was to shrug and give her a flash of the school boy grin she was rapidly beginning to love so much.

After their meal they ordered coffee and retired back to the reception area. Jenny chose to sit in the corner of a large leather sofa while Alan took the accompanying armchair. Jenny slipped off her shoes and slid her feet under her, reveling in the feel of the cool leather against her bare legs. Alan sat back in his chair with his arms along the rests and smiled.

"What?" Jenny asked when she realised Alan was smiling at the way she was sitting.

"Nothing." He said keeping the smile on his face.

"Go on, tell me." She insisted. "What are you thinking?"

"It's just so nice to see you so relaxed." Alan relented. "Especially after all that's happened recently. Plus you look so damn cute!"

Before Jenny could reply Raziq was back at their side offering them complimentary brandies. Jenny gracefully declined and went to slide her feet off the sofa, conscious that she was taking liberties with Raziq's hospitality. The restaurant manager held up his hands and insisted she stay as she was if she was comfortable. He then turned and walked over to the bar, clicked his fingers to get the attention of the young lad behind it and ordered the brandy for Alan in his native tongue. Soon a waiter was arriving with a tray containing coffees, brandy and after dinner mints. He placed them onto the low table in front of Alan and Jenny and then returned back to his station.

Alan leaned forward and picked up his brandy, cupping it in his hands. He gave it a gentle swirl in the glass before sitting back. He raised the glass to his nose to take in the aroma before taking a sip. Jenny, for her part, retrieved one of the mints and slipped it from its wrapper. Daintily she nibbled it around the edge.

The pair of them sat for a moment in silence enjoying the moment. It was Alan who broke the silence.

"I'm so proud of the way you stood up to Stella tonight." He said.

Jenny rescued a crumb of chocolate that had lodged in the corner of her mouth with her tongue before replying.

"I'm pretty proud of myself actually." She said taking up her coffee. "Mind you, I will admit to feeling a bit scared inside. For a moment I had a wild urge to run and hide. But I don't want to be *poor downtrodden* Jenny any longer. I've done that for all my life and it's made me miserable."

She reached across the gap between the sofa and the armchair and put her hand on Alan's

"You, Maisie and John have done that. You've stood by me; encouraged me; shouted at me ..."

Alan raised his eyebrows but Jenny let out a laugh.

"In a nice way, of course." She reassured him. "And at a time when I needed it."

Jenny went quiet for a moment trying to think of the words to sum up what she wanted to say to him. In the end she decided to keep it simple.

"What I'm trying to say is *thank you*." She said. "Thank you for your support and your belief in me. Thank you for rescuing me from my wretched life. Thank you for being there when I needed you. For all this."

Jenny raised her free hand and waved it through the air indicating the restaurant.

"But most of all, thank you for letting me love you."
She finished.

Alan took Jenny's hand and lifted it to his lips to kiss
it.

"It's me that should be thanking you." He said,.
"You have gone through so much to be here. I'm
honoured to have your love and will never take it for
granted."

Jenny pulled Alan's hand over to her own lips and
returned the kiss. They stared into each other's eyes
and both felt the deepest of love inside. Jenny finally
broke the silence.

"Let's finish these drinks and head back. I need to be
close to you."

Alan nodded across at the barman signaling for the
bill and then finished his drink. Having settled up they
sought out Raziq and thanked him for his hospitality.
He made them promise to visit again soon. Shaking
hands with the waiter who held the door open for
them, they left the restaurant arm in arm.

Chapter 50

The next few days were thankfully uneventful. However, there was one moment of unpleasantness when Barnes had the bare-faced cheek to turn up at the pub early on the Thursday night. Luckily, Jenny was still upstairs getting ready when her husband walked in. By the time she came down to the bar John had packed him off with the clear message that he was no longer welcome anymore and if he came anywhere near the Red Lion again the landlord would contact the police. With a tirade of bad language directed at John and Maisie Barnes had left, slamming the pub door behind him.

Jenny had heard the commotion downstairs and came tentatively into the bar. John was standing, arms folded across his chest, staring resolutely at the door.

"The nerve of some people." Maisie said and then smiled when she saw the look of concern on Jenny's face. "Oh don't worry, dear. John's sent the rat packing. I don't think we'll see him in here again."

Jenny was aware that the few customers that had come in for early-doors were now looking at her. With her head held high she joined Maisie behind the bar and began to tidy the shelves as if nothing had happened. Before long the customers had lost interest and returned to their own conversations.

The warm weather continued and the pub became busier the closer to the weekend it got. Alan spent as much time as possible with Jenny in between. With Barnes now barred from the pub Jenny told Maisie that she would like to take on more work to help out. At first she wanted any extra money due to her to go towards her upkeep but neither the landlord nor landlady would hear of it. Instead, they insisted that Jenny put the extra aside towards her new home with Alan. After her first Friday night shift, Alan wanted to take Jenny into the town to celebrate. However, Jenny said she was too tired and didn't feel up to it. As a compromise, Alan got her to agree to a celebratory take-away and invited John and Maisie to join them. Both agreed and while John cashed up the nights takings, Alan rang through to the Indian restaurant and ordered a selection of dishes for them to share. Maisie and Jenny set about getting plates and cutlery together.

Once the food arrived Alan insisted on picking up the bill and the four friends sat down to eat, enjoying one another's company until the early hours of the morning.

Jenny awoke the following morning alone but content. Alan had left them to return to Marjorie's so that he could unpack what little belongings he had managed to retrieve from the house he'd shared with Stella. Once up and dressed, she came downstairs to find that the postman had brought John and Maisie the letter they had been expecting ever since their meeting with the brewery representative. The letter gave notice that they had four weeks to vacate the premises and find alternative accommodation. John was already on the telephone to his brother who had offered them a place to stay until they could find somewhere of their own.

Jenny found Maisie in a somber mood. She was standing behind the bar staring across the room as she cleaned a glass. Sensing Jenny behind her she turned to look at her. Jenny noticed the tears in the landlady's eyes.

"Are you alright?" She asked.

Maisie indicated towards the letter now sitting on the bar. Jenny picked it up and began to read it. Having finished it she placed it back on the bar.

"So it's finally official then?" Jenny said.

The landlady nodded.

"We knew it was coming" she said, "but it's still a bit of a shock to see it there in black and white."

Jenny moved over to the landlady and gave her a hug. Maisie accepted the embrace for a moment before breaking away.

"Anyway, look at me all teary-eyed." She said dabbing her eyes with the towel in her hand. "We'll be alright. John's already got us somewhere to stay. His brother's."

She nodded towards the landlord who, handset to ear, gave Jenny a smile and a *thumbs-up*.

"It's you I'm more concerned about." Maisie continued.

"Oh, don't you worry about me." Jenny said forcing a smile. "I'll be ok. I'm sure Alan will help. Besides, look on the bright side. It's not as if I've got a lot of possessions to take with me. And what I have got are mostly still packed in my suitcases from my move here. No, I'll be fine."

Maisie laughed. Jenny gave her a puzzled look.

"Listen to Little Miss Positive Attitude here!" The landlady said good-heartedly. "The girl that started here a few months ago would have crumbled at that news. Now look at her!"

Jenny folded her arms across her chest and feigned indignation.

"The girl who started here a few months ago would never have dreamed of leaving her husband in the first place." She replied, giving an air of prim and properness. "So that girl wouldn't have been staring at homelessness now would she?"

Jenny finished by pulling such a meek and mild face that Maisie howled with laughter. John, in the meantime, had replaced the handset on the counter behind the bar and was staring in disbelief at the two women in front of him.

"It's nice to see you two girls in a good mood despite us all being thrown out onto the streets." He said trying to sound stern but failing miserably.

Jenny and Maisie looked at each other and then burst into a further bout of uncontrollable laughter. John, recognising that he was going to get no sense from either of them, shook his head and went down into the cellar where he knew he'd have more luck talking to the beer barrels than the two howling women above.

Maisie and Jenny shook with laughter and for the rest of the morning, if one of them got themselves under control they only had to look at the other to start off again.

By the time the pub had opened that lunchtime Maisie and Jenny were all laughed out. Having heard the constant barrage from up the steps all morning John had busied himself down in the cellar making a tidy cellar an immaculate one. He was determined that whoever came to take over the pub after him would have no cause to accuse him of keeping a slovenly cellar.

When he was sure that the hilarity of the morning was over and done with he emerged from his sanctuary. Maisie looked up from checking the till float and smiled lovingly across at him. He returned the smile and went over to unlock the external doors. As he did so he saw Alan walking across the car park. The two men acknowledged each other before John disappeared into the beer garden to ensure that all was in order there.

Alan walked into the bar to be greeted by a smiling Jenny. She skipped across the room and threw her arms around him. Before he could speak she planted her lips on his and hugged him close. When she did let him go he just stood there with a silly grin on his face.

"It's nice to see you, too." He declared when he finally came back to his senses.

Jenny gave him a smile that melted his heart before slipping behind the bar to pour him a pint.

"Now that's what I call service!" He added.

John came back into the bar grumbling to himself.

"What is it, my love?" Maisie asked frowning.

"Them damn kids!" John growled. "They've nicked one of the umbrellas again. If I ever catch them I'll show them a trick with an umbrella they've probably never seen, I swear!"

Maisie walked over to the landlord and planted a kiss on his forehead.

"Now don't go getting yourself all hot under the collar." She said softly. "In a few more weeks you'll not have to worry about no umbrellas again, will you? Nor no pub. Your time will be your own."

Alan looked across at Jenny who picked up the letter from the brewery and handed it to him. He scan read it before handing it back.

"I'm sorry, Maisie." He said. "Are you sure you don't want me to help you fight this?"

Maisie shook her head.

"Oh no, dear." She sighed. "We've resigned ourselves to retiring. Besides, we've arranged to go and stay with John's brother for a while. He says there's more than enough room for us and he wouldn't hear of us going anywhere else."

Maisie looked across at Jenny.

"If you want to help put my heart at ease, find somewhere for this young lady to stay." She continued.

Jenny dropped her eyes to the bar, conscious that they were all looking at her. When she raised them again she looked determined; defiant even.

"Like I said to Maisie earlier I'll be fine. I'll find somewhere." She said

"That's what I came to tell you." Alan said looking excited. "Marjorie has offered to put you up until we can find somewhere more permanent."

Maisie clapped her hands in glee and fairly jumped across the room to Alan. Before he knew it the landlady had her arms around him and was hugging and kissing him. Feeling a little embarrassed he looked across first at John who just shrugged his shoulders and then Jenny who just shook her head. In the end, he decided all he could do was stand there and let Maisie get whatever she needed to out of her system.

"That is such good news." She finally said letting him go. "You don't know how much of a weight that is off of my mind."

"There's only one snag." Alan said looking a little embarrassed.

"What's that?" Jenny asked.

Maisie started to look a little cross.

"Well, Marjorie's only got one spare room and I'm in it." Alan said. "It would mean either I move out or we share a room."

"Oh well if that's all it is of course she'll share the room with you." Maisie announced looking relieved. "It's nothing more than she's being doing with you here before now."

Jenny felt herself getting a little bit warm with embarrassment at all the talk about her bedroom arrangements.

"Maisie!" John reprimanded his wife. "You're embarrassing the poor girl."

"Nonsense!" The landlady overruled him. "It sounds a perfect solution. She'll do it!"

Alan hardly dared look at Jenny but when he did she sheepishly nodded her head.

"That's agreed then!" Maisie announced. "When can she move in?"

Chapter 51

Jenny smiled to herself as she stood looking out to sea. She remembered how excited she had felt when she realised that she was going to be living with Alan, if not in their own home, at least on a more permanent basis than they had been doing. She also remembered how scared she had felt, too. A small part of her had been afraid that their relationship wouldn't work out and that she would be left all alone. She had thrown everything away to be with Alan, however bleak it had been. But even then she knew that the alternative, a return back to the house she shared with Barnes and her son, had become unthinkable. Now, with the advantage of hindsight, she knew that those fears had been unfounded.

John and Maisie had insisted that Jenny should go with Alan there and then to start her new life with him. However, Jenny would have none of it, telling them both that she was determined to stick with them until the bitter end. Alan, gallant as ever, agreed to her wishes stating that Marjorie's offer was for Jenny to move in whenever she felt ready to.

The final few weeks in the pub for John, Maisie and Jenny were filled with mixed emotions. Maisie tried to make light of the situation doing her best to portray an air of excitement about retiring and all the things she and John were going to do once they had time to themselves. The landlord played along with Maisie's attempts to be cheerful but on more than one occasion Jenny caught him staring wistfully across the pub from the bar or sitting quietly by himself in the beer garden once it was empty of customers. Leaving the pub was hitting him hard but he was too proud to show it in company and too considerate of Maisie and Jenny's feelings to play on it.

Jenny was kept busy helping Maisie pack away her and John's belongings and before long the living quarters upstairs was festooned with cardboard boxes and tea chests. On her days and evenings off, Alan did his best to take Jenny's mind off the situation by taking her away from the pub. Sometimes they would visit the various restaurants Alan was eager to introduce her to while others they went walking in the peace and tranquility of the countryside; anywhere where she didn't have to think about John and Maisie's impending move.

On a couple of occasions Alan took Jenny to Marjorie's house where the author did her best to make her feel welcome and told to make herself at home. It was obvious to Jenny that Marjorie was truly excited about her coming to stay.

On one of these visit, Marjorie announced that she would soon be going on a book signing tour of the country so they would have the freedom of the house to themselves for a couple of months. However, she assured Jenny that she would still be there when she arrived to help her settle in. Alan told them that this was a relief as he, also, needed to go away for a few days and he didn't want Jenny to be left on her own in a strange house. Marjorie assured him that she would not leave on her tour until he was back to which Jenny informed them both kindly that she was quite capable of looking after herself and didn't need babysitting.

"My dear Alan," Marjorie had said smiling, "I wouldn't dream of going off gallivanting without making sure your young lady is well and truly ensconced here. Besides, we can get to know each other better and have a little girlie time."

Marjorie winked at Jenny which made her smile.

"Seems like I'm surplus to requirements then." Alan said good-naturedly.

"Only for a few days." Marjorie replied patting Alan's hand. "You two lovebirds have a lot of catching up to do."

The author winked at Jenny again, this time causing her to blush a little. Alan smiled his cheeky schoolboy smile which made Jenny redden further.

John decided early on that he didn't want to leave the pub in a blaze of glory. So when it came to the last shift the pub was quite quiet. Alan came over to have a last drink with them and when the final customer left at eleven the landlord decided to close up early.

"That's that then." John said with a nod of his head. "The end of an era."

Jenny and Maisie busied themselves cleaning and tidying the bar while John made one last trip downstairs to close up the cellar. When he re-emerged he was holding an unopened bottle of Cognac. He retrieved four glasses and then invited Maisie, Jenny and Alan to join him for a drink. They moved over to the table in the window and sat down. John placed a glass in front of them and poured a generous measure in each. He raised his glass and proposed a toast.

"To the future. May it be rewarding and full of happiness."

The other three repeated and raised their glasses before taking a sip. Maisie looked across at Jenny, a glint of mischief in her eye.

"What?" Jenny asked looking puzzled.

"I was just remembering that first brandy you had here, dear." The landlady explained nudging Jenny's arm gently with her elbow. "Damn near blew your head off it did if I remember rightly. Now look at you. Drinking one of the finest Cognac's like you're a professional. How times have changed, eh?"

Jenny let out a giggle as Alan raised his glass.

"To changing times." He announced.

The others followed suit.

Jenny decided she did not want to be outdone so she raised her glass too.

"To the best friends … no, family … a girl could ever want." She said feeling a lump in her throat.

Alan placed his hand over hers and squeezed it while John took off his glasses and began to clean them; his eyes a little more moist than usual before raising his Cognac and tipping the glass towards Jenny.

"To Alan and Jenny." Maisie said raising her glass. "May the love they've found last forever and may they live in happiness from this day forward."

The other three friends brought their glasses up to Maisie's and acknowledged the landlady's toast.

They sat in silence for a few moments before Maisie stood up.

"Right then." She said with enthusiasm. "Who's for some crisps?"

Alan raised his arm quickly followed by Jenny. John, with a look that said *what the hell* completed the set.

Chapter 52

Alan stayed the night with Jenny and helped pack the removal van with John the following day. Most of their belongings had to go into storage until they could find themselves a new permanent home but they had filled a number of suitcases with clothes to tide them over in the meantime.

When all was loaded the four friends had a last look around the inside of the pub. John closed the door behind them and locked it. Jenny hugged Maisie close to her while the landlord and Alan shook hands.

"You make sure you stay in touch now you hear, dear." The landlady said before whispering in Jenny's ear. "Remember what I said about being like a daughter."

Jenny felt the tears welling in her eyes as she nodded her head.

"And you've been more than a mother to me." She whispered back.

The two women broke away from each other and Jenny turned to John.

"I'm going to miss you so much." She said as she embraced the landlord. "You've been so good and kind to me. I'll never forget it."

She kissed him on the cheek and then stepped back.

The driver of the removal van jumped up into the cab and slammed the door to indicate he was impatient to move on. Maisie gave Alan a quick peck on the cheek.

"You look after her." She said looking serious. "She's very precious."

Alan smiled and nodded back at her before John grasped his wife by the hand and led her to the car. As they got in the driver of the van started up its engine. Jenny pulled out her handkerchief and blew her nose as her tears began to fall down her cheeks. Alan put his arm around her waist and pulled her close to him for comfort. The van pulled off and, with a toot of his horn, John followed it off the pub car park. Alan and Jenny stood in the early afternoon sunshine and waved after them. Jenny could not take her eyes off the car and it was only when it disappeared around a corner that she finally nestled her head into Alan's chest and let her emotions escape.

Alan stood there silently stroking her hair and letting Jenny cry herself out. Slowly the crying turned to intermittent sobs until finally Jenny turned her face up to him. He took his thumb and gently ran it over her cheeks to smooth away her tears.

"I'm going to miss them so much." She eventually said feeling a dull ache in her heart. "I don't know how I'm going to cope without them.

Alan looked down into her eyes and smiled.

"I'm here for you now." He said, his voice soothing and compassionate. "I'll always be here for you when you need me. And any time you want to visit them we'll go; no questions asked."

"You're a beautiful, kind man." Jenny said cupping Alan's face in her hands. "And I love you so much."

She pulled Alan's lips to hers and took comfort in their softness.

When they broke from each other Jenny let out a sigh and looked behind her.

"I'm going to miss this place, too." She said. "I never would have guessed when I first stood trembling in that doorway that my life was going to change forever. What an adventure it would be."

"And it's not over yet." Alan replied. "You're about to move into the next chapter of your life, a much happier life I hope, with me. So let's get you to Marjorie's and settled in.

He reached down and took Jenny's hand in his and together they walked away from the pub.

Chapter 53

When Alan and Jenny arrived at Marjorie's house the author was in the window waiting to greet them. Alan had rung on ahead to let her know, out of courtesy, that they were on their way and he could tell by the author's voice that she was excited at Jenny's arrival.

By the time they had retrieved Jenny's two suitcases from the boot of the car and were walking up the path, Marjorie had opened the front door and was hurriedly coming down the path to meet them. Before Jenny could object, the author had taken the suitcase she was carrying from her and was leading her by the hand towards the door.

"I've been so looking forward to you coming." Marjorie chattered as they entered the house. "I've spent the last few days spring cleaning the place so it's ready for you and Alan has promised me he has got your room ready.

The author looked across at Alan who dutifully nodded back at her.

"Wonderful." Marjorie exclaimed and put Jenny's suitcase at the foot of the stairs.

Alan placed the suitcase he was carrying next to it.

"You shouldn't have gone to so much trouble on my account." Jenny said feeling a little embarrassed that Marjorie should put herself out to this degree for her.

"Nonsense." The author said waving away Jenny's remarks. "It needed doing anyway so you were just the motivation I required."

Jenny looked across at Alan who raised his eyebrows and smiled back at her.

"Now then," Marjorie continued, "I've made a little bit of afternoon tea for us all so if you can be a dear, Alan, and put the kettle on I'll get Jenny settled in the lounge. We can bring the rest of her things in later."

Jenny looked across pensively at Alan before speaking.

"Erm ... I've not ... that is ..." She tried to say feeling quite embarrassed.

"What Jenny is trying to say is that she travels light." Alan said jumping to Jenny's rescue and nodding at the two suitcases.

"Oh I see." Marjorie said with no hint of judgment in her voice. "That's excellent then. We can all sit down and relax. I'm sure it's been a traumatic morning for you both and you would value putting your feet up for a while."

Jenny suddenly realised how emotionally drained she did actually feel and the thought of doing absolutely nothing for the afternoon became exceedingly appealing.

Marjorie took Jenny's silence for agreement and took her by the hand.

"That's settled then." She announced leading Jenny down the hallway.

Alan followed partway before turning off into the kitchen area. By the time he returned to the lounge to join the two women Marjorie had Jenny sitting in a reclining seat; shoes off and feet up. He let out a chuckle as he walked into the room to which Jenny responded with a dazed look and a shrug of her shoulders. Marjorie was busy clearing space on a low level glass-topped coffee table apparently preparing it for the imminent arrival of the afternoon tea. She gave it a quick satisfied nod before excusing herself and disappearing out of the room.

"Comfortable?" Alan asked gently mocking.

"Very." Jenny replied a little sleepily. "I could get used to all this pampering."

Alan sat down in the corner of a three seated sofa next to the recliner and reached out to hold Jenny's hand. He was just about to speak when a voice called out from the kitchen.

"Alan, be a dear and help me with the tea tray."

Alan released Jenny's hand, pulled himself out of the cushions and headed in the direction of the kitchen. He met Marjorie in the hallway carrying two plates of sandwiches and cakes. She smiled at him and disappeared into the lounge.

Alan located the tea tray and returned to the lounge. When he entered Marjorie was standing by the fireplace, plates deposited on the coffee table, holding her finger across her lips. Alan glanced over at the recliner. Jenny, head resting slightly to her left on the cushioned backrest and chest gently heaving, sat fast asleep.

Chapter 54

Jenny woke later that evening and found herself in a double bed. She was fully clothed, minus her shoes, and felt snug under a lilac coloured duvet. The pillows around her head felt soft and comforting.

The curtains were drawn but she could tell that it was still reasonably light outside. With a stretch she sat up and plumped up her pillow behind her, taking in the spacious room that she assumed was now to be hers and Alan's for the foreseeable future. It was tastefully decorated with plain painted walls of cream and contrasting lilac curtains that matched the bed linen. There was a dressing table in the corner with a large mirror resting on it through which she could see herself sitting there in bed. She couldn't help giggling at herself as she saw the queen-like figure staring back at her from the other side of the room.

There was a high backed white wickerwork chair in front of the dressing table and the furniture was completed by a double wardrobe off to her left. Sitting in front of it were her unopened suitcases.

Jenny stayed there in bed for a moment enjoying the feeling of security it gave her before sliding out from under the duvet. Her stocking feet landed on the plush softness of the cream carpet and she almost groaned with pleasure at the way it seemed to envelope her toes.

She went over to the dressing table and looked into the mirror. Her clothes were ruffled from sleeping so she adjusted them to make herself look presentable and then left the bedroom to go downstairs.

As she walked down the corridor Jenny could hear the low murmur of conversation coming from Marjorie's lounge. She walked into the room feeling a little embarrassed.

Marjorie and Alan were sitting side by side on the sofa with a map of what looked like the UK spread out in front of them on the coffee table. They both looked up as Jenny entered and Alan smiled at her.

"Hello, sleepy head!" He teased. "Feeling better after your nap?"

Jenny nodded.

"I don't know what came over me." She said. "I felt a little drowsy so thought I'd close my eyes for a moment while you were bringing in the tea. Next thing I knew …"

She shrugged her shoulders in bewilderment and then looked around the room for a clock before continuing.

"Just how long have I been asleep?"

"Nearly two hours." Alan replied.

"Really?" Jenny said raising her eyebrows, genuinely surprised.

Alan nodded.

"I feel so rude." Jenny said looking over at Marjorie. "I'm so sorry, Marjorie. You went to all that trouble of putting on afternoon tea for me and I slept right through it. You must think me really ungrateful."

"Don't be silly." Marjorie responded smiling as she shooed Jenny's apology away with a flap of her hands. "I think no such thing. You've had a busy and traumatic morning. It's no wonder you were tired. Besides, it was only a few sandwiches and cakes. They'll keep. In fact I've taken the liberty of plating a few up for you. I thought you might be hungry when you woke up."

Jenny felt a little overwhelmed by Marjorie's kindness but promised herself that she wouldn't become emotional about it. She really did want to get out of the habit of getting tearful every time someone acted kindly towards her. Besides, she realised that the sleep had done her some good and she now felt quite relaxed and refreshed.

"In fact, would you like a bite to eat now?" Marjorie asked as she stood up. "You must be ravenous."

Jenny was about to politely decline when she was suddenly aware that she did feel quite hungry so she nodded.

"Wonderful." The author said clapping her hands. "I'll just pop into the kitchen and fetch them for you. I'll put the kettle on too."

"Let me." Jenny said moving to stop Marjorie. "I can't keep having you wait on me and being a nuisance."

"I wouldn't dream of it." Marjorie said kindly. "It really is no trouble at all. Now you sit down next to Alan and I'll get it all sorted."

Before she had chance to argue, Marjorie sidestepped Jenny and was out of the lounge and into the kitchen from where Alan and Jenny could hear her quietly singing to herself as she filled the kettle.

Jenny sat down next to Alan.

"She really is a wonderful woman." Jenny said staring wistfully at the door.

"She is that." Alan replied nodding.

Jenny turned her attention to the coffee table.

"What's this you've been looking at?" She said pointing to the map.

"Marjorie has been showing me where she is going on her book tour." Alan explained sitting forward. "She's going on quite a journey and to some fascinating places too. We've just been having a look at some of the sights she wants to take in while she's out there."

Jenny studied the map and saw that there were a few places circled. When she examined it closer she could see some of the places of interest they had earmarked for Marjorie to visit; Stonehenge; Blenheim Palace; Hadrian's Wall. These were just some of the places that Jenny recognised the names of. Some of the others she had never heard of.

"It all looks very exciting." She said thinking how marvelous it would be to be able to visit these places.

Alan seemed to read her mind.

"Marjorie's asked if we want to join her for part of the tour." He said. "I told her I'd speak to you and see if you were interested."

"Can we? Really?" Jenny asked, her eager eyes staring into Alan's.

"Of course we can." Alan answered smiling, ecstatic that Jenny was keen on the idea. "We'll arrange where the best place is to meet up with her and when she's going to have some free time to spend with us."

Jenny reached over and squeezed Alan's hand. She still couldn't believe how exciting her life had become since she'd met this kind and gentle man.

Alan began to fold the map up to free up the coffee table ready for the impending arrival of the tea tray. As he did so, Jenny settled back into the sofa.

"So, how did I get from here to the bedroom then?" She asked when Alan had stored the map safely in a magazine rack at the side of the sofa.

"I carried you up and tucked you in. You looked very cute snuggled up under the duvet."

"You could have slid into bed with me." Jenny said with a cheeky little giggle.

Alan laughed.

"Believe me, it was tempting." He said. "But you were dead to the world and I didn't want to risk waking you."

Jenny reached over and squeezed Alan's hand.

"Ever the gentleman." She said with fondness in her voice.

"Well, it wasn't just that." Alan said pulling her hand to his cheek. "Marjorie came up behind me with your suitcases and then started fluffing around with the curtains and stuff. I could hardly jump into bed and ravish you in your sleep with her in the room, could I?"

Jenny widened her eyes in feigned shock at what he'd said and punched him gently on the arm with her free hand.

"Why you cheeky ..." she began but before she could finish Alan placed his mouth over hers and kissed her passionately.

When he pulled away Jenny felt giddy and a little flushed. Alan's kiss always seemed to have the effect of stirring her in a way she would never have thought possible from a kiss just a few months ago.

"Besides," Alan continued, "we'll have plenty of time for that later when we're alone."

Jenny felt herself getting hotter at the thought of being alone with Alan in that comfortable double bed and was just about to tell him so when Marjorie re-entered the room carrying the tea tray. She glanced at Jenny and her face took on a concerned look.

"Are you alright?," she said, "You look a little flushed. Is it too warm in here for you? I can open a window for you if you wish."

Jenny tried hard not to giggle, a feat made harder when she saw Alan's now familiar school boy grin plastered across his face.

"No, really, I'm fine." She replied. "I'm just a little embarrassed about making you run around after me. That's all."

"Nonsense." The author said. "It's my pleasure. It's nice to have guests in the house to pamper to. So let's please not hear any more about it"

As if to draw the conversation to an end she passed Jenny her plate of sandwiches and began to pour the tea.

With Marjorie's back to them Jenny took one of the sandwiches and, looking at Alan seductively, licked her lips before nibbling on the bread. The author turned to give Alan his tea and then stopped, once again looking concerned.

"Are you sure it's not too hot in here?" She said staring at him. "Only, you look a little flushed now as well, Alan."

"I'm fine, honest." He said as he took the cup from Marjorie.

The author looked at him for a moment and then turned back to the coffee table. Alan glanced over at Jenny who gave him her sweetest innocent look before winking at him.

Alan took a quick sip of his tea.

Chapter 55

Over the next week or so Jenny did her best to familiarise herself with Marjorie's home. She insisted on helping out with the daily chores telling the author that if she was to continue staying there she must be allowed to pull her weight. Besides, Jenny pointed out, if Marjorie was soon to go off on her book tour then she would be leaving her home at her mercy. It would be best all round if the author allowed Jenny to get used to what needed to be done and where everything was while Marjorie was still there.

Once Jenny had found her way around the kitchen and worked out how to operate the oven she announced to Alan and Marjorie that she was going to make them a meal. It was, she said, to be a way for her to say *thank you* to them both for their kindness.

Despite their protests Jenny insisted and would not budge from her stance until they agreed. Seeing that Jenny was determined to do this for them Alan and Marjorie finally gave in. So it was that it was arranged that the following Friday night they would all sit down and eat a meal together prepared by Jenny.

Having badgered Alan and Marjorie into accepting the meal Jenny then began to secretly stress about what to make for them. Though she had made meals for her husband and son before, those had never been anything too exotic. Bangers and mash or fish fingers and chips hardly seemed appropriate for what she had in mind so she wracked her brains as to what she could prepare.

As luck would have it, she was thumbing through one of Marjorie's women's magazines when she came across a recipe for spaghetti bolognaise. Jenny thought the picture in the magazine looked wonderful and tasty and was just what was required. She made a list of the ingredients she would need and then turned her mind to shopping.

Living in the village Jenny had not gone into town very much, choosing to buy what meagre family food they could afford from the convenience store. The odd occasion when she had ventured into town she had always been accompanied by Barnes who would never let her out of his sight for one moment. Not once had she ever gone into town on her own. The upshot of all this was that what was probably a normal regular occurrence for most people suddenly took on greater significance in Jenny's eyes. However, the more she thought about it the more she was determined to tackle the issue head on.

Alan had arranged to play golf during the Friday daytime so Jenny asked him if he would mind dropping her off at the supermarket on his way to his game. Alan picked up on her trepidation and offered to help.

"Why don't you wait until I've finished and then I can come shopping with you?" He said. "You don't have to do it on your own."

Jenny went quiet for a moment. It would have been so easy to say *yes* to Alan and she was just about to open her mouth to do so when she stopped herself. She couldn't keep acting as if she was defenseless and needed everyone to do things for her. There was a whole wide world out there that she needed to cope with and she was determined to do so. Besides, if she continued letting Alan protect her from that world and not allow her to do anything on her own would she actually be any better off than she had been with Barnes; as well intentioned as Alan's actions were towards her. No, she had to stand on her own two feet and this would be a part of that.

"No, Alan. Please just drop me off." She said reaching for his arm and smiling. "I need to do this on my own. I'm a big girl now and it's time I stopped being scared of my own shadow. Besides, I think I'll have a little wander around town. There was a coffee shop I went to with Maisie which I wouldn't mind visiting again. I might even take Marjorie's book with me and read."

Alan could see the determination in Jenny's face and loved her more for it. As much as he wanted to be there to protect her every minute of the day he didn't want to crush her bid for independence.

"Do you want me to pick you up after?" He asked.

"That would be nice. Thank you" Jenny said and leaned over to kiss him.

When she woke up on the Friday morning Jenny found that she was actually excited about her trip into town. Alan, to his credit, had tried to play the whole thing down by not mentioning it at all during the intervening days. She jumped out of bed and quickly got herself washed and dressed. She was eager to get on with it and was mildly frustrated when Alan sleepily took his time to get ready.

When they finally left the house Jenny grabbed her handbag and virtually frog-marched Alan to the car, such was her enthusiasm. She waited impatiently while he fumbled with the car keys before eventually getting the door open for her. She sat in the seat, buckled up and placed her handbag on her lap; staring straight ahead through the windscreen. Alan joined her and couldn't help but smile at her as he searched for the ignition.

"Boy, you are keen!" He chuckled as he started up the engine.

"I have a lot to do today while you're off playing golf." Jenny replied sounding serious but not condemning. "Now please drive."

"Certainly, ma'am!" Alan said laughing and tipping Jenny a salute before pulling away from the kerb.

Jenny sat in silence all the way to the supermarket. Alan chatted away trying his best to fill the quiet that had descended in the car and make the atmosphere a little more light hearted. When he finally pulled up on the supermarket car park Jenny remained motionless in her seat.

"Are you alright?" Alan asked looking slightly concerned.

Jenny nodded her head.

"You still want to do this?" He asked gently.

Jenny nodded again; a little slower this time.

"I can still cancel my golf if you want me to come with you." Alan suggested kindly. "I don't mind."

This seemed to break the spell for Jenny.

"No, please don't!" She blurted out. "I'll be alright. I have to do this."

She leaned over and kissed him on the cheek, no longer feeling the excitement of the early morning.

Before he could say another word Jenny was out of the car, her handbag over her shoulder, and closing the door. He wound down the window.

"I'll pick you up from here at lunchtime, ok?" He called out to Jenny as she walked away from him. Without turning around, Jenny raised her hand to him in acknowledgement and continued on walking towards the town.

Alan sat in the car until Jenny disappeared from view willing her to keep walking. He half expected her to come running back but was pleased when she didn't. He hoped she was going to be alright. He knew how much courage it had taken her to do this but he also knew that if she managed to get through the day unscathed, it would be a major boost to her self-confidence.

He started up the engine and, with slight trepidation, drove off.

Chapter 56

Jenny felt a change in the wind. Though still warm enough to be comfortable she could feel the heat of the sun slowly beginning to fade. She pulled her cardigan tight around her and wrapped her arms across her chest.

It was times like these when she missed Alan the most. He always had the knack of doing the right thing at the right time and Jenny just knew that he would have had his arms around her to keep her warm long before she had felt the temperature drop.

Jenny closed her eyes and tried to imagine him there with her; strong and manly yet kind and gentle. Her heart, as if in league with the sinking sun, felt heavy as she struggled to remember his touch; his smell; even the sound of his breathing. She missed him so much and feared that the further she moved away from his departure, the dimmer her memory of him would become.

Living without Alan was the hardest thing she had ever had to do in her life, even compared to all the other hardships she'd had to endure through her life. He had always been able to balance being there for her when she needed him and letting her find her own way when necessary. Like that first trip to town on her own and how hard it had been walking away from him and the safety of the car that morning.

All the excitement she had felt when she woke up on the day of her shopping trip seemed to drain away from her during the car journey into town; to the point that she did not think she was going to be able to get out when Alan parked up outside the supermarket.

As unintentional as it was meant to be on his part, Alan's offer to give up his golf rather than comforting Jenny, had the effect of making her feel wretched about herself. Yet again she saw how Alan was willing to put her well-being before his own needs. In contrast, Barnes had never given up anything for her in his life and Jenny doubted that the selfish brute would even know how to think of anyone else but himself. As a result she was still coming to terms with the fact that not all men were like the beast she had married. With this in mind, Alan's suggestion was the catalyst she had needed to force herself to leave the vehicle.

Once out of the car, it suddenly seemed to become a magnet doing its level best to pull her back into it and its relative safety. Jenny knew it would have been so easy to have given in and let it drag her back so, in an attempt to overcome its pull, she took a determined step forward. She quickly followed this with another; and then another. Before long she was walking away from the car concentrating hard on each step she took rather than giving in to the urge to sprint back to the car.

When Alan had called out to her about picking her up later she knew she had to keep walking. If she had stopped and turned to acknowledge him then she knew she would have been lost the moment her eyes met his and would be back in the car without hesitation. So, keeping her back to him, she waved her hand with as much of a casual air as she could muster and carried on towards the town. As she did so, Jenny could almost feel Alan watching her as she neared the corner that would take her out of the view of the supermarket.

When she finally turned away from him, Jenny suddenly felt cut off from the safety of her new world. All the air seemed to escape from her lungs and her legs began to lose their strength. She became light headed and frantically glanced about her searching for some protective haven she could latch on to before her legs collapsed from under her and left her in an embarrassing heap for all the town to see. The panic and dread that she had felt when she first stood outside the pub seemed to manifest itself again. To her relief she spotted an unoccupied bench not too far from her across the pedestrianized high street and managed to force her leaden legs to transport her to it. Jenny dropped to the slatted seat and sat there for a moment gradually getting acclimatised to the town centre and its surroundings.

She felt exposed to all and sundry. Her old feeling of insecurity tried to force itself through the new but fragile self-confidence she had begun to build up since meeting Alan. Gradually, she began to realise that nobody walking around the town was showing any particular interest in her as they were too intent on going about their own busy lives. Inhaling deeply, she began to relax until she could feel her breathing begin to return to normal and the strength flow back into her legs.

Curiosity started to overcome her anxiety as she studied the area around her. There was a bank behind where she was sitting; a chemist off to the right in front of her and a pizzeria to the left. Starting to feel calmer she began to concentrate on why she was in town in the first place.

"That's it." She said to herself nodding. "Think about what you're here to do and that will take your mind off where you are."

Realising she was talking to herself she quickly looked around her to see if anyone had heard. To her relief it seemed that no-one had.

Jenny gazed down the street and could see more banks and a number of charity shops. A glance up the street and, hey presto, not too far away she recognised the coffee shop she'd visited with Maisie.

"Coffee!" She whispered. "I'll have a coffee while I get my wits together."

This time she wasn't so lucky. A young boy holding his mother's hand walked by and looked across at the strange woman quietly talking to herself. Jenny smiled at him feeling a little embarrassed. He narrowed his eyes and stared back at her looking a little unsure before trotting to his mother's side and hugging closely into her hip. Jenny shrugged her shoulders and decided it was time to move on before someone reported a *crazy woman* sitting on a bench in the middle of town.

She got up from the seat and tested her legs. They supported her well and now seemed to be ready to take her wherever she wanted to go. Trying to look assured, she walked off in the direction of the coffee shop.

There were a few tables free outside on the street in front of the coffee shop but Jenny decided that she wasn't quite ready to sit in full view of everyone yet. Instead, she went towards the big glass double doors. She started to go in but then stopped and stood in the doorway for a moment. She'd never been in a place like this on her own before and suddenly her nerves threatened to return. However, an old man came out of the coffee shop and held the door open for her.

"There you go, Miss." He said politely.

"Thank you." Jenny said, her voice sounding calmer than she thought possible.

"It's a pleasure." The old man replied and tipped his hat at her. "I'm glad to be of service. Good day to you."

Feeling obliged not to seem rude to the old man by turning tail and running she took a deep breath and went inside.

The gorgeous aroma of coffee beans hit Jenny's nostrils straight away and she inhaled deeply, marveling at the strong scent. She could vaguely remember the layout from her previous visit with Maisie and surveyed the tables around her. The coffee shop was by no stretch of the imagination full and she saw plenty of places to sit.

Jenny joined the queue waiting to be served behind a teenage couple who, arms draped around each other's shoulders, seemed to be in the process of devouring each other. Such was the extent of their concentration on this act that they were oblivious to the waitress behind the counter, a woman Jenny estimated to be about her own age, frowning while waiting to take their order.

Jenny took it upon herself to gently tap the young lad on the shoulder and, when he turned to look at her, indicated with her eyes that their order was required. With a smile of embarrassment he separated from his girlfriend and proceeded to request their drinks. When they had finally moved away from the counter the waitress turned her attention to Jenny.

"Thanks for that." She said smiling then almost wistfully added. "Oh, to be young and in love again, eh?"

Jenny smiled back and thought of Alan, thankful that the realms of love were not reserved just for the young.

Jenny ordered her coffee and decided to treat herself to a slice of the chocolate cheesecake that was in the glass cabinet in front of her almost imploring her to buy it. She paid the waitress and then looked around again. The teenage couple had found a table for two and were once again engaged in heavy petting.

Jenny looked up passed the counter to where she could see a second room which contained a number of leather armchairs and sofas. She picked up her tray, made her way up a couple of steps towards it and sought out one of the comfortable looking chairs. There was one free in the corner of the room that looked nice and secluded so she chose that. She placed her tray on the wooden table in front of it and then sat.

For a second or two she sat there taking in her surroundings. Soft instrumental music was quietly playing in the background and those customers that had chosen to sit in this area were either deep in conversation or engrossed in various pieces of reading material.

Jenny sat back in the chair, reveling in its comfort and felt the trauma of the past few minutes begin to dissipate. Slowly she began to feel relaxed and, as she grew in confidence, she took out Marjorie's book from her bag and began to read. Before long she was far too engrossed in the story to worry about being on her own in the coffee shop.

Jenny spent a good hour reading in the chilled out surroundings of the coffee shop. She had nestled in the leather armchair and even slipped off her shoes so she could slide her legs underneath her. Every so often she would take a sip of her coffee and after one particularly invigorating chapter, stopped to eat her cheesecake. Having polished this off and finally finishing her drink, she inserted her bookmark in the fold of the novel and closed it. She slipped it back into her bag and took a look around her.

While she had been reading there had been a change of clientele in the room. It had filled up a little more and there was the faint hum of conversation just slightly drowning out the music being played over the sound system.

Feeling thoroughly refreshed and at ease, Jenny stood up and placed her bag over her shoulder. She had surprised herself with how much she had enjoyed this timeout on her own and vowed that she would make sure she repeated it on a regular basis.

As Jenny walked back down passed the counter the waitress that had served her smiled across at her.

"Thanks." She called out from behind the till. "Come back soon."

Jenny thanked her back as she passed the table still inhabited by the love-struck teenagers; still wrapped around one another and their coffee still untouched in their mugs; unquestionably cold by now.

Jenny looked across at the waitress and then nodded towards the teenagers. The waitress shrugged her shoulders and smiled as if to reiterate what she had said earlier.

With a confident step, Jenny exited the coffee shop and set out to explore the town.

Chapter 57

Jenny wandered along the high street going from shop to shop intrigued by the variety of things that they had on offer. Still mindful of money she resisted the temptation to go on a spending spree, contenting herself with what she thought was called *window shopping*. On the odd occasion she did venture inside Jenny couldn't get over how friendly, in general, the shop keepers were.

After she had done one full circuit of the high street, Jenny decided that she should probably make her way to the supermarket and start thinking about the ingredients she needed to buy for Alan and Marjorie's meal. The sun appeared from behind a cloud and showered her with warmth. The nervousness of earlier had dissipated and she basked in the enjoyment of walking along the cobbled high street.

However, as she walked across the car park where Alan had dropped her off earlier, she got the familiar feeling of butterflies in her stomach. The supermarket seemed enormous in front of her and the open-mouthed entrance looked as if it was eager to swallow her whole. She stood on the paved area outside, her legs once again starting to betray her body and refusing to propel her forward. In seemingly fast-motion, the shoppers around her dived in and out of the supermarket. The scene played out so fast that once again Jenny began to feel giddy.

"You alright there, Miss?" A strangely familiar voice broke into the melee around.

Jenny turned her head in the direction of the source of the voice. To her surprise, there stood the old man who had held the coffee shop door open for her, smiling at her in a way that suddenly brought serenity back into the panic induced mayhem about her.

"Y…yes, I'm fine thanks." She murmured looking at the floor feeling embarrassed.

"I don't like supermarket shopping either." The old man said. "I really do hate the pushing and shoving that goes on in there."

He nodded his head towards the supermarket entrance.

"It seems that as soon as a perfectly rational human being enters through those doors they lose all sense of humanity; blocking aisles while they decide what to buy; ramming their trollies into you in an attempt to get passed. It's all so very jolly un-civilised."

Jenny didn't know whether the old man was trying to soothe her or scare her to death. But somehow his words did have a calming effect on her. She raised her head and smiled at him.

"It's crazy and I'm sure you'll think I'm silly," she began, "but I've never been in a supermarket before. I mean, on my own. I've been in with my husband, well ex-husband now I suppose, but never without him."

She waited for his face to betray his incredulity at her revelation but instead she saw warmth and compassion in it. Feeling a little more at ease she continued.

"I'm scared of going in there. It was easy when there were two of us. I'd stick to him like glue and never leave his side; even to the point of him shouting at me to get out of his way."

"Which goes to prove my point entirely about the metamorphosis of mankind." The old man nodded knowingly.

"Oh, no." Jenny carried on. "He was like that outside the supermarket too."

"Hence him now being your ex-husband." The old man said, his warm smile returning to his face.

"I don't know why I'm telling you all this." Jenny said turning her head a little in embarrassment. "You must think me a very silly woman."

"On the contrary." The old man said placing his hand lightly on her shoulder. "I think you are a very brave woman to come here and face your fears. That takes courage."

Jenny could feel herself starting to blush a little with a different kind of embarrassment.

"I think what is needed here is a little strategy." The old man said after a moment's thought. "May I escort you inside?"

Jenny was about to object but the old man held up his hand to stop her.

"It would be my honour to walk you over the threshold." He said. "Then hopefully once you are inside you will feel a little easier about the place."

Jenny smiled and nodded.

"The honour would be all mine." She said and encircled his arm around hers. "But on one condition."

The old man frowned at her.

"You promise not to turn into an ogre once we go through those doors!"

The old man let out a hearty laugh.

"I promise." he said.

Jenny started towards the entrance and then stopped.

"I don't even know your name." She said

"It's George." The old man replied.

"Nice to meet you, George. I'm Jenny."

"Nice to meet you too, Jenny." George said smiling. "Ready to shop?"

"Ready to shop." Jenny confirmed and George escorted her through the entrance.

Once inside, with George on her arm, Jenny felt her fears drain away. They navigated the first few aisles together until Jenny had convinced George that she was happy to continue on her own. Before they parted Jenny thanked him for his kindness. George held her hand, lifted it to his lips and kissed it. She gave him a peck on the cheek and they then went their separate ways.

Contrary to what George had said, Jenny actually found the supermarket exciting. Like her experience of the high street, Jenny found herself wandering the aisles wondering at the array of items on display. When she had been there before with Barnes she had not taken any notice of what was around her, spending most of her time staring down at the floor. But now, her new found awareness had her marveling at the shelves laden with all sorts of goodies.

As she sauntered around she took out the list of ingredients she needed to make the meal and soon had an armful of goods. She was juggling them into a more comfortable, manageable position when a young female shop assistant, seeing her plight, arrived at her side with a shopping basket.

"Here, I thought you could use this." The young girl said offering Jenny the basket.

Jenny gently dropped her items into it and then took it from the girl.

"Thank you." Jenny said smiling.

The young girl smiled back and then continued on down the aisle in search of someone else she could be of assistance to.

Relieved of the weight from her arms, Jenny set off towards the clothes section. She had decided that she wanted to buy Alan a little gift to show him how much she loved him. She found the tie section and started to sift through what was on offer. She had never bought a tie for anyone before. Barnes always bought his own clothes, not trusting her to choose something appropriate. But she soon found one that she was pretty convinced would match a favourite shirt of Alan's. She removed it from the rack and placed it in her newly acquired basket.

Slipping the handles of the basket into the crook of her elbow she made a last check of the ingredients list. She seemed to have everything she required. Even so, there was a nagging at the back of her mind telling her that she had forgotten something.

Jenny stood there for a moment thinking hard when it suddenly came to her.

Wine! She thought. *I need a bottle of wine.*

Smiling at having teased out the nag she then began to frown. She wasn't a wine connoisseur but knew enough to realise she needed the right wine to compliment the meal. She couldn't hide the fact though that she had no idea whether she needed red or white, let alone what type of each. In a state of perplexity she made her way over to the alcohol aisle hoping that there would be something, or someone, there to guide her. She even hoped that George may still be around because she was convinced that a gentleman such as him would know the right one to get.

Jenny arrived at the alcohol aisle and was dismayed to see the vast variety of wines on offer. There was shelf upon shelf of bottles from every imaginable wine growing country out there. Not only were there no end of reds and whites but her mind was further complicated by the introduction of rosés.

Jenny groaned.

To make matters more frustrating there wasn't a shop assistant in sight.

Why does this have to be so complicated? She thought to herself.

She placed her basket on the floor and stood there with her hands on her hips surveying the aisle. She was just trying to work out in her own mind how she was going to decide on which bottle to choose when a strong hand grabbed her roughly from behind and turned her around. She found herself staring right into the bloodshot eyes of her husband.

"What the hell are you doing here?" Barnes snarled.

Jenny could smell stale alcohol on his breath and it brought back memories of her days with him. She tried to step back but he now had a firm grip of her wrist.

"Let me go!" She cried out trying to struggle free.

Barnes grinned at her menacingly and she felt a chill run down her neck. His face was unshaven adding to the menace.

"Well. Well, Well!" He laughed. "The little mouse has found herself some spirit, eh?"

"Get your filthy hands off me." Jenny said quietly but firmly, intent on not causing too much of a scene. "If you don't I'll scream."

Barnes let go of Jenny's shoulder and grabbed her cheeks; squeezing them tight.

"Don't even think about it!" He growled in her ear, his breath hot and rancid on her cheek.

Jenny's eyes darted up and down the aisle looking for help but there was no-one around. She couldn't help but laugh inside at the absurdity of it all. Here she was, in a shop full of people and she was in what seemed to be the only empty aisle in the supermarket.

Barnes picked up on her searching eyes.

"There's no-one to help you out this time." He sneered. "I hear that interfering old landlord has been sent packing and that new boyfriend of yours hasn't the balls to stand up to me."

Barnes went quiet for a moment and then turned Jenny's face to his.

"Here's what's going to happen. You're going to walk out of this place with me, nice and quiet, and then you're coming home where you belong. You're going to forget all about that fancy man of yours and get back to being my wife."

Jenny tried to speak but Barnes' grip on her face prevented her from doing so.

Barnes' eyes dropped to Jenny's chest.

"I've missed you, Jenny." He said, a drop of saliva forming at the corner of the mouth. "I've missed you so much."

Jenny remembered all the loveless nights Barnes had taken her and the thought of going back to them made her feel sick. She would kill herself before letting

Barnes anywhere near her again and tarnish the beauty she had had with Alan.

She began to struggle again.

"I think I like this new feisty you." Barnes said thrusting his groin firmly against her leg.

Jenny felt him hard on her thigh and fought harder.

"Never!" She said through her clamped teeth.

"We'll see about that." Barnes growled and then started to force her down the aisle back towards the entrance.

"What's going on here?" A voice familiar to Jenny shouted out.

She peered over Barnes' shoulder to the source of the voice and saw George standing there looking horrified.

Without letting go of Jenny Barnes turned around.

"Move on, granddad." He said menacingly. "You don't want to get caught in the middle of a husband and wife's lovers' tiff."

George stood his ground.

"I believe you're Jenny's ex-husband which gives you no right to treat her like this." The old man said.

This only served to increase Barnes' bad temper further and he squeezed Jenny's jaw a little tighter causing her to cry out. George took a couple of steps forward.

"I'm warning you, granddad. Come any closer and you'll regret it."

Barnes stuck out his chin and glared at the old man but George refused to back down.

"And I'm warning you that if you don't release Jenny this instance YOU will regret it." George said crossing his arms and glaring right into Barnes' eyes.

"Do you really think you have the strength to take me on, old man?" Barnes sneered at George cockily.

"No, but I have." Came a voice from behind Barnes.

Barnes turned towards the new voice just in time to see Alan's fist power through the air and smash into the bridge of his nose. With a horrible crunch his face seemed to explode in a spray of crimson fluid. Taken completely by surprise he released Jenny and went sprawling across the floor of the supermarket; coming to a stop at George's feet.

"May I?" The old man said looking at Alan questioningly.

"Be my guest!" Alan replied.

Not needing to be told twice, George launched a swift kick into Barnes' groin causing him to squeal out in further pain. Not knowing where to hold, his nose or his now throbbing testes, Barnes lay there whimpering.

Attracted by the noise, two burly security guards finally came running around the aisle.

Barnes looked up and saw his opportunity.

"Dese doo hooligans assaulted me." He groaned wiping blood from his nose with his sleeve while gently caressing his bruised genitals. "Arrest dem."

"I think you'll find we were saving this young lady from your brutish gasp." The old man spoke up.

"Is this true, George?" One of the security guards asked the old man. "Did you two assault him?"

"We may have used a little force to persuade him to let go of this lady here." George replied. "But no more than was necessary."

Alan couldn't help but smile at the little twinkle in George's eye when he said this.

"You know George?" Jenny asked rubbing her face where Barnes had been grasping her. "You called him by his first name and we haven't yet introduced ourselves."

"Of course we know George." The second security guard chipped in. "He was the store manager here for thirty years before retiring last year."

Jenny looked across at the old man, astounded by this new revelation.

"Guilty as charged." George said with a sheepish look and a shrug of the shoulders.

"Are doo going doo arrest im?" Barnes whined from the floor.

"If George here says it was you that was causing trouble then that's good enough for us." The first security guard said. "Do you want us to arrest him?"

"Yeth!" Barnes piped up.

"I'm not speaking to you so shut up." The security guard growled at Barnes before turning to face George.

"Well?"

"That rather depends on Jenny here." The old man said.

Everyone turned to look at Jenny who shook her head.

"I just want him out of my sight!" She sighed.

The two security guards nodded and then shook Alan's and George's hands in turn.

"Say *hi* to Cynthia for us." The second security guard said to George before helping his colleague pick up Barnes from the floor and frog-march him out of the store.

"Tell her to come in soon with some more of those wonderful cupcakes." One of them called over his shoulder. "We miss you bringing them in."

George nodded and then turned his attention back to Alan and Jenny. Jenny introduced him to Alan, not missing the opportunity to tease the old man about his failure to come clean about who he really was. George shrugged good-naturedly and then bid them farewell, their gratitude ringing in his ears.

"Are you alright?" Alan asked holding Jenny close to him and kissing her forehead.

"A bit sore and shook up but I'll live." Jenny replied. "Where did you come from anyway?"

Alan laughed.

"I've been sitting on the car park for the last half hour waiting." He said. "I finally decided I ought to come and look for you. I think it's a good job I did!"

"Thank you." Jenny said.

"For what?" Alan said frowning.

"For coming to my rescue." Jenny said.

Alan smiled.

"My pleasure." He said.

Jenny smiled back at him then frowned remembering why she was in that aisle in the first place.

"What's the matter?" Alan asked looking concerned.

"Please help me choose a wine to go with the meal tonight." She said with pleading eyes. "I haven't a clue what I'm supposed to get."

Alan laughed good-heartedly and picked up Jenny's shopping basket.

"Come on." He said. "Tell me what you're making and let's see if we can't find a bottle or two."

Chapter 58

Jenny made Alan promise that he would not tell Marjorie what had happened at the supermarket. She did not want to spoil the author's evening as she was desperate for it to be a success.

Alan offered to help her make the meal but Jenny insisted that she be left alone. It was her way to say thank you for the love and support they had given her. Marjorie also tried to help out but, again, Jenny declined the offer. The author reluctantly agreed but then put in a request that, if possible, could Jenny make a couple of extra portions as she was having a friend over for lunch the following day and it would help her out immensely if there was enough food for that. Jenny said she was happy to do that and then banned everyone from the kitchen while she cooked.

Half way through Alan popped his head in and announced everything smelled good. He told Jenny that he and Marjorie had set the table and were waiting with anticipation for the food to arrive.

"Erm, what time are we planning on eating?" He asked sniffing the aromas emanating from the cooker.

"About seven thirty, why?" Jenny asked.

"Just wondered." Alan said and before Jenny could quiz him any further he disappeared into the dining room.

Jenny was just putting the finishing touches to the meal when she heard the kitchen door open behind her.

"I'm nearly finished." She called out as she stirred the bolognaise sauce to make sure it was cooked thoroughly. "A couple more minutes, that's all."

"I'm pleased to hear that. I'm famished, dear." A familiar voice replied.

Jenny stood there for a moment, rooted to the spot. Slowly she turned around to be met by the rotund, grinning face of Maisie. She launched herself across the kitchen and threw her arms around her old friend. As she hugged Maisie she peered over the land lady's shoulder and saw John standing there, complete with sheepish grin.

"What are you two doing here?" Jenny asked when she had finally composed herself. "Not that I'm not pleased to see you."

"We were invited for a meal." Maisie said. "Alan rang us and told us you were cooking. He said we were welcome to join you all so we decided to come down. That's alright isn't it?"

Jenny smiled at Maisie.

"Of course it's alright. I'm just a bit shocked at your sudden appearance that's all."

Jenny released Maisie and went over to hug John.

"It's so good to see you both." She said feeling a lump start to grow in her throat.

"Now don't go all emotional on me." John said kindly, his own eyes a little moist.

Jenny laughed and then ushered them both into the dining room. Marjorie and Alan were already seated and the table was set for five people.

"You sneaky people." Jenny said directing her comments at Alan and Marjorie. "You kept that a secret."

"Nothing to do with me." Marjorie replied holding her hands in the air. "It was all Alan's idea."

Jenny looked across at Alan.

"Guilty as charged." He said. "I just thought it would be nice to meet up again."

"It's more than nice." Jenny said hugging Maisie again. "It was very thoughtful of you and thanks."

Jenny guided John and Maisie to two of the empty seats and then disappeared back into the kitchen while Alan poured them both a drink. Before long, she'd returned with the food and they were all merrily chatting and enjoying themselves.

After the meal, which they all agreed had been splendid, Alan and John took themselves off to the kitchen to do the washing up, leaving the three ladies to chat. Maisie was in awe of Marjorie and was keen to know all about the author's writing. At one point, Marjorie excused herself from the table and went off in search of Alan and John. Jenny was grateful for this considerate act as it gave her time to catch up with what Maisie and John had been up to since they had left the pub.

Maisie informed Jenny that they had finally found themselves a place to live. It was very nice them living with John's brother but they were constantly falling over each other. So, it had been a relief to finally find a place of their own. Maisie told Jenny that she and Alan were always welcome and that they should bring Marjorie with them some time. The house was an old convent so was big enough to accommodate them all. Besides John had big ideas of turning it into a B&B; the idea of retirement not resting long in the landlord's head.

Very soon Marjorie returned with a tray of coffee and after dinner mints she had *found* in one of her cupboards. Jenny scolded herself that she hadn't thought to buy some whilst shopping but the author told her not to be so hard on herself. She had been the most perfect of hostesses.

Marjorie also brought in a copy of her book and presented it to Maisie. The land lady was lost for words and said so. John hinted that this was a first for a very long time. They sat, drank their coffee, ate their mints and chatted away until John regretfully pointed out that he and Maisie ought to be making tracks. They were staying at a small hotel on the other side of town and needed to make an early start next day back home on account of builders arriving.

Jenny got a little tearful as they said their goodbyes but Maisie made her promise to visit them soon. As they drove away Jenny nestled into Alan's arms on the doorstep.

"That really was a very thoughtful thing to do." She said squeezing him tightly to her. "You really are a lovely man."

"Come on." Alan said. "Let's lock up and get to bed. It's been a busy old day in more ways than one."

Jenny suddenly felt weary but happy. Despite the altercation with Barnes in the supermarket the day had been a success on so many levels. She had taken steps to overcome her fear of doing things on her own; she had seen the kindness of others; and Alan had once more proved how much he loved her.

Yes, she thought as she drifted off to sleep in Alan's arms, *today has been a very good day indeed.*

Chapter 59

To her surprise, Jenny woke the following day feeling a bit deflated. She couldn't quite put her finger on why but when she spoke to Alan about it he thought it was probably due to the stress and excitement of the previous day having left her drained. After the busy day she'd had, she was now faced with an empty day of nothing to do.

"What you need," he said as they sat opposite one another at the breakfast table, "is something to fill your days with."

Jenny saw the logic in this but had no idea how to address it. She was reluctant to get a new job as she was still uncertain where they would end up living. She didn't want to be messing people around if she could help it. However, the need to carry on earning so that she could contribute towards saving for their new home was also at the forefront of her mind. When she presented this conundrum to Alan he told her he would support her in anything she wanted to do but suggested that she didn't rush into a new job straight away. He thought that she would benefit from some time to recharge herself after all the stress she had had to endure over the last few months.

"What you could do with is a hobby." He suddenly announced as they sat eating their cereal.

"I have a hobby." Jenny replied looking puzzled. "I read."

"No." Alan continued. "You need a hobby that will get you out of the house and into the fresh air.

He looked thoughtful for a moment and then his face lit up.

"What about golf? I can teach you how to play no problem."

Jenny stared at him and shook her head.

"I can't do that." She said. "That's your escape. You don't want me tagging along. Besides, you have your friends to play with."

Alan sat back in his chair and sighed.

"No-one's ever available to play these days." He said sadly. "I have a feeling they've all been warned off associating with me by Stella."

"But you played with one of them yesterday, didn't you?" Jenny said looking bemused.

"He didn't turn up." Alan said shaking his head slowly. "I didn't say anything to you because you had enough trauma at the supermarket to contend with."

Jenny reached over and held Alan's hand.

"I'm so sorry." She said. "You should have told me.

She put his hand to her cheek and nestled into it. Yet again he had unselfishly done his best to protect her by putting her needs above his own.

"We need to be honest with each other." Jenny said softly. "We need to share the bad as well as the good. You are always putting me before yourself but I want to be there for you when you need me too. Don't feel you can't tell me anything, no matter how down I seem."

Alan shrugged his shoulders.

"It's no big deal." He said stroking her face gently.

"But they're your friends. Surely they are man enough to stand up to Stella."

"And risk getting their wives into trouble with Stella? I don't think so." Alan said with a look of resignation. "I wouldn't really class them as friends anyway. Just acquaintances. It's no big loss, honestly. We're not particularly close. The only thing we have in common is golf and they're much better at it than I am. Whatever friendship we had has run its course. So, as you can see, I could do with someone to play with. That is, if I can find somewhere to play."

Jenny screwed he eyes up and looked at Alan.

"What else aren't you telling me?"

Alan shut his eyes, took a deep breath and then opened them again.

"As I was on my own I decided to go to the driving range where I was told my membership had been revoked. Something to do with not paying my green fees. Stella is big pals with the captain of the club so I can guess who's behind that too. As much as I debated with him that I'd paid my fees he made it clear that I am no longer welcome there. There was no use arguing about it. Besides, all this negativity towards me would have had a detrimental effect on my game anyway."

Alan forced a smile as he tried to make light of the situation.

Jenny shook her head and looked down-hearted.

"Why does Stella keep doing this?" She sighed. "Why does she keep causing so much trouble? Surely she can see that you're not going to go back to her. Why can't she just give up?"

"That's not Stella's style unfortunately." Alan said ruefully. "She'll keep fighting to the bitter end or until she gets what she wants. Which, incidentally, is not necessarily to get me back. I think she's passed that now. I think she's just hell bent on tearing us apart now. Very childish, I know but all very Stella. I blame it on her being an only child. Anyway, whatever her reasons they won't be pleasant ones. The sooner we can move away from the area the better."

Jenny stood up and went over to Alan's side of the table. She sat in his lap and pulled his head gently into her chest.

"You don't deserve this." He said.

"*We* don't deserve this." Jenny replied.

The two sat there in silence for a while until Marjorie came bowling into the kitchen.

"Well, aren't we the two lovebirds?" She said smiling enthusiastically before catching the downcast look on their faces.

"Oh." She said frowning. "Whatever is the matter? You look like you lost a pound and found a penny."

"It's nothing." Alan answered sitting up.

Marjorie wasn't going to be fobbed off so easy so she looked at Jenny.

"Jenny?" She said with raised eyebrows.

"It's Stella." Jenny started with a sigh. "It looks like she's got to Alan's golfing partners. None of them seem available to join him when he suggests a going for a round. Not only that but it looks like she's had Alan thrown out of the club too."

"Is this true?" Marjorie asked Alan.

"Seems that way." He said nodding.

"Hmm. That's not good." The author said. "She's a sly one that wife of yours. That's for sure."

"You can say that again." Alan said stern-faced.

Marjorie stood there for a moment and then disappeared out of the kitchen. Alan and Jenny returned to their silence, both contemplating Stella's actions. From the hallway they could hear Marjorie's muffled voice talking to someone on the telephone. Before long, the author was back in the kitchen.

"That's that settled then." She announced proudly.

Alan and Jenny looked at each other, puzzled as to what Marjorie could have been talking about. Jenny was the first to ask.

"What's settled?"

"Stella is not the only one with some influence in this area." The author said with an uncommon look of smugness on her face. "She's not the only one with friends in high places."

Alan shook his head, still bemused by Marjorie's strange behaviour.

"What are you talking about?" He asked. "What influence and what have you sorted?"

"Well," The author began, "you know that new exclusive golf club that has just opened outside town?"

Alan nodded. In truth, he had been reading about the new club with envy and had broached the subject of joining it to Stella numerous times. The fees were a lot more expensive than the club he presently played at but the facilities were second to none. Rumor had it that, once established, it was going to make a play for holding the Ryder Cup in the future. Stella, for reasons that now became clear, was adamant that he stayed where he was.

"It just so happens that the owner is a very big fan of mine." Marjorie continued. "He would be more than delighted to make you a member and, as he's there most days, you are more than welcome to join him and his friends for a round."

Jenny's face was beaming as Alan stared at Marjorie, not knowing what to say. Then reality jolted him back.

"That's very good of him but there's no way I can afford the fees. Not now."

Jenny now looked disappointed.

"You don't have to." Marjorie said smiling. "I explained that you might not be living here for much longer so he said you can play for free as long as you like. Just don't let the other members know."

Jenny's eyes nearly popped out of her head.

"But ..." Alan began but the author cut him off.

"No *buts*." She said. "You've helped me out along the way to me getting published so this is my way of saying *thank you* to you."

Jenny launched herself off Alan's knee and threw her arms around Marjorie.

"Thank you. Thank you. Thank you." She said laughing.

Alan stood up and joined them. Jenny stood aside allowing Alan to hug Marjorie.

"You are a special lady." He said as he let go of her.

"And you, sir, are a special man." The author replied.

"Oh yes, yes, yes." Jenny cried out clasping her hands together and bringing them to her chest as she jumped up and down.

Alan and Marjorie stared at her wondering what had gotten into her. She seemed far more excited than the situation warranted.

"You know what this means?" Jenny said with a huge sigh of relief.

Alan and Marjorie shook their heads.

"This means I won't have to learn golf!"

Alan looked at the girl merrily hopping about in front of him and burst out laughing.

After the hilarity of the moment had abated Marjorie disappeared off to a meeting with her publisher leaving Alan and Jenny alone in the house. Alan raised the question again about a hobby for Jenny but she assured him she was happy as she was for the time being. In the future, she promised him, she would look to something more active than reading but for the time being she was happy to take things easy and build up her confidence in her own time.

Chapter 60

Jenny felt a warm glow inside her that combatted the cooling sea breeze as she thought about how, from the moment that she had first stepped into the Red Lion and met Maisie and John, her life had been changed for the better by entering the lives of such wonderful people. Despite the heartache and tears she had suffered during the years preceding that moment she had learned to put her faith and trust back in people. She came to realise that not everyone in the world was as mean and despicable as her ex-husband and son. Jenny had also learned, with the love and support of her new found friends, how to live her life in happiness for the first time ever; this despite the backdrop of Stella's best endeavors to bring her sadness.

And through all this, the most loving supportive person in her life had been Alan; something he was to prove time and time again with no greater example of which he was to do for her over the next few days following that breakfast gathering.

Alan and Jenny spent the rest of the day enjoying each other's company. They sat and talked about everything and nothing, content with just being with each other. Alan made them a light lunch and they settled down to watch the afternoon movie; fittingly a romance to which Jenny could cuddle up to Alan on the sofa. She laid her head on his shoulder and, feeling as secure as she'd ever felt, dozed off to sleep.

Jenny woke with a start. She was alone in the lounge lying flat out on the sofa covered by a blanket. The television was off and there were muffled sounds of pots being moved around coming from the kitchen. She sat up slowly, stretching the sleepiness from her limbs before standing up and heading into the kitchen to see what all the activity was. She found Alan concentrating on a set of instructions from a recipe book he'd found in one of Marjorie's cupboards.

Alan sensed her behind him, turned and smiled.

"Feeling better after your nap?" He said.

Jenny nodded and looked around the kitchen

"What's going on here then?" She said still sounding sleepy.

"I thought I'd prepare the evening meal for when Marjorie gets home." Alan said. "We can all eat together."

"Any surprise visitors I should know about?" Jenny asked scanning Alan's face for the slightest twitch that might indicate he was hiding something.

"No, not tonight." He replied laughing. "Though I do have some news to tell you and Marjorie."

Jenny stared at him with a quizzing look.

"What are you up to now?" She said narrowing her eyes.

"All in good time." He said and turned back to the work surface to continue preparing the meal.

Jenny was just about to protest when she heard the sound of the front door opening. She peered into the hallway in time to see Marjorie entering with arms full of boxes and papers.

"Here, let me help." Jenny called over and quickly joined the author.

"Thank you." Marjorie said sounding a little out of breath. "My publisher has given me all this to approve before we set off on the tour."

Jenny relieved the author of one of the boxes and set it down at the bottom of the stairs. Marjorie pushed the front door to with her foot and then placed her own box next to it. She sighed as she slowly shook the tension out of her arms.

"Just give me a moment to recover and I'll get started with dinner."

"It's all in hand." Alan's voice called out from the kitchen. "You have half an hour to get freshened up and be ready."

Marjorie looked at Jenny and raised her eyebrows. Jenny shrugged her shoulders in reply.

"Jenny, can you help me with the veg." The voice from the kitchen continued.

Jenny smiled at the bewildered author before disappearing into the kitchen to join Alan. Marjorie sighed and, feeling surplus to requirements, went upstairs to shower.

Jenny enjoyed helping Alan with the meal. She was amazed at how adept he seemed to be in the kitchen and his ability to cook. . Alan told her that this was the result of all the years he spent fending for himself while Stella was away from home building her power base. In contrast, she couldn't remember Barnes ever stepping into their kitchen unless it was to retrieve a beer from the fridge. And hell would freeze over before he would ever consider cooking a meal

"That was lovely." Jenny said as she sat back in her chair and sighed contentedly.

"Indeed it was." Marjorie said. "Compliments to the chef."

"There's plenty more left if you want seconds." Alan offered.

"I couldn't eat another thing." Jenny said shaking her head. "I'm full to bursting."

She placed her hand on her stomach to reiterate how full she was.

"I'm pleased you liked it." Alan said smiling. "It's a long time since I was able to cook for someone. I quite enjoyed it. Mind you, my glamorous assistant did wonders with the vegetables."

Jenny shook her head.

"I only peeled a few carrots and potatoes." She said turning to Marjorie. "Alan is the one who should take all the credit."

"Well, it was lovely." The author said as she nestled back into her chair. "There's no doubting it. You two make a wonderful team."

Jenny reached over and slipped her hand into Alan's. He gently squeezed it. Marjorie sat watching them for a moment and then leaned forward, put her arms in front of her and placed them on the table.

"Now then." She said looking serious. "I have news for you. I had a productive meeting with my agent today and the dates of my book tour have now been confirmed. We shall be hitting the road at the end of the month and I'll be away for the best part of six weeks."

"That's wonderful!" Jenny said letting go of Alan and reaching out to hold the author's hand. "I'm so pleased for you."

"Thank you, my dear." Marjorie said. "It is all rather exciting."

Alan pushed his chair back and stood up.

"This calls for a celebration." He said and disappeared in the direction of the kitchen.

Jenny looked lovingly after him. He was soon back with a bottle of champagne and three glasses. He uncorked the bottle, the *pop* causing Jenny to giggle, and slowly filled the glasses. When the bubbles had subsided he passed the drinks around and then raised his glass in the air.

"To Marjorie. May the book tour be successful and sales be plentiful." He said with a grin.

"To Marjorie." Jenny said and took a sip of her drink, the bubbles fizzing up into her nose causing her to gently sneeze.

"Bless you." Marjorie said. "And thank you both for your good wishes."

Alan nodded his head and then looked serious himself.

"I, too, have news." He said looking somber. "I have to go away next week for a couple of days to attend to some business. Marjorie, I was hoping that you would be able to look after Jenny for me while I'm gone. It should only be for one night all being well.

"Can't I come with you?" Jenny said frowning at Alan.

"Unfortunately not." Alan said winking at Marjorie.

"But ..." Jenny began.

"It's alright." Marjorie interjected. "You'll be fine with me here. Besides, I could do with some help organizing what I need to take for the book tour."

Jenny looked from the author to Alan and then back again.

"Why do I get the feeling that you two are plotting something?" She said furrowing her eyebrows.

"I'm sure I don't know what you mean." Marjorie replied looking innocent.

"Nor I." Alan added. "It's just a short visit to hopefully conclude some business, that's all. I'll be back before you know it."

Jenny stared at them both, trying to read their faces. Both were giving nothing away. Alan started to collect the dishes together.

"Right. Washing up." He said.

Jenny moved to help him but Marjorie stopped her.

"No." She said. "I'll help him. You make yourself comfortable in the lounge. Go on."

With a shooing motion the author ushered Jenny out of the room towards the lounge. Jenny sat herself on the sofa and watched as Alan and Marjorie disappeared into the kitchen wondering what on earth they could be cooking up now.

Chapter 61

For the next few days Jenny quizzed Alan about what business it was that he was hoping to conclude and, more importantly, why it was necessary for him to be away to do it. However, Alan would not reveal what it was. Despite numerous requests for her to go with him he adamantly insisted that he needed to go alone and that she should stay with Marjorie.

Likewise, if Marjorie was aware of what Alan was up to then she was not forthcoming with any answers either. In the end, with an air of exasperation and resignation, Jenny gave up asking.

Alan left Marjorie's early on the Tuesday morning and told Jenny that she could expect to see him back late the following day. The night before his moods seemed to swing from overly excited to mildly anxious. Lying next to him in bed Jenny began to get concerned and asked him if they, as a couple, were alright. Had he got any misgivings about her? Was he going away because he needed some space? To Jenny's surprise Alan laughed heartily at this and told her that if the business he was hoping to conclude came off then they would be more than alright. Jenny tried to push him again on what it was but Alan just placed his fingers gently on her lips to quieten her. Then, as if to quell her fears, he made tender but passionate love to her. When he left in the morning she was asleep and she vaguely remembered feeling the brush of his lips on her forehead.

*

Jenny spent the next two days helping Marjorie get ready for her book tour. To her surprise, and no little pleasure, this entailed spending the second day shopping for clothes. Marjorie decided she needed a new wardrobe and what better way of taking Jenny's mind of Alan's absence was there than a little bit of retail therapy.

Jenny found that she was beginning to feel a lot more relaxed around the town now. Her earlier fears had all but dissipated, especially being in the company of such a town celebrity like Marjorie. Everywhere they went the author was recognised and given good wishes for the success of the book.

Jenny also found that she enjoyed helping the author choose her outfits.

"I want clothes that portray me as business-like but without losing my femininity and definitely not being too opulent." Marjorie said when they entered the first boutique of the day. "I don't want to come across as too aloof but as someone everybody can relate to. I'm well aware of my humble beginnings and don't want to give myself airs and graces."

Jenny laughed at this causing Marjorie to look puzzled."

"What's funny?" She asked.

"I'm sorry." Jenny said trying to get her laughter under control. "But, next to Maisie, you are one of the most down-to-earth people I know. I can't imagine you being in anyway aloof. Everyone will love you."

Marjorie smiled.

"Thank." She said. "I don't what to come across as better than anyone else. I'm so lucky to be in this position."

"You won't." Jenny replied. "I'm sure of it. You're not that kind of person."

Marjorie smiled gratefully at the comment.

The two women then set about the task of selecting clothes for the author. At each boutique Marjorie modelled and Jenny gave her an honest opinion. By mid-afternoon they were loaded up with at least six different outfits.

Marjorie announced that she wished to go into one more shop before calling it a day. Despite feeling a little jaded, Jenny was having such a good time she agreed. In truth, her feet were starting to ache and she was looking forward to putting them up when she got back.

The author led Jenny into an expensive looking boutique just off the high street and started perusing the garments. Jenny had never seen such exquisite clothes. The fabrics and colours were chic and vibrant causing her to only wonder how much they must cost.

"Oh, Jenny, what about this one?" Marjorie called out from across the room. "How beautiful is this?"

Jenny looked over to the author who was holding up the most gorgeous short sleeved dress she had ever seen.

"Wow! That is so lovely." She said joining Marjorie and feeling the fabric.

She turned to the rack and started searching through the sizes.

"What are you doing?" Marjorie asked kindly.

"I'm looking for your size." Jenny replied, her head buried in the rack. "That one looks a little small for you."

It was Marjorie's turn to laugh this time causing Jenny to peer out looking bemused.

"What?" She said.

"It's not for me, dear." The author chuckled. "It's for you."

Jenny looked puzzled.

"For me? I can't afford anything like that."

She returned her attention to the rack but Marjorie tapped her on the shoulder.

"Try it on and see." She said. "Just for me."

Jenny turned and looked wistfully at the dress.

"It is beautiful." She said.

"Go on." Marjorie said gently thrusting the coathanger into Jenny's hand.

Jenny paused for a moment and then took the dress from Marjorie. With a quick nod in the direction of the changing room the author indicated that she should change into it. With a look of resignation, Jenny disappeared behind the curtain.

Ten minutes passed and Marjorie was starting to get concerned.

"Are you alright in there?" She called out. "Do you need any help?"

There was a rustle from behind the curtain and then Jenny finally emerged looking pensive.

"Let me see." Marjorie said and stepped back to get a proper view of the girl in front of her.

The author put her hand to her mouth and gasped. Jenny stood there feeling a little self-conscious.

"What is it?" She asked. "What's wrong?"

Marjorie shook her head.

"Nothing is wrong." She finally said. "Nothing at all. Quite the contrary actually. It's just that you look absolutely stunning in that dress. It's almost as if it was made for you."

Jenny's face reddened a little and she shyly glanced down at the floor.

"Oh, Jenny. You must have that dress. You really must. You will blow Alan away with it."

Jenny looked up at Marjorie and sighed.

"I can't afford it." She said. "I looked at the label in the changing room and it is far too expensive for me. I was nearly too scared to put it on in case I damaged it and had to pay for it. It's a beautiful dress but ... no."

"I could ..." Marjorie began but Jenny shook her head.

"No, Marjorie. Thank you but you can't. You've already been too kind to me." Jenny said firmly. "Besides, everyone keeps treating me to things I can't afford and they have to stop. I can't keep taking money off everybody. If only for my own peace of mind."

Marjorie saw the resolute look on Jenny's face and admired her for it. She decided not to pursue the issue.

"If you're sure?" She said. "I really don't mins."

"I'm positive." Jenny replied smiling before disappearing back behind the curtain.

This time she was only a few minutes before she remerged with the dress neatly returned to its coat-hanger.

"Now then." She said. "Can we go home and eat? I'm ravenous."

Marjorie smiled at her and nodded. Jenny looped her arm around the author's and led her back out of the shop.

Jenny was pleased to see Alan's car on the drive when they pulled up outside Marjorie's house. Quickly she jumped out and helped the author retrieve the days shopping from the boot, eager to see Alan and find out what he had been up to. As the two women entered through the front door Alan's voice called out from the lounge.

"I'm in here."

Marjorie and Jenny carefully placed the clothes over the bannister and went to join him. Alan was sitting in the armchair and looked a bit nervous. Jenny's heart sank a little, fearing bad news despite all his reassurances before he left. He stood up and looked at Jenny then indicated that she sit down. Jenny obliged.

"How did trip go?" She asked, the words a struggle as her mouth had gone dry.

Alan's apparent nervousness seemed to increase.

"I'll know in the next few minutes." He replied.

Jenny looked at him warily.

"Why?" She managed to force out.

"Well." He began. "It's like this."

Jenny felt her heart racing in her chest wishing Alan would say what he needed to and hoping he would say nothing. What he did say could not have been further way from what she was expecting.

"That cottage we liked. By the coast. We're going to live in it."

Jenny burst out crying.

Chapter 62

Alan was crestfallen. Jenny was in floods of tears and he felt miserable. How could he have been so dumb as to expect Jenny to be happy with not being consulted about the cottage? He'd been a fool to think that he could just stroll up after two days away and expect Jenny to be over the moon about him securing it for them.

He sat down next to her on the sofa and put his arms around her.

"I'm sorry." He said trying to comfort her. "I thought it would be a nice surprise for you. I know how much you loved the cottage. I should have talked it through with you before I did something as stupid as committing to it for us. Please, please forgive me. I've been such a fool."

Jenny looked up into his face and frowned.

"What are you talking about?" She said, slowly gaining control over her sobs.

"I'm sorry I've upset you." Alan replied starting to feel a little emotional himself.

Jenny shook her head.

"You haven't upset me." She said.

"But I thought ... the tears ..."

"I didn't know what to expect with you going away and being so secretive with Marjorie about it." Jenny whispered. "A crazy part of me even thought you would end our relationship when you got back."

"Why on earth would I do that?" Alan asked, genuinely confused. "I love you. I want to be with you forever."

"I understand that." Jenny said. "More than ever now. But you have to understand that with what's happened to me in the past it's still hard to fully trust anyone, even someone who obviously loves me as much as you do. I still get scared that this is all a dream that will end very soon."

"I just wanted it to be a surprise for you." Alan said.

"It was certainly that." Jenny said smiling and holding Alan's hand. "And a wonderful one too. One I never expected at all."

"So, you're pleased?" Alan said looking hopefully at her.

"Of course, I am." Jenny replied smiling and threw her arms around him.

Alan breathed a sigh of relief.

"Thanks goodness for that." He said.

Alan then described how he had gone back to the cottage to talk to the woman owner. She had remembered him and Jenny and said what a lovely couple she thought they were. Alan told her that they could not afford to buy the property outright but proposed renting it with a view to buying in the long term. The woman admitted to being frustrated that she could not sell and that she had been considering the rental option. The upshot of it all was that she had agreed to rent it out to Alan and Jenny, fully furnished, on a temporary basis until they were in a position to buy. The monthly payment was reasonable and Alan had agreed that any maintenance of the property would become his responsibility.

Marjorie, who had stood quietly throughout, clasped her hands together in front of her and raised them to her chest.

"Oh, this is so wonderful!" She said, struggling to hold back her own tears. "It's so romantic. Almost like a fairytale."

Jenny peered up at the author.

"Maybe you could write a book about it." She said cheekily.

"I might just do that." Marjorie replied and beckoned for Jenny to join her in a hug.

Jenny stood up and wrapped her arms around the grinning author.

"I'm so pleased for you." Marjorie said holding Jenny tight. "Now you can start building a real life together."

"I'll never forget how kind you have been to me." Jenny said holding Marjorie at arm's length and looking her in the eye.

"Nonsense." The author replied. "It's been my pleasure."

Alan stood up.

"We should celebrate." He announced. "After all, it's not every day you get to move house. Get your glad rags on and let's go out for a drink."

In no mood to argue, Jenny nodded and quickly disappeared to change leaving Marjorie and Alan alone.

"That really is a wonderful thing you've done." The author said. "She deserves the best."

"And I will do my utmost to make sure she gets it." Alan replied looking serious.

Marjorie hugged him and whispered into his ear.

"I know you will." She said.

She held him there for a moment before letting him go.

"Now then." She said looking perplexed. "I need to get changed. We have some serious celebrating to do."

She went out of the room leaving Alan there alone. He puffed out his cheeks and let out a big sigh.

Yes he said to himself. *I'm going to make sure she gets the best in life.*

With that, he disappeared upstairs himself to get changed.

Chapter 63

Alan started the process of renting the house the very next day. As a moving in present, Marjorie insisted that she paid any fees resulting and wouldn't take *no* for an answer from either Alan or Jenny.

Alan, keen not to leave any doubt in Jenny's mind as to his intentions, made sure that she was involved in all the decisions that needed making. They assured Marjorie that they would honour their promise to look after the house while she was away on her book tour but aimed to move in to the cottage as soon as she returned. A moving in date of a week after Marjorie's return was agreed.

Marjorie had been on her book tour for three weeks when Alan and Jenny joined her for a long weekend in Salisbury. Jenny had always wanted to see Stonehenge so they decided this was a perfect place to go. They booked a couple of nights in a reasonably priced hotel and then met the author in a local book store on the Saturday morning where she was signing copies of her novel. After the signing, the three of them paid a visit to the prehistoric landmark. Jenny thought that the site was mystical and that she could almost feel the magic of the place permeating up from the ground.

The friends had a meal together that evening and then Jenny and Alan departed for Marjorie's home late the following Sunday evening. When they arrived back, the post was sitting on the doormat waiting for them.

Alan picked up the bundle of letters and sifted through them. Naturally, the majority were for the author but there was one letter addressed to him. It was from Stella's solicitor.

"I don't believe the cheek of that woman." Alan said waving the opened letter in the air and looking angry.

"What's it say?" Jenny said looking concerned.

"My dear wife is demanding that I pay back all the money I have in my account on the grounds that it was all given to me by her." Alan said flabbergasted. "But a lot of that money is mine saved from the sale of my garage."

"Surely she can't do that?" Jenny said.

"I don't know. I need to find out." Alan said trying to control his anger. "If she does take that money then we will have nothing to pay the rent with. We could lose the cottage."

Jenny looked horrified. Once again her dreams looked set to be shattered.

"Why can't she just leave us alone?" She said looking crestfallen. "Why can't she just let us live our lives?"

"Not her style." Alan said suddenly looking weary. "She won't rest until she feels she's won."

"But won what?" Jenny said, desperation in her voice. "You've already said she doesn't want you back. So what's there to win?"

"I don't know." Alan replied. "I'm afraid there's no sense in searching for reason where Stella's concerned."

"There must be something we can do?" Jenny said as she sat down on the sofa.

Alan sat down next to her and took her hand in his.

"I promise you this, Jenny." He said. "Whatever it takes I will make sure you get that cottage."

Jenny nestled her head into the nape of Alan's neck and wept.

The following morning Alan re-acquainted himself with an old school friend who had qualified as a solicitor and arranged to see him regarding Stella's letter. After reading it, the solicitor sat back and smiled.

"I don't know which cowboy she got to draw this up but it's not worth the paper it's written on." He said. "There's nothing here to say that the money wasn't given to you legally or with any provisos. Therefore, unless evidenced to the contrary the money's legally yours."

"So, she can't make me give it back then?" Alan said, the reassuring words of his old friend going some way to soothing the tiredness he felt through not sleeping a wink the previous night.

"Not on this alone." The solicitor said shaking the letter. "You didn't sign any agreements about the money, did you? What it could be used for? Things like that."

Alan shook his head.

"No. A regular amount was transferred into my account for *living expenses.* Her words." Alan explained. "I don't think she wanted me to know how much she had in her account; not that I'm the slightest bit interested, you understand. So she got me to set up a separate account."

"Interesting." The solicitor said rubbing his chin with his hand. "Do you think she has something to hide?"

"I've no idea." Alan said. "Like I said, I'm not that interested."

The solicitor nodded and say quietly for a moment thinking.

"So you and ..." He referred to the letter. " ... Stella? Separated?"

Alan nodded.

"Irreconcilable?"

Alan nodded again.

The solicitor look pensive again before continuing.

"Divorce?"

"Oh yes." Alan replied without even having to think about it. "Without a doubt."

"When?"

"As soon as possible, I hope." Alan said looking determined and thinking of Jenny.

"New lady in your life?" The solicitor persisted.

Alan nodded.

"Is she the cause of the break up?" The solicitor said looking serious. "Sorry, but I've got to ask."

"No. We were apart way before I met Jenny. Just living in the same house."

"Ok." The solicitor said. "You know you could be entitled to half Stella's money if you divorce?"

"Like I said, I don't want her money." Alan said angrily. "I just want to keep what is mine and for her to leave us alone."

"Well, you can make it a condition of the divorce that she lets you keep your money and leaves you alone in exchange for you not pursuing half her money." The solicitor advised. "If she doesn't agree you can petition for half of what she has."

"But I don't want it?"

"She doesn't know that, does she?" The solicitor said smiling. "Play her at her own game."

"I don't know. She's pretty powerful."

"Look, Alan, if this ..." He held up the letter again. "... is the standard of legal representation she has then it'll be a breeze. I'll tie this so-called legal expert in so many knots he won't know his decree nisi from his decree absolute. Trust me."

"If you're sure?" Alan said a little warily.

"Oh yes." The solicitor said nodding. "I'm sure."

Alan thought for a moment.

"Ok, what do I have to do?"

Chapter 64

Dusk was really starting to set in on the cliff top and Jenny new that the time was getting close. The sun was setting into the sea and she knew that soon she would have to say good-bye. She thought back to that letter of Stella's and how receiving it had been the start of something good in their lives as oppose to the anxiety it had first caused. Perversely, in the end they had Stella to thank for a lot.

True to his word, the solicitor managed to broker a divorce settlement that allowed Alan to keep the money he had and get an undertaking from Stella to let Alan and Jenny live in peace. Even when she sacked her incompetent legal representation and tried to employ someone who was a bit savvier the damage had been done. So, not wanting to risk losing half her fortune, Stella gave in and signed the divorce papers.

Elated with the way his friend had dealt with Stella, Alan then tasked him with brokering Jenny's divorce. After hearing about all the years of abuse she'd had to put up with the solicitor had no trouble in giving Barnes an ultimatum. Sign the papers or his mistreatment of Jenny would be passed on to the authorities. Barnes being the coward he was, did the one and only decent thing he could and signed.

So it was that not long after Jenny and Alan moved to the cottage, decree absolute pending, they were both free of their respective marriages.

On the day of moving Jenny and Marjorie shed not only tears of sadness at their parting but also tears of joy at the promise of the new life Alan and Jenny were embarking on. Once again Jenny found herself leaving a home where she had found love and friendship. However, unlike when she had left the Maisie and John's pub full of anxiety at the uncertainty ahead, this time she was leaving full of hope and anticipation.

Marjorie stood and waved them off from the pavement outside her house. As they drove away, Jenny waved back and remembered that first time she had visited for the party. How mixed up she had felt on the way home but also how she had vowed to be with Alan. Somehow, with no little heartache, she had managed to keep that vow. At times she thought it would never happen but here they were now, driving to a new life together with nothing but the future in front of them. As Marjorie disappeared from view Jenny thought that she would never be as happy as she was at that moment again.

It didn't take Alan and Jenny long to settle into the cottage at all. Right from the first moment they walked in they felt at home and as if they belonged there. They made a few practical adjustments to furniture placements but on the whole didn't feel the need to change things around too much. Alan spent a lot of time pottering around in the garden making it a haven for them to sit out in.

At night they would light the candles which they had spread around in various nooks, crannies and hanging from trees turning it into a magical place of tranquility. They would sit drinking wine and talking about the future until the air became too chilled even with the protection of jumpers, blankets and crackling chiminea. Then they would retire to bed and make love, eventually falling asleep in each other's arms.

To supplement the money Alan had, and to try to raise funds to buy the cottage, each of them took on a part-time job. Jenny put her new found skills to use by working in a quaint pub in town three nights a week while Alan helped the local garage out during the holiday season when it became overrun with holiday makers misbehaving cars.

Any opportunity they could get they took a picnic up to the cliff top and sat reading or just enjoying each other's company. Invariably they would stay there all day until the sun set into the sea, never ceasing to marvel at the colours that accompanied it.

It was on one such occasion that Alan announced his wishes.

"I love it so much up here." He said holding Jenny close to him as they gazed out to the horizon and the setting sun. "Promise me that when I die you'll scatter my ashes up here. Scatter them out over the cliff."

"Alan, I ..." Jenny began.

Alan softly but firmly interrupted her.

"I'm serious, Jenny. Promise me."

Jenny stared out to sea for a moment and then turned to gaze into Alan's eyes.

"I promise." She whispered.

Alan nodded and smiled at her.

"Thank you." He said.

"But you have to promise not to leave me ever." Jenny said looking serious. "Please don't leave me alone. I couldn't bare it."

Alan laughed.

"I'll try my best." He said holding her close. "That's the best promise I can make."

Jenny nestled herself further into Alan's arms so that he could hold her tighter. In silence, they watched the sun disappear below the horizon.

Marjorie was a frequent and welcome visitor. As a result of her book tour her novel reached stratospheric heights in the literary world. She was invited onto a number of talk shows and became something of a minor celebrity. Not long before the anniversary of Alan and Jenny moving into the cottage she released her second novel which was tipped to be even more successful than the first.

Alan and Jenny's life was idyllic until one day her son Stuart turned up on the doorstep.

Jenny was making Alan's breakfast in the kitchen. They'd been particularly late going to bed the previous night having been up to the cliff top until well past sundown and then sitting out in their garden until the early hours enjoying the warm weather. As a result they were a little slow at getting up and going but as it was Sunday they didn't feel any rush.

Alan was in the sitting room reading the paper while Jenny went about making them both a bacon and egg sandwich. She'd already placed their coffee cups on the tray and was about to add the bacon sandwiches when there was a knock at the door.

"I'll get it." Alan shouted out.

Jenny felt a twinge of annoyance at the possibility of their breakfast being disturbed but set about quickly tidying the kitchen.

Alan came through looking serious and Jenny raised her eyebrows querying his look.

"There's someone here to see you." He said, not looking pleased at all.

"Who?" Jenny asked bemused.

She hadn't really made many friends since moving to the cottage and from the look on Alan's face she didn't think it could be a surprise visit from Marjorie or Maisie.

"Hi, Mum. How you doing?" A voice she recognised came from the doorway.

Jenny looked across at the youth that stood in the doorway and sighed heavily.

"Stuart. What are you doing here?"

"That's a nice greeting for your son who's come all this way to see you." Stuart said trying to look hurt but only looking more obnoxious.

"Even so, what are you doing here?" Jenny repeated trying hard not to feel intimidated in her own home.

"I thought it was time I came to visit you." He said then looked around him. "Nice place you've got here. Must have cost a penny or two."

"What do you want, Stuart?" Alan asked trying to control his anger.

"I've come to see mum if that's alright with you?" Stuart snarled in Alan's direction.

Alan felt the hairs on his neck bristle.

"Stuart!" Jenny shouted across the kitchen. "You act civilly in this house and show some respect to Alan. If you can't behave properly then you'll have to leave."

Alan looked across at Jenny and saw the resolute look on her face. If it had been possible for him to love her more, then the way Jenny stood up to Stuart would have filled his heart further. Stuart, for his part, was visibly taken aback.

"It's alright, Jenny." Alan said. "Stuart's not going to cause us any trouble, are you Stuart?"

Stuart shook his head and seemed lost for words.

Jenny nodded, seemingly satisfied with the outcome of her outburst.

"Right then, Stuart." She said. "Let's start again. Exactly why are you here?"

"Erm, I want to have driving lessons and dad won't give me the money." Stuart said slightly hesitant. "He said you're loaded so come and see you."

"Why, the cheeky b…" Alan began but was cut off by Jenny's raised hand.

"How much do you need?" Jenny asked.

"£200 will get me passed in a few weeks." Stuart said sheepishly.

"£200!" Alan said astounded. "You've got a nerve."

Jenny shushed him again and turned her attention back to Stuart.

"I need to do the intensive course so that I can pass quickly. I want to go to college but to get there means driving." Stuart quickly explained.

"And what about a car?" Alan piped up. "How are you going to afford one of those?"

"Dad knows a few people from where he worked." Stuart carried on. "Says he can get me a cheap one."

"There's no way your mum can afford that amount of money." Alan said trying hard to put a lid on his anger.

"But you're loaded. Dad says." Stuart said with no little bravado. "Plus he says you left me so you owe me."

"Well, you can tell your dad ..." Alan started but Jenny slammed her hand on the table making him and Stuart turn to face her.

"Stop arguing!" She cried out. "I'll not have it in my home. I'll give you the money if you just go away."

"But ..." Alan began again only to be halted by Jenny putting her hand in the air.

"No, I've decided." Jenny said.

Stuart turned to Alan a smiled cockily.

"And don't you think I'm a soft touch for it either!" She shouted at Stuart. "This is the one and only time you ask me for money. Ok?"

Stuart nodded, his eyes full of anticipation as Jenny left the kitchen. He looked at Alan and smirked at him making Alan bristle with rage.

"If you were my son I'd ..."

"You'd what, old man?" Stuart said daring Alan to make a move.

Alan considered it but was prevented from doing so when Jenny came back, cheque in hand.

"Which driving school do I make it payable to?" Jenny asked.

"Don't you have cash?" Stuart said frowning.

Jenny glared at him.

"No. I don't. It's a cheque or nothing. You choose."

Stuart could see by the stoic look on his mother's face that she was serious.

"Ok, make it out to me then." Stuart said smiling.

"I don't think so." Jenny replied staring at her son. "Tell me which one or I rip the cheque up and that'll be it."

The smile left Stuart's face as Jenny placed her fingers over the edge of the cheque ready to tear it in two.

"Wait! Wait!" He called out as he reached into his jeans for his wallet.

He pulled out a business card and passed it to his mother. Jenny scanned it and then wrote the name of the driving school on the cheque. She held it out to Stuart who went to take it off her. She quickly pulled it back before he could take it.

"No more, Stuart. I mean it." She said

"Sure, mum. Whatever you say." He replied and quickly took the cheque off her when she offered it again.

Stuart examined it for a moment as if checking to see if it was real and then placed it in his wallet. Alan stared at him fuming but knew there was nothing he could do about it.

"Thanks, mum." Stuart said with little gratitude in his voice. "Got to dash. My mate's waiting outside."

With that he turned tail and marched out of the cottage.

Jenny stood there waiting for the backlash from Alan. However, he just shook his head.

"It's a small price to pay to get him out of our hair." Jenny tried to explain.

"Oh, Jenny. He'll be back." Alan said looking disappointed. "This is just the start. Mark my words."

"But he is my son when all's said." Jenny tried to justify.

Alan sighed deeply and looked forlorn.

"We've not seen the last of him, you'll see." He said sadly.

Unfortunately for Jenny, he was not wrong.

Chapter 65

The air was tense around the cottage for a couple of days after Stuart had left. Alan did his best not to be angry at Jenny and she, for her part, tried to smooth things over by being extra attentive to him. Neither seemed keen to talk about the problem but both knew that until that particular boil had been lanced then life couldn't really get back to any semblance of normality.

It was Alan that broke the ice first.

"I'm sorry about losing my temper with your son." He said. "But I didn't like the way he turned up unannounced and expected you to give him money."

"I'm sorry, too." Jenny replied taking hold of Alan's hand. "I hate us not talking. It doesn't seem natural."

Alan gently squeezed Jenny's hand.

"I know." He said. "It's just I don't want to see your good nature taken advantage off."

"Guilty conscience, you mean." Jenny said softly.

"I keep telling you. You have nothing to feel guilty about."

"But he's my son." Jenny tried to explain. "No matter how bad he's been in the past I can't escape that fact. And I do feel guilty about leaving him with his father even despite that fact."

"I understand that." Alan said. "It's your caring nature that makes me love you so much. But it concerns me that he will be back for more. And if he is, will you be strong enough to say *no* to him."

Jenny bit her lip and sighed.

"Maybe he'll stay away now." She said.

Neither of them truly believed that.

*

To Alan's great annoyance Stuart developed the habit of turning up like a bad penny when least expected. To his relief, it wasn't as regular as he expected. Jenny did her best to stand up to him but in the end her guilt got the better of her and she gave in.

Stuart was canny enough not to push his luck too much. His demands, though unwarranted, were never excessive. The odd £30 here. The occasional £50 there. All mounted up and all left Alan feeling bewildered and downhearted.

Jenny always paid out of her own money and never once asked for Alan's support. She didn't think it right that Alan should pay for her guilty conscience though she knew that, despite his thoughts to the contrary, he would have offered the money if needed.

Then the visits seem to stop. Two months went by since his last visit. Then three. Then six. Marjorie, on one of her visits, informed Jenny that she'd done a little snooping in the village and it seemed that Stuart had moved away and was at university. All she could hope for as his mother was that he'd finally found his way in life and that he'd put his obnoxious past behind him. She wasn't to see him for at least another year.

Alan and Jenny had both been divorced for the best part of two years when, on Valentine's Day, Alan proposed. Not having to think about it Jenny said *yes* and they were married the following month.

They both opted for a small ceremony at the town's registry office. Maisie, John and Marjorie were invited and they finished the day off with a meal at the local pub Jenny worked at.

John spent the evening talking with the landlord and swapping tales of the trade. He kept telling him how Jenny was a natural and that he had trained her well; something her existing boss concurred with.

Jenny and Maisie chattered away talking about all the latest shopping trips they'd been on while Marjorie filled Alan in on her latest novel; her third to be released.

At the end of the night they said their *good-byes* and went their separate ways. Jenny and Alan returned to their cottage where they spent their first night as a married couple.

As she lay in his arms after they had made love, she sighed gently.

"You ok?" Alan asked as he stroked her hair.

"Perfect." She said snuggling deeper into his chest. "Absolutely perfect."

"I still have to pinch myself that you're mine." He suddenly said. "I still can't believe it even after all this time."

Jenny sat up and looked at him, deep adoration in her eyes.

"You are the most wonderful thing that has ever happened to me in my life." She said, her eyes welling. "And I don't ever want to lose you."

Alan pulled her gently down to him.

"I'm not going anywhere." He whispered in her ear. "You've got me for eternity."

He gently squeezed her to him and, contented, they both fell asleep.

Chapter 66

Jenny felt her eyes begin to moisten. She wasn't sure if it was the cool wind being whipped up by the setting sun or the growing reality of what she was about to do. She picked up the rucksack, slowly walked to the edge of the cliff top and looked down. The tide was fully in and the waves were crashing against the rocks below. Not long now and it would be done. No, not long now.

Six months after their wedding Jenny got a call from Maisie. John had taken a tumble and badly broken his hip. He had been taken to the local hospital where they decided they needed to operate on him to repair the damage. Jenny listened to Maisie with growing concern. Beneath her bravado, Jenny could detect the undercurrent of fear in her old friend's voice. So, despite Maisie's protestations to the contrary, Jenny arranged to go and be with her overnight to keep her company.

Alan himself had not been feeling too good but was in agreement with Jenny that she should go. Jenny packed her overnight bag ready to depart the following day. As she planned on going early she organised for a taxi to pick her up so as not to disturb Alan who, very man-like, had taken to his sick bed.

"Are you sure you're ok with this?" She asked for the umpteenth time. "I don't have to go. I can stay and look after you instead."

"I'm fine, really." Alan said putting on his best brave face. "Nothing a day in bed won't cure. You go and I'll see you in two days."

Not particular sure she was doing the right thing but conscious of how Maisie could do with some support, Jenny finally decided she would go.

Jenny set her alarm clock to give her plenty of time and was up and ready when the taxi arrived. Alan was fast asleep and gently snoring so she kissed him on the forehead and quietly closed the bedroom door. As she left the house she pulled the collar of her coat around her against the chill and walked down the pathway. The taxi driver met her by the gate, took her bag from her and placed it in the boot. They were soon driving down the road to the station.

The train journey to Maisie took just under four hours. Thankfully Jenny only had to change trains once early on in the journey leaving her plenty of time to sit and read Marjorie's new novel. She still couldn't believe she had the privilege to know someone so famous and it always gave her a thrill when she took her book out and saw Marjorie's photograph on the back cover.

Jenny also took the time to reflect back on her life with Alan since they had moved to the cottage. Never had she felt so in love with someone and felt her life was complete. Stella had finally given up trying to break them up and Barnes, as all cowardly bullies tend to do once they've been stood up to, had sloped off into the shadows. Jenny felt a contentment that had only been possible with the arrival of Alan in her life.

She felt warm inside and marveled at how far she had come in such a relatively short period. She had emerged from those dreadful dark days of fear and suppression with Barnes to a fulfilling life of calmness and confidence. Sometimes she wondered how different her life could have been if she had met Alan earlier but never dwelt too long on it for fear of not appreciating what she had there and then.

She remembered the timid person she was who would tremble at the thought of being out alone in town; at the mercy of anyone and everyone. Yet, here she was now, travelling across country on her own and not thinking twice about it. All because of the love of a good man and the friendship of people that believed in her. Her heart felt full of love for Maisie, John and Marjorie but most of all, Alan. Her knight in shining armour, her Sir Galahad who had saved her from the dragon that was her marriage. It was his love that had seen her through the dark days and it was his love that would enrich her life for the rest of their days together. And she would love him with all her heart as long as she continued breathing.

Chapter 67

Maisie met Jenny at the station and the two friends went straight to the hospital to see John. He was undergoing his surgery and she was keen to be there when he came around. They sat in the relative's room on the ward and waited for news of the operation. Jenny held Maisie's hand and tried to comfort her as best she could. After what seemed like an eternity the surgeon finally came to see them.

"All went well." He announced with a smile on his face. "Your husband sailed through the operation and we managed to repair the damage. We'll keep him in for a week or so to make sure there's no complications but I'm sure he will be alright now."

Maisie stood up and hugged the surgeon.

"Thank you." She said releasing him and wiping a tear from her eye. "Thank you so much."

"You are most welcome." The surgeon said looking a little embarrassed.

"When can I see him?" Marjorie asked.

"He's in recovery now and will be back in his room soon." The surgeon explained. "He'll be a little groggy for a while and probably sleep most of the day. He should be more with it tonight so I suggest you go home for a while and come back later."

Marjorie thanked him again and the surgeon disappeared out of the room. Jenny put her hand on her friend's shoulder and then suggested they find somewhere for a bite to eat. Marjorie, relieved that all had gone well, allowed herself to be guided out of the hospital to her car.

*

Marjorie and Jenny returned to see John that evening. He was sitting up when they arrived and looked a little drained. However, his face lit up when he saw Jenny.

"What on earth have you been up to?" She said as she went over to the bed and gave him a big hug.

"Being a big clumsy ox is what he's being doing." Maisie said before John could open his mouth.

John rolled his eyes to indicate that this wasn't the first time he heard that particular description of himself and just lay his head back in his pillow; too drained to find a suitable retort.

"How are you feeling?" Jenny asked sitting down on the seat by the bed and taking hold of John's hand.

"A bit sore." John replied. "And a bit groggy. But I'll live."

"And so you'd better." Maisie said trying to sound stern but only betraying her concern in her voice. "Don't think you're leaving me so soon."

John shook his head.

"I only had a fall, Maze." He said sighing. "It's not as if it's life threatening."

"A man of your age has to be careful." Maisie said frowning. "All sorts of complications could set in."

"Well, they wouldn't dare set in with you around would they, my love?" John said and then winked at Jenny causing her to snigger behind her hand.

"Oh, I see." Maisie said looking at Jenny and narrowing her eyes. "Ganging up on me now, eh?"

"Sit down and take the wait of your feet." John said smiling. "You're tiring me out just standing there."

Maisie pouted her lips and then turned to retrieve a chair lying free next to one of the nearby empty beds.

She pulled it up to the bed opposite to Jenny and took hold of his other hand.

"Really, my love." She said, the concern Jenny knew was inside finally leaking onto her face. "How do you feel?"

"Like I've been kicked in the leg by a horse." John replied grimacing. "And a ruddy great horse at that."

In unison, Jenny and Maisie patted John's hands in an attempt to soothe him.

Chapter 68

Jenny stopped over with Maisie that night. She telephoned Alan when they had returned from visiting John to see how he was feeling. Although he told her that he was fine Jenny detected the strain in his voice and promised him that he would be severely pampered on her return. They said their good nights and then hung up.

Jenny insisted on Maisie putting her feet up while she made them a light supper. Maisie was too tired to argue so didn't. She directed Jenny to the kitchen and told her to use whatever she could find in the fridge and cupboards. Jenny had a good rummage around and pulled cheese and biscuits accompanied by a bowl of salad. However, when she returned to Maisie her friend was fast asleep and gently snoring. She found a blanket lying over the back of the sofa and, carefully removing Maisie's shoes, covered her. Not wanting to disturb her, Jenny took herself off to bed where she soon fell asleep herself.

Jenny woke the following morning feeling a little disorientated. It took her a moment or two to remember where she was before getting out of bed and going downstairs. Maisie, now in her pajamas and dressing gown, was already in the kitchen sliding croissants into the oven. Coffee was warming in the percolator and an array of jam-jars were lined up on the worktop.

"Did you sleep alright, dear?" She asked.

Jenny nodded.

"I'm sorry I fell asleep on you last night. I must have been tired." Maisie said.

"That's alright." Jenny replied. "I understand. You made it to bed then?"

She pointed at Maisie's dressing gown

"Oh yes, I woke up and found myself alone in the lounge," Maisie began, "so I took myself upstairs."

The strong aroma of coffee hit Jenny's nose.

"Mmm. That smells good." She said

"Well, take a seat and let's have breakfast." Maisie said nodding at the breakfast table. "Then I'll get you to the station and you can get back to that poorly husband of yours."

Jenny sat down and thought of Alan. She couldn't wait to be back with him and to feel his arms around her.

Maisie dropped Jenny back at the railway station and waited with her until the train was ready to depart. The two friends hugged and Jenny made Maisie promise to give John a kiss from her when she visited.

"I don't think I've kissed John myself in years." Maisie said pretending to look shocked. "But if you insist."

"I insist!" Jenny said laughing. "And don't think I believe you're telling the truth about that for one minute."

Maisie shrugged her shoulders and then gave Jenny a last hug. Jenny held her tight and then let her go. She quickly boarded the train and sat in a window seat where she could see Maisie. As the train pulled away the Maisie waved and Jenny felt a lump in her throat. She waved back and, once out of sight of Maisie, wiped a tear away from her eye. She settled back in her seat and got out Marjorie's book. She was determined to have it finished by the time she got back home.

*

The taxi pulled up outside the cottage and Jenny leaned over to pay the driver. She felt excited to see Alan and impatiently waited for the driver to retrieve her bag from the boot, a feeling particularly enhanced by her bladder needing to be relieved. Before he had driven away Jenny was inside.

The cottage was strangely quiet when she entered. The heating wasn't on and it felt uncomfortably cold.

Jenny called out to Alan but got no answer. She put down her suitcase before checking the kitchen and lounge. He wasn't in either.

Calling his name again she went upstairs. Their bedroom door was closed so she quietly opened it in case he was asleep. She smiled to herself making a promise that she would slip into bed with him and make love to him when he woke up.

She peered in at the bed and frowned when she saw that the bedclothes were drawn back having been slept in but empty.

She walked in and looked around. There was no sign of Alan. She felt the sheets and they were cold.

"Alan." She called out again getting more concerned.

Listening intently for any sound she went over to the window to see if he was working in the back garden. Even as she did so she couldn't help but think something was wrong. Alan wasn't the sort of person to leave the bed unmade in a morning; even with Jenny gone. She looked out but there was no sign of him.

Now she really was getting worried. Something didn't feel right.

She tried to calm herself. Maybe he had woken feeling better and decided to go to work. Maybe he was late and left the bed until later. That had got to be it, surely.

Jenny decided she would call the garage and check to see if Alan had turned up there. First, she really did need to pee.

She went along the corridor to the bathroom admonishing herself for getting jumpy about Alan. She put it down to John's misfortunes being on her mind and that she was desperate to see Alan.

Shaking her head, she opened the bathroom door. She was greeted by the sight of Alan, still dressed in his pajamas, crumpled on the floor. He was lying on his back with his head, slightly cocked to the side, underneath the hand-basin. His lifeless eyes were staring at the pedestal to the toilet.

Jenny dropped to her knees beside him and screamed.

Chapter 69

Jenny thought back to that moment when she found Alan lying there. She'd quickly pulled herself together but even then she knew he'd gone from her. Alan had already started to feel cold and his body to stiffen.

She'd sat down beside him and lifted his head into her lap, stroking his hair as she rocked him back and forth as if the sheer motion of doing so would bring him back to her. But in her heart of hearts she knew he was gone.

The tears came, slowly at first and then in uncontrollable sobs. Then hysteria returned and once again she started screaming. The local postman found her cradling Alan in her arms and called for the emergency services.

When the police arrived they had to gently prise Alan from Jenny because as much as she knew he was gone, she couldn't find it in her to let him go. Slowly and patiently they finally got her out of the bathroom and into the bedroom where, grief stricken and in shock, they slowly extracted out of her what had happened.

The coroner determined Alan had been dead for some hours before she had got home. Days later he'd explained that Alan had had a massive heart attack, the sort that, even if she had been there, Jenny wouldn't have been able to save him from. He told Jenny that she should not admonish herself for not being with him – she did. She should console herself that it was quick and without suffering – she couldn't.

Marjorie came and stayed with her during the immediate time after; helping with the funeral arrangements and all that went with Alan's departure. She even notified Stella who, though Marjorie would never tell Jenny this, showed no feeling and seemingly smirked down the telephone line.

Maisie and John attended the funeral, at the local crematorium; John on crutches but not allowing anything to stop him being there. A small service but all who needed to be there were.

Jenny had been presented with Alan's ashes by a very somber man in a black suit and told to take her time deciding where she wanted Alan interring. But Jenny couldn't bear the thought of being parted from him. They had been through so much together for them to be separated now.

For the best part of twelve months Marjorie, Maisie and John had tactfully and lovingly talked to Jenny about laying Alan to rest. And for all that time she had been deaf to them.

Then one day, standing on the cliff top grieving for her beloved Alan, his words came back to her. She remembered her promise to him.

It was clear then what she had to do.

She had brought him to the cliff top where they had spent so many happy hours together. Where she felt his presence in the breeze; heard his voice in the rustle of the bracken. Where they could be together forever.

She took the urn from the rucksack and looked down at the sea below.

Yes, it was here. Together.

She unscrewed the top to the urn and held it out in front of her over the edge of the cliff. Slowly she turned her wrist until Alan's ashes released into the sea breeze.

Tears ran down her face but she made no sound until, as the last of the ashes floated away she looked out to the sun setting in the sea.

"Good-bye, my love until we are together again." She whispered

Looking down into the swell of the sea she thought she could see him smiling back up at her. And she smiled, too.

Yes. It was here where they would be together forever.

The End

For more information on Phil's Writing please go to the website:

https://sites.google.com/site/philswriting/

or Facebook Group:

https://www.facebook.com/groups/196499010414296

Made in the USA
Charleston, SC
20 December 2014